Praise for *Drumveyn*:

"Raife adds her dynamic new voice to the likes of Rosamunde Pilcher and Barbara Erskine with this well-crafted and emotionally powerful debut novel." —*Romantic Times*

"Alexandra Raife has achieved something quite unusual—a warm, friendly, involving story with a page-turning quality that emerges less from plot than from the characters, who are perceptively drawn, real and (oh, bliss!) likable. A lovely book."
                                        —Reay Tannahill

"*Drumveyn* had me hooked from the first page. A delightful book which I enjoyed enormously. Alexandra Raife is certainly a gifted storyteller."   —Barbara Erskine

"A richly satisfying story where a large and varied cast of people is set against a vividly familiar background. I found it unputdownable. I hope Miss Raife has many more such novels in her."   —Mary Stewart

Mountain
Heather

Alexandra Raife

Previously published in Great Britain as *Grianan*

A SIGNET BOOK

SIGNET
Published by the Penguin Group
Penguin Putnam Inc., 375 Hudson Street,
New York, New York 10014, U.S.A.
Penguin Books Ltd, 27 Wrights Lane,
London W8 5TZ, England
Penguin Books Australia Ltd, Ringwood,
Victoria, Australia
Penguin Books Canada Ltd, 10 Alcorn Avenue,
Toronto, Ontario, Canada M4V 3B2
Penguin Books (N.Z.) Ltd, 182–190 Wairau Road,
Auckland 10, New Zealand

Penguin Books Ltd, Registered Offices:
Harmondsworth, Middlesex, England

First published in the United States by Signet, an imprint of Dutton NAL,
a member of Penguin Putnam Inc. Previously published in Great Britain
by Michael Joseph Ltd under the title *Grianan*.

First Signet Printing, December, 1998
10 9 8 7 6 5 4 3 2 1

Copyright © Adrienne Lewis, 1997
All rights reserved

PUBLISHER'S NOTE
This is a work of fiction. Names, characters, places, and incidents either are
the product of the author's imagination or are used fictitiously, and any
resemblance to actual persons, living or dead, events, or locales is entirely
coincidental.

Part One

Part One

Chapter I

It was a long time since Sally had been to the Edalmere cottage. The road looping up on to the eastern
Lakeland fells was still a single track but dark now
with new tarmac, litter bins at every passing place.
She even met cars coming down, glimpsing faces red
from a day in the sun of early May. Edal village had
spread to at least twice the size she remembered, lines
of new houses straggling out along each of its arms.
She was glad Aunt Janey had arranged for the key to
be left in the door. She could not have faced calling
to collect it from Ann Jackson, who used to clean the
cottage for Aunt Ursula and still kept an eye on it,
and who would have exacted her due of gossipy noth-
ings about whatever domestic arrangements she had
made, about the family, and about Sally's own long-
ago visits here.

At the southern end of the narrow lake the tarmac
ended in a car-park, with a map in a glass-fronted
case, fire warnings, the green-and-white pointing arms
of signposts. There was a row of bungalows beyond it.

Sally nearly turned back. She didn't want it to be
like this, didn't want change, didn't want people. It
had been disconcerting to find today, with decisions
behind her and the break finally made, that the whole

wretched fiasco with Julian had filled her mind with
renewed agony. Humiliation and anger eating into her,
she had registered little of the journey and felt exhausted now. But there was nothing to go back to,
and as she wasn't ready yet to meet Aunt Janey's
searching eyes and stringent comments, the cottage
would have to do as a staging-post. At the very least
it would provide solitude and freedom from demands.

Once past the bungalows, with their half-grown
shrubs and lawns already suffering from too much
mowing on low cut, the track following the lakeshore
was more familiar, though metaled with rough stone
which Sally thought was new. The old whitewashed
farmhouse on the bend looked the same but was
clearly occupied now, chimney smoking, a muddy estate car at the door, a child's bike propped against the
wall. It was now called, Sally saw, Edal Bank. She was
filled with swift irrational resentment. In former times,
when she had come here for childhood holidays with
her parents and later with Janey, this house had always been shut up and deserted.

Now the track seemed narrower as it entered the
plantations which from this point clothed the shores
around the northern end of the lake, thickly planted
to the water's edge. Bars of sunlight flickered mad-
deningly across her face as the track swung closer to
the lake and the trees thinned, then she was driving
blind in dense shade as it turned away again. There
was a sudden slashing burst of light from the sun balancing itself on the ridge of the great hills to the west.
She didn't remember this open space, which gave a
view of the whole length of the lake and the high
northern fells. But she was too tired, too empty of
interest to feel anything but exasperation—at the un-

expected intrusion of people into this once-secluded place, at the minor irritations of the sun in her eyes, the ache in her shoulders after the unbroken spell of driving, the sweatiness of her thighs clamped together for long hours without moving.

She didn't even like the cottage much, she remembered wearily. Well, it was only intended as a stepping-stone between the disaster her well-adjusted life in the south had turned into and the hard work and challenges ahead. She turned into the steep-pitched driveway (had that PRIVATE sign always been there?) and came out onto the grassy ledge where the little house faced west into the eye of the sun. As she stepped stiffly out, shaking her skirt free of her legs, lifting her heavy hay-colored hair out of her collar, automatically tucking her shirt down into her broad leather belt, sweet air met her, smoothing across her face like cleanser, filling her nostrils with the tang of resin mingled with the scents from Aunt Ursula's once-loved garden. With a long sigh of relief she leaned against the warm wing of the car and, tilting back her head, closed her eyes. The sunset light spreading its last brilliance along the dramatic skyline glowed through her eyelids, warmed her face. Tension seeped away. A few days alone here, with nothing to do, nothing expected of her, then Grianan, and no need to look further for the whole of the summer.

After a moment, she reached into the car for the keys and went to open the boot, noting the grass which now grew where gravel had been. Aunt Janey came here when she could get away from Grianan, which wasn't often, but no one else ever used the cottage as far as Sally knew.

The fancy little wrought-iron gate whined at her

touch, the fleshy cables of buttercups reached across
the path, dandelions had rooted in the cracks of the
steps. A sudden rush of loneliness took her by the
throat; a mixture of a nostalgia she hadn't expected
to feel and dread of the empty future.

Nothing had been changed in the kitchen. Carved
pine rioted everywhere; Beatrix Potter china crowded
the dresser shelves; there still in their places were the
terracotta garlic baker, the automatic egg boiler (with
piercer) in the shape of a chicken. Gaudy tulips
rammed into a too-small vase were deciding whether
to turn up or down. The cuckoo clock had been
wound. Damn Ann Jackson.

Sally dumped down the coldbox of food she'd
brought from the car and went through to the hall.
The door to Aunt Ursula's room was open. Shrouding
the bed was the familiar beige silk counterpane with
its faded satin-stitch bamboos. Aunt Ursula had died
in this bed; Uncle Teddy too for all she knew. Sally
would rather sleep on the kitchen table with the Pig-
ling Bland condiment set.

She tried the small room she had always been given
as a child and was met by the smell of cold unstirred
air. Dead flies lay on the peeling paint of the windowsill. Tatters of sun-rotted cream linings hung from the
edges of faded floral curtains. She could live with that.
She went out to the car to fetch her bag and duvet.
Adult equivalent of taking your teddy with you everywhere? She didn't care.

Settling in didn't take long. She hadn't brought
much with her and basic food supplies had been left
in the fridge as promised. The boiler was switched on,
the house warm. Too warm, too cluttered. Every surface was busy with objects. Everything possible was

ruched, gathered and flounced. Net curtains hid the view down the shining length of Windermere. This single piece of elaboration suddenly loosed in Sally all the suppressed anger of the day. She felt stifled, desperate with the need to be outside, to have space around her, breathe cool air.

The two main choices for walks had always been to take the steep path up through the trees behind the house and come out onto the fell, or to go along the lakeside track to reach the open southern shore. Sally had no energy tonight to face a climb and took the lower track. She had forgotten already that the house down the lake was now inhabited and was taken by surprise to meet two children playing in the lane on their bicycles, riding across planks they'd laid over the ditch, a brown-haired boy of perhaps ten, a younger sister with red-gold curls. They both answered politely when she spoke to them, pausing as she passed.

Sally found she couldn't wind down. She had enjoyed coming here as a child and had looked forward to seeing the place again, particularly to being on her own here, but she had a strange feeling that it was refusing to accept her, its beauty as two-dimensional as a painting, denying her admittance. She sat on a rock and watched a pair of mallard with nine dots of ducklings bob on the glinting ripples above the sandy beach; on the island a hundred yards away the cormorants were drying their wings; in the shadows under the farther shore she caught the white gleam of the swans. None of it meant a thing.

She had come here to be free, however briefly, of time and people, past and future. To sleep, eat, walk, idle. It sounded simple, but how first to subdue the churning thoughts?

Shivering as a small wind came off the water, bored
with the ducks, after a few minutes she pushed herself
up off the rock and turned to go back. Food, bath,
bed. Sleep? That she could not be sure of.

The lane was empty, the children gone. A battered
pickup had joined the estate car outside the house. Its
bonnet was up and a man was standing beside it turning something over in his hands, holding it up to the
light, too intent on what he was doing to notice Sally
passing. He was tall and lean, with curly red hair
darker than his daughter's, big oatmealy sweater sagging as he leaned forward and replaced whatever part
he'd taken out. That was all she saw, but in one of
those waves of longing that swept Sally still she felt
an acute envy for the woman in the neat white house,
with her husband, her children, her home in this lovely
place, secure, looked after.

Then she mocked the facile image impatiently. This
man, however attractive he had looked in that one
swift glance, probably wouldn't have two words to
string together, the lucky wife would be ploughing
through the washing-up, the children watching telly
and squabbling. Well, that was as facile as the first
image, honesty made her admit. The truth was these
people had their life together, as a family, whatever it
was like, while she was about to return alone to an
alien little dwelling, ill-suited to her mood, feeling up-
rooted, dispossessed and without armor of any kind.

She woke late, still feeling tired. This had not been
the plan but there was nothing to lure her in the day
ahead. She dawdled about, having a long shower and
washing her hair in Aunt Ursula's fussy bathroom, the
outer world shrouded by polka-dotted net. But in this

place the landscape could not be ignored for long. The brilliance of the spring morning, the clean lines of the hills, the emptiness and silence woke a spark of enthusiasm. She was here; she had left the high-tech, high-spec, emptily resounding house in the suburbs of Reading for good; it was sold and gone. Idleness and introspection would do no good. She would walk down to the village for bread as they always used to, look in and thank Ann Jackson for getting the cottage ready—and make sure that she understood she wouldn't be needed again while Sally was here.

Would it be warm enough later to swim? Would the old wooden jetty still be there in the bay below the cottage? A memory came back of lying on its silvery sun-warmed planks, the smell of lake water in her nostrils, the tiny peaceful sound as it slapped gently against the pales.

As she walked, gradually sounds impinged, birdsong, lambs' cries from the fell high above, a tractor working somewhere down toward the village. And a nearer engine, coming along behind her. She stepped up onto the bank to let the vehicle pass. It was the pickup from Edal Bank. She lifted a hand to acknowledge the raised hand of the driver but didn't look at him, not ready for encounters yet. But you're going to shop in the village, you fool, you're going to have to speak to someone.

"It was so sad about your auntie, and going so soon after your uncle too. One week she seemed just the same as ever, the next—well, as I said to Garth—"

Garth! Was that surly bruiser Mr. Jackson really called Garth? But Sally knew the thought was cloaking another less comfortable one, that she had not made the time to come and see Aunt Ursula before she died.

". . . and how is Miss Buchanan these days? It's a while since we've seen her but of course she's a busy person with the hotel to look after and it is quite a drive down here."

It was always a surprise to hear Grianan called a hotel. It was more like a house where Aunt Janey allowed chosen friends to stay, gave them a rough time if they didn't behave and then made them pay for the privilege.

"You'll see some changes here," Ann Jackson was saying.

"I certainly do. The village seems to be double its previous size."

"Oh, there's folk coming in from all over. Retired couples mostly, though there's a few young ones. You'll see we've got a new school."

She sounded quite proud of it. Sally thought the sprawl of ugly one-story buildings surrounded by asphalt a poor exchange for the dignified stone school-house with its grassy playground by the river surrounded by thick hawthorn hedges. It was now a craft gallery.

"And you're staying with Miss Buchanan for the summer, she tells me," Ann Jackson ran on. "That'll be grand for you both."

Be bloody hard work, more like, Sally inwardly retorted, but even that prospect held a certain comfort. Janey's letter asking her to help, an unprecedented request, had jolted her at last out of the futile existence she had found herself in after Julian—but thoughts of him had made yesterday a harried nightmare. She wouldn't think about all that today.

Changes indeed. There were several cars in the car-park at the lake foot, and as she started along the track she saw groups of walkers ahead of her, the crude colors of their weatherproof clothing intrusive against the light, spring colors of the broad-leaved trees along this part of the shore and the darker mass of plantations.

Where were these purposeful groups heading? Surely they didn't intend to use the path behind the cottage to reach the fell? But they passed the drive and kept on along the lane, which as Sally recalled petered out in mud and bramble thickets after a quarter of a mile. She had enjoyed "exploring" around the shore as a child, though probably she hadn't gone as far as she imagined, but once she had grown too big to duck under the branches of the tight-packed conifers it hadn't been much fun. Had a path been opened right around the lake now? She felt outraged at the idea, then laughed at herself. She hardly qualified as an inhabitant.

She scraped together a lazy lunch, prowled around looking for something to read, though she couldn't recall ever seeing Aunt Ursula with a book in her hands and Teddy had never got beyond Hammond Innes, then mildly guilty because it would never have been allowed in the afternoon in the past, she switched on the television. Golf, cartoons, swimming with tur-tles or a mad crackling blur. She made do with the turtles, curled up in a rocking chair filled with hard little cushions piped in different colors. For all the entertainment the turtles provided she might as well have chosen the blur.

Then with an exclamation of disgust she leaped up, leaving the chair rocking madly to and fro. Thoughts

of Aunt Janey were close today, Grianan looming.
This was supposed to be a transition period, wasn't
it? A training period, even! What was the word? Fa-
miliarization. Positive thinking, woman. She'd follow
those walkers and see what had happened to this quiet
place where no one came.

Chapter 2

A lot of work had been done along the track north of the cottage, trees and bushes trimmed back, a ditch dug, stone bottoming laid in the muddy patches. Sally could see that vehicles came along here. A view had been opened up to High Rigg. After half a mile a new footpath branched off, logs set across it to make steps, a split-log railing curving above the drop. A signpost read "Harter Fell and Haweswater Reservoir."

Steps, handrails, signposts—no wonder the place was crawling with people, Sally thought angrily, then realized there wasn't a soul in sight. How many years since she had been here, and she expected not an inch to have changed. At least this path meant no one would try to reach the fell via the cottage.

She kept to the lower track, trying to visualize it as it had been, soon coming to the point where a small beck came down, now crossed by a wooden bridge. This was the place where the path had died and Sally had been in her own private territory. A favorite route had been to climb the narrow ghyll to a tiny waterfall. Surely that wouldn't have changed—but could she get up to it still? With an impulse to recapture some fragment of a past long jettisoned she turned off among the bushes, thinly clad with early foliage, and began to thread her way up the bank. Hidden, secret, sparkling in sunlight filtered through leaves, the fall splashed down into its rocky cup. The fallen branch that used to form a rudimentary bridge had long ago rotted away. Determined to reach the same boulder from which she used to sit and watch the fall safe from grown-up eyes, Sally saw that above her head a solid-looking branch would let her swing across. She eyed the rush of water with new respect. Well, who was there to care if she fell in, got soaked or broke her neck? She took the few steps back that the crowding bushes would allow, and jumped for the branch, letting go at the top of the swing and arching out toward a flat stone. She barely made it, and there was a scrambling moment before she got her weight forward and her fingers around a rock. As she clutched it, getting her breath back and giggling, a voice above her commented mildly, "Most people find it easier to use the bridge I've built for them."

Sally's feet slipped and floundered among the loose stones as she straightened and, still clinging to her anchoring rock with one hand, freed the other to push back her heavy hair. A few feet away, camouflaged against the trees in a rust-brown sweater and worn cords faded to a yellowish olive-green, regarding her with amusement, stood the man she had seen last night outside the old farmhouse.

Laughter seized her. A responsible, competent, well-heeled career woman of thirty-one swinging from the trees. "Recapturing my childhood," she explained, looking for a way up the bank. "Never a good idea."

He came forward and, smiling, reached down to pull her up. "Can be fun though. And if this was a childhood haunt of yours then you must be Ursula's niece."

How had he worked that out? Aunt Janey, of course. "Sally Mayn—" But suddenly, in this place, in transition between two phases of her life, Sally came to a decision she had been circling around for weeks. It was time to leave behind her English surname, her father's name. "Sally Buchanan," she said firmly.

"Mike Danaher." If he had noticed the amendment he gave no sign. "I live in the house along the lane."

"I saw you there as I passed yesterday evening. Doing something to the pickup."

"Distributor cap." He was still looking at her with enjoyment, as though welcoming the entertainment she provided on an uneventful afternoon. "And I passed you in the lane this morning."

"Oh, yes, of course." Had he noticed that she had not looked at him, evading contact?

"You'll see some changes here if you haven't been back for a while," he went on easily.

"Don't tell me you're responsible for them?" she demanded, suddenly making the probable connection.

"One or two. Though you can't say I've done much tampering up here," he observed, looking around at the sequestered little place.

"So what were you doing up here?" she asked.

"I was working just below. Hearing some strange creature blundering about in the bushes I thought I'd better investigate."

"Elephant or bear, I suppose."

"I didn't expect something in the simian line, certainly."

They laughed and the thought flicked across Sally's mind that it was the laughter of friends. Mike Danaher's lean face, made longer by the fact that his dark-red springy hair was already receding above the temples, his natural high color deepened by the all-year-round tan of the outdoor man, his hazel eyes alive with amusement, already seemed strangely familiar.

"A simian lunatic," said Sally resignedly, trying to remember what she had yelled as she leapt.

"I wouldn't have missed it," he assured her, his grin widening.

The Danahers had owned the house at the lake foot for years, Sally recalled, and quite a lot of ground with it. "Are you living here all the time now?" she asked. "I always remember the house being empty."

"We came back after the children were born. Michael's ten now."

That long since I've been here, she thought, with a pang of renewed guilt. "And do you farm here? Do you own all this? I don't remember."

"Most of the land up here belongs to the North West Water Authority. Used to be the Manchester Corporation. The lake was one of their reservoirs back in the 1880s. But you'll know all about that."

Sally shook her head. "I don't think I know much about anything, or I've forgotten if I ever did."

"Several of the small lakes in this area were part of their scheme. Then when they made the big new reservoirs like Thirlmere they sold off some of their ground up here. My grandfather came over from Ireland in the twenties—tired of all the aftermath of the Black and Tan war—and bought the farmhouse and some land at the southern end of the lake and cleared the trees. He farmed it, but it was too small to be economical."

"Were there trees right around the lake at one time?"

"Corporation policy. Dense planting right to the water's edge helped to prevent evaporation and increased water extraction. You still see it elsewhere, and it's currently the subject of a major conservation battle."

"So why do you work on their footpaths?"

They had fallen, oblivious now of their surroundings, into this conversation which absorbed them just as anything they had started to talk about would equally have absorbed them, settling without discussion on the big, flat-topped rock where Sally always used to sit.

"These days they're very keen on opening up the land to walkers and so on," Mike went on. "And they've moved away from the old style of solid blocks of conifers and made rules about planting broadleaved trees, creating access and what they are pleased to call 'amenity developments.' I wanted a means to live here full-time. I was brought up in Kendal after my father gave up farming and leased the land, but I'd always wanted to come back here one day. At the time when my father died I didn't have the knowledge or the interest to try to start up the farm again. I'd trained as a civil engineer and done a pretty mixed lot of jobs in different parts of the world. So now I'm a sort of warden, pottering around clearing ditches and building bridges and counting birds for people like the RSPB—and keeping an eye on vandals who don't keep to the paths."

Sally turned her head to smile at him, a smile of pure pleasure. Every separate element of this moment was good. The shining ribbon of water spilling down the rock face with the white churn of foam at its feet, the skittery sunlight that came and went through the whippy branches of indigenous birch and hazel along the beck, the absolute sense of peaceful seclusion and the strange and equally strong sense that time had ceased to matter, that this moment could be held and savored—and that for this man beside her, unknown half an hour ago, the feeling was exactly the same. His full attention was turned to her, those clear hazel eyes which were so striking and alive were very intent.

She made a serious effort to keep the conversation on a normal, unexceptionable, social level. "So you knew Aunt Ursula and Uncle Teddy?"

"Not terribly well." A small reserve there? "I saw more of your aunt after your uncle died. I used to look in to make sure she was all right."

"That was good of you." Sally paused. "I never came to see her. When she was alone. When she was ill." She had not voiced that guilt before.

"You were living in the South?" It was a question; he wasn't offering her an excuse.

"In Reading." How could she put all she would have liked to tell him into a few bald sentences? Then suddenly it all seemed too remote, too painful and petty and exhausted for this place and this moment.

"And you're going up to see Janey?" He had this easy way of carrying her forward over difficult moments. And his familiar use of her aunts' Christian names was agreeable and somehow comforting.

"Yes. I'm going to Grianan." She caught the quick turn of his head and knew that in spite of all the years of absence, the selfish absorption in the life she had created for herself, she was still unable to say that name without love. "Just for the summer," she added, as though needing to make her independence clear.

"That was Ursula's home—and your mother's?"

"Yes, my mother was the youngest sister. Rose. She married a doctor."

Her tone was so dismissive that only as she went on did Mike realize this was not some earlier marriage, as he had assumed, but that she was referring to her own father. "He's a consultant hematologist now, very successful and very busy, still teaching as well as looking after his private patients and doing research. There are a lot of new treatments being developed these days for coagulant disorders . . ." She recited this with a terse bitterness she could not suppress. Mike made a small movement as though he wanted to protest, then checked it.

Sally took a steadying breath. "Sorry. I don't talk about him usually."

"And you don't use his name."

So he hadn't missed that. "As of today. As of just now, actually. I'd always wanted to be a Buchanan." What would Janey think? Would it please her or would it jar on her peculiar sense of absolute honesty?

"Oh, God, not another rabid Scot."

"Like who?"

"Never mind. Go on about your family."

"Well, my mother decided she'd had enough of blood when I was eight and left." Again Mike looked as if he would like to soften the harsh offhandedness of her words, but he didn't interrupt. "My father established her very definitely in my mind as the one at fault, abandoning us for no reason and so on. I adored him at that stage and never saw enough of him so I was thrilled to get so much attention from him all of a sudden. In theory I was given the choice of who I wanted to live with and I chose to stay with him. I can't tell you how callous I was to my mother." She dropped her head into her hands for a moment, closing her eyes against the uncomfortable memory. "Then I discovered—only it took me a long time to realize it—that I had just been a weapon for my father to wound her with. Afterwards I was the prize when the battle was won. He took no notice of me at all after that." She heard her voice thin to bleakness and lightened it with an effort, continuing rapidly, "Oh, there was the usual setup—housekeepers, boarding school. Privileged in the general scale of things."

"Did you keep in touch with your mother?"

Had he divined in some way that this was the part that mattered?

"Not very successfully," she told him, trying hard to be matter-of-fact, keeping her eyes on the fluid patterns of the sunlit water. "She went off to Australia and married a mechanic. He has his own garage now in a town called Orford, a tiny place outside Goulburn in New South Wales. She's now called Rouse. Rouse Brumby, that is."

Mike laughed, but his eyes watched her attentively. "Go on," he said.

Sally found that suddenly she wanted to put it all into words, the long-ago disillusionment which she had grown so used to burying, and that here, now, she could attempt it. For this unknown man seated beside her in the secluded windless corner, where she felt quite separate from the train of everyday events and carried back to childhood simplicity, would listen, would hear what she was saying.

"Oh, it was my own fault, I suppose. I had this dream all the time I was growing up of one day going out to Australia to find her—big reconciliation scene. When I finally went, taking a year out before university, it was a complete non-event. To start with, there were four little Brumbys. Not so little either, the eldest was ten. They were a big, noisy, close-knit mob, enjoying life, very laid back. I was critical, bored and intolerant. I couldn't accept that my mother really wanted to be part of it. I made the mistake of talking to her as though we two knew better and the rest of the family were just an ignorant crowd of yobbos. God, I can't believe how crass I was." She shook her head, her mouth tight, carried back even after all this time to that misery of separateness and arrogance and baffled need.

"How long were you there?"

"Three months. I hated every moment of it. I know I was too ready to find fault but it was a pretty one-horse place. I never found anyone I could talk to. I kept hoping that there'd be some point of contact with my mother but in the end I came to the obvious conclusion—she didn't actually like me and couldn't wait for me to take myself off again."

"You would remind her too much of your father."

"I'm sure that was part of it." There seemed no strangeness in him making such an observation.

"Do you still live with him?" Mike asked.

"I hardly ever see him now. Even when I was growing up I spent as little time at home as I could, once I'd accepted that his interest was centered elsewhere. I went mainly to Grianan—I was mad about the place in those days. Sometimes I came here after Teddy had retired and he and Aunt Ursula were living here all the time, but Grianan was my great love."

"Has the family owned it for long?"

"It was built by my great-grandfather. Janey inherited it because she was the eldest and unmarried and because she had looked after my grandfather when he became crippled with arthritis."

"And now she runs it as a hotel?"

"After a fashion." The term always seemed incongruous when applied to Grianan and Sally grinned fleetingly to think of Janey's highly individual style of doing things. "I'm going to help her for the season." Beyond that she could not look, and perhaps her tone said so for Mike asked no more questions.

They sat and talked, comparing childhood visits here, finding that much ground each had thought private had in fact been shared. They talked about their travels. Mike had been in Australia too, for a couple of years, and they had both stopped off in Malaysia on the way home, following the same track down the eastern side of the peninsula. Sally, doing sums, decided that he must be older than he looked, probably in his early forties.

As they talked the sun moved around till the high screen of Sitkas at their backs left them in chilly shade. Mike had made no reference to time, work or having to get back, and Sally had been content to leave that to him. Now he said, "Come on, you're shivering," and rose to his feet, half offering a hand to pull her up. She smiled her thanks but didn't take it. She sensed that he didn't want to take a step toward physical contact and she felt the same. That was something outside the pleasure they had so astonishingly found of minds instantly in tune. But he hates this extraordinary little interlude being over as much as I do, she thought with certainty as in silence she followed him down the slope, ducking under the bushes, catching the springy branches he held back for her, jumping the drainage channel onto the track where the pick-up was waiting.

"Like a lift home?" Mike offered formally.

Sally hesitated. She wanted, most simply, to go on being with him. But sitting beside him in the pickup, heading toward his home, perhaps meeting his children in the lane . . . It wouldn't really matter and yet, that was his life. This meeting, the amazing simplicity of being with him and talking to him, for how many hours, had been perfect in itself.

"No, I'll walk back, thanks."

He nodded, his eyes on hers. She had the feeling he had read her thoughts and accepted them exactly as they were.

He turned to the van. It was over. To her surprise Sally found that, beneath the obvious surface regret, she didn't mind. It had been good. She counted herself lucky to have shared those quiet hours with him.

His hand on the open door of the van, Mike turned and said, "I'm going out after foxes this evening. Would you like to come?"

The moment scored itself into Sally's brain. She was aware of everything around her, the gloom of the track finely lanced by pencils of light from the lake where the evening sun spread gold across the calm water, the soft brown of the fallen needles under the trees, the piney smell of dank trapped air among the branches, the black sodden pile of twigs and debris Mike had been clearing from the ditch, the mud drying on the handles of the tools in the back of the pickup. She was conscious of the beat of her heart. Mike was not going to allow this good thing they had found to vanish.

She hadn't answered but he said, "I'll come by at about half eight."

She walked home in a mood of lightness and simplicity. No questions presented themselves. She would just let things be. Which didn't prevent her from singing in the shower, or from putting on her favorite sea-green shirt which matched her eyes.

She had just begun to cook supper when she heard the creak of the gate. So long as that wasn't Ann Jackson—or Garth even, come to do some work in the garden which he was supposed to look after.

Mike stood grinning on the step, the complete hard man in combat jacket and boots, rifle slung over his shoulder. It was less than an hour since they had parted.

"Thought I'd watch you eat your supper."

Laughter, delight, a feeling of certainty which reason couldn't shake, rose in Sally giddily. "You idiot. Come in."

"I knew you'd be pleased," he said complacently, propping his gun beside the corner cupboard and looking around him. "Nothing much has changed in here, I see."

"Isn't it a nightmare?" But in this mood of carefree happiness the words were tolerant, benevolent even. "And perhaps you can tell me what this thing is supposed to be? I'm totally baffled by it. Is it a dolls' wardrobe? But it opens at the top." It was about two feet high and nine inches wide and had a little barred window with a checked curtain.

"God, you're ignorant. Don't you know a baguette box when you see one?"

"*A baguette box?*"

"Ursula was very proud of that. It was one of Teddy's last presents to her. The fact that she couldn't get baguettes nearer than Kendal didn't worry her at all."

"She really did go over the top. Look at this Jemima Puddle-Duck kitchen timer."

"Dear old Ursula, how she loved all this kitsch. I've always thought it was good of Janey not to sweep it all away."

Probably didn't have time, Sally thought, but suppressed the cynicism. "Would you like some supper? You can't have had much time to eat. I was just about to make an omelette."

"Thanks, but I've had something."

"Then would you like coffee, or a drink?"

"A beer?"

"Now that I didn't bring."

"Thoughtless. What are you drinking? Don't tell me, dry white wine."

"Precisely."

"Coffee then, thanks. Is that all you're proposing to eat?"

Oh, man, do you think I can concentrate on food?

"Is shooting foxes part of your conservation role?" Sally enquired, as they sat for the first time at Ursula's tricky table where unwary thighs tended to jam painfully under pine scrolls and twirls.

"Don't give me a hard time. It's a question of choosing which predators you want to encourage. Or balancing the numbers of predators so that they all get their share. If the foxes take all the food there'll be nothing left for the kestrels or peregrines. And keeping the numbers down stops the farmers muttering about losing lambs. It's part of the job for me. Does the idea bother you?"

"No, I was brought up on all that in Glen Ellig."

Memory of going out after foxes with Jed. Not the moment to think about that.

The Edalmere foxes were safe enough that night. Though Mike led the way to a bank where he knew a vixen had cubs and they dutifully lay waiting in silence for signs of activity, Sally thought that if Mike's mind was as far as hers from the job in hand his reactions would be too slow for even the most unwary target to be in danger.

When the light had finally gone under the trees they made a move, going down to sit in the dusk on one of the cleared rocky points above the lake, with only the most peripheral awareness of the regular quiet sound of ripples lipping stone, the white scuttering lines across the lead-colored water as a pair of duck came in to land, or an owl calling from the steep woods.

They talked compulsively, luxuriously. Sally had wondered, walking home earlier, whether they would ever be able to recapture the magical ease of the afternoon, but it had not deserted them. Once or twice she found herself wanting to move so that her shoulder was against Mike's; a simple instinct, part of the deep closeness of their mood. But each time she checked the impulse. It wasn't part of this. She wanted to change nothing, initiate nothing.

It was hours before they stirred and headed slowly back along the lane. They came to a halt at the bottom of the cottage drive.

"Smell that hawthorn," Mike said. Letting the heady scent wash over her Sally knew she would never be free of the associations of this moment.

Apart from pulling her up from the beck's edge this afternoon Mike hadn't touched her yet. She didn't know if he would touch her now and found that she was ready to accept whatever choice he made. She wanted everything about this to be just as he wanted it. None of the usual questions which are part of any new encounter, especially one charged with such powerful mutual attraction as this one, seemed to exist. There was no weighing of possibilities, no looking ahead, only acceptance and a great contentment.

"I'd better walk you to your door."

A few more moments together in the cool early darkness, standing by the little iron gate—and suddenly the conventions came pushing in. There was no reason to assume that Mike was in the same dreamy non-seeking state that she was, Sally reminded herself, oddly flurried.

"I shouldn't really ask you in for coffee, should I?" she said, intending the words to be light and matter-of-fact but merely sounding awkward. "Your home territory." She had wanted him to know that she respected it but was afraid she had struck a clumsy and false note.

But Mike understood. "Thanks for that," he said and bent his head to give her two or three swift little kisses down cheek and jaw. The minutest pause, a similar light kiss on her lips, and he had turned, going down the slope with his rapid long-legged stride, leaving Sally—mature, experienced, almost married—as vividly conscious of the touch of his lips as if no one had ever kissed her in her life before. The tingle of it spread through her veins.

Absurd, absurd, she thought giddily, running up the short path. But unquestionably delicious and glorious.

Chapter 3

A high fluting sound penetrated Sally's uneasy dawn sleep. Some wretched bird. She had had trouble getting to sleep at all and wasn't prepared to be dragged awake now. White light glared through the more-or-less-unlined curtains. The insistent sound came again. Whistling. In one leap she was out of bed, yanking aside the curtain. Standing against the trees across the roughly mown grass, gun slung on shoulder, grinning at her cheerfully, was Mike.

There was a brief fierce tussle with the sticking window. "What *do* you think you're doing, you madman?"

"Get the kettle on, woman, stop wasting time."

"Whatever time is it, anyway?"

But he was gone, heading around to the door.

Jesus, Sally swore to herself, banging a brush at her rough hair, grabbing up a frilly dressing gown she'd only packed because it was so light. Trousseau gear, she remembered, and for the first time there was no pain in the reminder.

"Where's the coffee then?" Mike demanded, coming in larger than life, bringing with him a waft of crisp dawn air and a male smell of hill clothes and gun oil which was headily evocative to Sally. Below the immediate pleasure of seeing him she felt the stir of a new eagerness for the life she was returning to. With an effort she made herself turn away to fill the kettle and not stand beaming at him like an idiot.

"Are you going out after that vixen again?"

"Been up there already. No sign of her."

"Good."

He laughed. "Yes, I can't say I'm in killing mode myself this morning. I only went out because I was having trouble sleeping. The cat was a bit startled to meet me as he was coming in." He sounded very light-hearted.

"I'm not surprised."

In the fussy kitchen they sat leaning forward across the table, drinking each other in with eyes, words and nerve ends. Once when Sally got up to give him more coffee Mike put his arm around her, comfortably, naturally, not drawing her toward him. That feels so normal, she thought, hooking her fingers into the shoulder strap of his jacket and leaning lightly back against his arm for a few moments as they talked. In the instant that her muscles began to take her weight again she felt his arm start to withdraw as though their brains were one. The need for touch had been acknowledged, but they had agreed they were not yet committed to it. Perhaps would not be. Sally was almost sure Mike had made his decision on that.

Without pause, it seemed, Ursula's maddening cuckoo burst from his little door and yelled at them. "He might end up sorry I brought my gun," Mike said once. It was his only reference to time. When he got up to go Sally made no protest or comment. But when he stood below her on the steps to say goodbye, their faces level, she could feel hers pinching. She felt small and cold.

"I'll come this evening," he said. The warmth of the relief which swept her shook her. It was a long time since physical reactions had been so emphatic.

In memory the day was a blur of peace and brightness, though in reality the sun hardly appeared and an east wind had brought a marked drop in temperature. Sally took her breakfast through to the sitting room where the sun was warm at the big window. Then with a new urge for space and simplicity, which she knew went a lot deeper than improving the view, she left her toast half finished and, dragging up a chair, began to strip away the swathing loops of net. It was a satisfying exercise. Knowing there was no one to care—Janey would definitely approve—she carried on around the house, freeing every window from its shroud. Then, enjoying the new feeling of space and light, she made fresh coffee and went back to the sitting room window.

The marvelous view from it tempted her to drive down to Windermere, associated vaguely in her mind with expeditions and treats. She didn't want to explore around the lake where Mike might be working. If she had not been in such an addled state she would have known perfectly well what she would find in the little town, plastered with signs and choked with visitors.

In her mood of large goodwill, however, she was prepared to accept it all, ambling and shopping with a mindless indifference to the commercialism and the crowds, and she drove home contentedly with the car filled with the smell of new bread (not baguettes), planning to have lunch and then catch up on some sleep.

She had just tipped her shopping out on to the

kitchen table when she heard the gate screech. Her heart leapt into her throat. It can't be, you fool.

The door opened and Mike's head came around it. "That looks promising. I was about to make myself a sandwich when it occurred to me I might do better here."

Where was his wife? Sally didn't ask. The children presumably were at school. "What a chancer. Still, it'll stretch to two, I suppose."

She carried the tray into the sitting room. His reaction didn't disappoint her. "You've let in the light. What a difference. Poor old Ursula and her frills."

"I went around the whole house."

"Good for you. I could never work out who she thought could see in. This house can't be overlooked from anywhere."

"Not overrun with neighbors, certainly. Apart from you, nothing nearer than those new bungalows at the foot of the lake. Wasn't that ground part of the farm?"

"It was. I sold the plots a couple of years ago. Needed some cash. I'll probably have to sell more before long." Thoughts there that she had no part in, and Mike's face was suddenly grim.

"And who lives there?"

"One young family, but the rest are elderly couples. A lot of people who come to the Lakes for holidays all their lives dream of spending their last years in some remote spot like this. Most of them move to the nearest town after the first winter."

He didn't stay long—he said he had to meet someone from the National Trust that afternoon—but as he left he told her, "Nine o'clock." Sally felt so high on the promise of those brief words that she knew sleep would be impossible. She threw the dishes into the sink and took off up the path to the fell.

She was less fit than she'd thought, in spite of regular workouts in the Sieber gym, and her thighs were aching and her knees trembling when she reached the ridge. But it was worth it. She had been in the South too long, she thought, gazing with delight at the high ramparts of Helvellyn away beyond the pass, though the jumble of peaks to the west and southwest were lost in cloud today. And soon she'd be in Glen Ellig. Much as she enjoyed this scene, and keener though that enjoyment undoubtedly was because of the feelings Mike had unexpectedly aroused, the glen was the landscape that truly moved her.

She had barely got back to the cottage and was running water to wash up, missing the sound of the gate, when a rap at the door made her heartbeat accelerate. It couldn't possibly be Mike this time—could it?

A tall, white-haired female stood there, tubular in baggy tweed skirt with a bulge at each knee and a dated quilted jacket, a spaniel crushed subserviently against her woolly calves.

"Elsa Callander," she announced in those ringing tones which imply that no further introduction can be needed. "Heard in the village you were here. Old friend of Teddy and Ursula's." She cracked her stick against the spaniel's ribs in the sort of habitual gesture with which one—one like her—swipes at nettles. The spaniel shrank in on itself, since it could press no closer to heel.

"How do you do? Won't you come in?" Sally asked, wondering as she spoke what sort of inexorable conditioning makes us incapable of saying, "I don't care who you are, go away."

Elsa Callander was not a kitchen table sort of visitor. In the sitting room she lowered herself without enthusiasm into one of the rocking chairs which flanked the fireplace. The dog crept behind it, evidently thinking poorly of the cover it afforded, and gazed at Sally with hopeless eyes.

Sally went back to the kitchen to scrounge around crossly for something to offer by way of afternoon tea, found a jar of plum jam and lifted off half an inch of grey-green mould with its wax seal, realized she was going to have to sacrifice her breakfast croissants and even found herself looking for cups and saucers. She rallied, swearing, to slap mugs on the tray.

They conversed: Teddy and Ursula, Teddy's career in the diplomatic service, Ursula's illness. "Of course she was so thankful to have me on hand for company. Someone she could *talk* to, you know. It makes all the difference, doesn't it? There are so few people of our sort here."

Sally felt a fierce resistance to the prospect of her referring to the Danahers. To Mike's wife. It was vital to learn nothing. They passed safely on to Aunt Janey.

"Naturally, one can't blame her for wanting to do absolutely *nothing* when she's here. Hotel life must be so demanding." Good for Aunt Janey.

"And I gather you have some frightfully high-powered job. I do admire all you girls so much. Of course nowadays the opportunities are there, aren't they? It was so different in my day. And I do understand that you must have found it very difficult to get away . . ." To visit your aunt, ill and suffering, widowed and alone.

"Of course my mother knew the Buchanans as a girl." Of course. "Such a fascinating family."

Oh, Mike, come back and talk to me. Tell me about

the hydro electric scheme you worked on in Uruguay and the road you built in the Sierra de Gredos—even talk to me about Australia and I'll forget my hang-ups about the place.

The plum jam tasted fusty. Sally was glad.

"So sad this delightful little house should lie empty. All the Beatrix Potter memorabilia, an amazing collection, it must be quite valuable." She clearly hated it. "Our dining circle gets ever smaller, alas. Do come and see us, won't you, while you're here? The second bungalow from this end." But at least these sounded like departing noises. "Now, how long will you be staying?"

Christ, she's getting her diary out, Sally realized with horror. The thought of missing Mike if he found time to come made her ruthless. "I'm really not sure but I'm afraid I'm here to escape rather." Automatically wrapping it up in her guest's language. "Things have been rather difficult lately"—a pretty piece of understatement—"and I was just planning to be thoroughly lazy. It's very kind of you but I'm sure you'll understand . . ."

Oh, you silly old bat, go, go. How dare you come here bursting in uninvited like this? Which really meant, How dare you knock at the door and not be Mike?

Sally didn't believe she would sleep with so many thoughts milling around in her head, but as soon as she hunched the duvet around her shoulders she was away, dreamlessly oblivious for three hours and waking when the alarm went off with the instant knowledge that something marvelous was about to happen. How long was it since she had woken feeling like that?

She was pottering about doing her makeup, not impressed by the effect the wind this afternoon and then bed had had on her unquellable hair, when a tiny sound penetrated her happy anticipation. A sound she didn't want to recognize or accept. She turned, brush in hand, to stare at the window, every atom of her rebelling at the sight of the first needle-fine streaks. But rain had been threatening all day; she had just been too besotted to relate it to herself and Mike.

He wouldn't come. He couldn't come. No one went out to shoot foxes in the rain. How could such an improbable excuse be offered or accepted? And if he didn't come tonight she was irrationally convinced that she would never see him again—which she at once recognized as a fair indication of her state of mind since he had already appeared twice today without warning. The branch of an unpruned japonica tapped the pane against a sky much darker than it had been this time yesterday evening. Yesterday, when she had first met Mike. That couldn't be only yesterday.

She sat on listlessly at the kitchen table after a meager and abstracted supper, then, angry with herself for listening for the sound of the gate, went through to the sitting room. He wouldn't come. But she didn't turn on the television.

It was nearly ten when he came and this time she couldn't resist asking, "But what are you meant to be doing?"

"Oh, I come and go, you know. It's a pretty flexible job." But he didn't enlarge on it, and Sally asked no more.

For the first time the ease between them was not complete. Perhaps it was because that doubt still hung between them, perhaps because they had moved to the sitting room where comfort came second to Ursula's mania for objects, or perhaps because questions were beginning to nudge closer. It was Sally who asked, "Would you hate walking in the rain?"

"I could stand it," was all Mike said, but she sensed his relief as they went out into the soft air, rich with garden scents against the ever-present background of spruce and pine. The thin rain barely reached them as they went in silence along the track, their eyes adjusting to the darkness, using the paler gap of sky between the trees to guide them.

Then Mike stopped and with one firm sweep of his arm drew Sally against him, and she responded as readily as a dancer, as though at that exact moment her body too had shared the same need. They stood close and still, their bodies fitting against each other with an aptness that seemed utterly familiar; stood for long, silent moments of intense awareness and strange peace.

What seemed extraordinary to Sally, when she looked back on it, was the absence of doubt or questioning. She accepted the embrace for itself, asking for nothing more, remembering afterward the spider-light fingers of the rain on her cheek and her skin feeling alive to it, the infinitesimal sound of the rain and the faint stir of the wind in the branches above them, the mingled scents of the spring night and her intense awareness of Mike's arms, the lean hard-muscled length of his body against hers, his cheek on her hair.

He didn't kiss her, simply held her for unmeasured moments. Then, by a decision transmitted from one to the other, but coming from whom neither of them could have said, they moved on—but this time Mike's arm stayed around her.

When they reached the cottage again Sally knew he

would come in; it didn't occur to her to wonder about it. They went through to the sitting room, taking a bottle of wine and a couple of cans of beer.

"Good, I'd hoped you'd remember those," Mike said, a remark Sally thought would repay examination later.

When they lit the mock-coal fire the room seemed suddenly normal, welcoming, theirs. And when Sally was about to sit down Mike said, "Not near enough," and reaching a long arm pulled her chair close to his.

"So what was wrong with Reading?"

The question cut across their easy inconsequential talk and Sally felt her head jerk around and knew she had given herself away.

"We've talked about big chunks of our lives but that's one that's been left out."

"Reading, well, how shall I put it—a settled, conventional, achieving existence with excellent prospects which came to pieces in my hands." She did her best to speak lightly but heard the effort in her voice, as though she was having trouble with her breathing. She had not talked of this to anyone.

"Do you want to tell me?"

"Oh, nothing spectacular, you know. The best-laid plans . . ." She could not go on.

Mike's hand, long and brown, with darker freckles across the back, its palm leathery smooth with manual work, took hers, folded it in his. "Your job was there?"

"Yes, with Sieber Research, just outside Reading. The place is the window-dressing part of the company, where all the big meetings and conferences are held, beautifully kept grounds, all that stuff. Oh, God, you don't want to hear this." She broke off, feeling help-

lessly bogged down by these details which brought her
no nearer to what would be so painfully hard to
explain.

"Just take your time. I want to hear. How long were
you there?"

"Six years. I went in as a junior administrative officer—did business studies at university, nothing intellectual—then a couple of years ago I landed the senior
admin. post."

"You were young for that."

"I know. It was a lucky break, just a combination of
circumstances. Though the job isn't all that challenging
once you've been around the loop a couple of times.
Glorified PA, really."

"Only a lot better paid."

"Indeed." Perhaps it was easier after all to keep to
the mundane for a while. "It was like belonging to a
big club. You know what these huge firms are like."
Mike didn't argue. "Everything's laid on—swimming
pool, squash, badminton, tennis, gym. Very good food,
and nowhere else near enough to go for lunch anyway.
It all tended to get a bit incestuous, I suppose. You
could have an entire social life without ever moving
outside the Sieber net."

Mike said nothing, stretching out his long legs to
the fire, apparently prepared to listen to incoherent
trivia all night if necessary.

"I met someone. Well, I'd known him vaguely for
some time, but suddenly he was around more." She
checked. This was like having a stick in your hand and
preparing to ram it into a wasps' nest with nowhere
to run to.

"He worked there too?"

Grasp that. "Yes, he was a research chemist, one

of a very élite crew. I didn't come across him much in my job in the normal way of things. Then he was involved in a major presentation I was doing; we had to work together quite a lot . . ." Her voice tailed away. This was so far from what she wanted to say, what she needed Mike to know.

"What happened, Sally?" His keen narrow face looked compassionate, his striking, clear hazel eyes intent and perceptive. "What went wrong?"

"He was divorced." She spoke rapidly now. "That all happened three years ago—well in the past. We started going out together about a year ago, more now. It all seemed so good, lots in common, lots of things we liked doing together. We got engaged last summer. I'd been about to buy a house though I hadn't started looking, and we decided I should go ahead with that and we'd live there. Julian's wife was still living in their old house and he kept saying she'd be moving out soon and they'd sell and then his capital would be free and he would pay off my mortgage. We were going to be married in February, then somehow—I can't describe it—the glow seemed to fade. Julian was suddenly busier, had less time to spend with me. He was abroad for a while and when he came back and I was absolutely longing to see him it—I don't know—it just fell flat. There was nothing more tangible to it than that."

Mike pulled her chair hard up against his and put an arm around her shoulders. Sally felt reassurance and comfort flow into her. "The thing was," she said baldly, "he'd started seeing his wife again. He'd had to go and look at some problem with the house—and they'd just—well, he'd gone on going to see her—and then he—"

"Decided he wanted to go back to her."

Sally nodded dumbly, unaware that she was clutching his hand tightly.

"You poor girl."

"The worst part was," she said, having difficulty with her voice again, but determined to get this into the open at last, "he was so good about it. So conscientious. He actually decided for a while that he should stay with me and go through with our marriage. He even waited to tell me, when it was perfectly clear that he couldn't live without Mandy, until after Christmas, so that he wouldn't spoil the holiday for me. Can you imagine anything more ludicrous? How decent can you get?"

"He must have been a bit out of touch with reality." A note of anger in Mike's voice was welcome balm.

"Oh, completely. He was a well-meaning dreamer. He genuinely considered sticking to me and trying to make things work. Only, when he finally saw that wasn't a good idea—presumably Mandy was able to help him there—I was the one who didn't stick to the rules of good behavior. I decided that for once I'd put up a fight and not be turned down. Only you see, Julian was an essentially honest person, and when I demanded to know why he was going back to Mandy and what was wrong with me, he told me. He preferred her in bed. There's not a great deal you can say to that."

"Oh, Sally." Mike's arm tightened around her.

"Well, that was it. Nothing to fight about. No one could have been more honorable or kind about breaking off an engagement. You couldn't fault him. In other words, he was still the nice guy I'd loved." Her voice wavered and she closed her eyes tightly. "Anyway, I decided it would all be too difficult staying on at Sieber and of course he couldn't leave. I thought I could go on living in the new house and find another job in the area. All my friends were there. But they weren't, really. They were all tied up with Sieber and basically I'd left the club. It all just fizzled out naturally. My fault as much as anyone's, because I wanted to be on my own. Another problem was, I didn't like the house. Julian liked everything to be ultra efficient. Technology was there to be put to use. My original idea had been to find a cottage that hadn't been too badly pulled about. So there I was in a very expensive steel and glass monstrosity, all alone with the engagement presents. What a pathetic tale."

"Come on," Mike said gently, and she gave a rueful nod, acknowledging that the note of cynical self-contempt hadn't been necessary. She lifted their linked hands and pressed her forehead against them, closing her eyes, letting the present seep back.

"You've sold the house?"

"It was much sought after," she assured him more lightly.

"And you're going back to Scotland to live?"

"I'm not sure that I'd have managed to haul myself out of that mess on my own initiative," she confessed. "I couldn't whip up the competitive edge you need to fight for jobs in today's market. But just when it was beginning to dawn on me that I was in trouble Aunt Janey wrote and asked if I'd consider helping her this summer. She's never needed help before—or never asked for it. It seemed the obvious answer; a summer at Grianan won't leave me much time to feel sorry for myself. After that—well, to be honest, I don't have the faintest idea."

"You don't have to yet, do you? Isn't that the point? You'll have the breathing space you need."

If life with Aunt Janey could ever be called a breathing space. And then there were the other questions she had been pushing away. How to tell Janey what had happened? She had never explained and her aunt had never asked. And would Janey think she had been blind and naïve about Julian, cowardly about throwing up her job so readily? Whenever she thought of Janey Sally found she was measuring herself once more against the standards Janey had set, and it felt as though she was returning to Grianan with remarkably little to show for the years she had been away.

Chapter 4

No whistling outside the window the next morning. Sally slept on and on, undisturbed. It had been very late when Mike left, with one swift comprehensive hug and not even the light little kisses of the previous evening.

Sally lay relaxed and peaceful, her mind ranging idly over their conversation last night. She felt as though the dark nightmare of helpless rejection which was all too familiar, the humiliation and acute sense of isolation, had stopped pressing in upon her and had become an everyday matter that could happen to anyone, had happened to her and could be dealt with.

Just talking to someone. That was all it had taken. Or just talking to Mike. Beneath the tough exterior, the fitness and energy, there was a capacity for understanding and sympathy which she trusted implicitly. How incredible really this meeting had been; the instant pleasure and confidence in each other, then the tacit shared instinct to let it be simple, unstated, perfect in its own right.

Would she see him today? But she knew she would. They had moved on a long way now.

She was still drifting around eating muesli and banana and warming up the last of the croissants when the sound of a hoarsely protesting engine grinding up the short drive shattered the silence and her mood of undemanding contentment. Going frowning to the door, Sally was in time to retrieve a note from under a stone on the doormat before the squat, glowering bulk of Garth Jackson came rolling toward the steps.

"The wife sent you this up. Makes it for the shops. And she said were you wanting anything?"

"No, everything's fine, thank you," Sally assured him with the best smile she could manage, burning to read her note, accepting from him a little tub with a red check cover which he jerked at her disdainfully.

"I'd best be doing that grass around the back then. Been waiting for a while, has that."

"Oh, no, please don't bother. I'm sure it's fine. I really wanted—" Peace and quiet, you moronic troglodyte.

Garth Jackson, a man unshakably convinced that no one else knew anything about anything, from mowing grass to running the National Health Service, had already gone to drag a Flymo out of his sagging rust-eaten van.

You pig-headed creature, Sally fumed, recognizing defeat. Going back into the house she looked at the offering in her hand. Rum butter. Could anything be more revolting? Without a second thought she pitched it into the bin. Outside the Flymo coughed and roared into life. The quality of life at the cottage had suddenly deteriorated. She pulled the note from her pocket.

"Come and build bridges." Did that have any particular meaning? Whether or not, she would go.

Leaving everything as it was, and not bothering to mention to a deafened and engrossed Garth that she was going, Sally fled down the drive with a lovely feeling of irresponsibility and escape. Even a long straggle of bored-looking schoolchildren in gumboots and cagoules trudging resentfully along the track could not deflate her. She overtook them, nodding to the glum girl in charge, who didn't nod back. No wonder the children looked extinguished with boredom.

Turning back when she had passed the path to the fell, Sally saw with relief that the group intended to go up it. Their leader was commanding and exhorting with raised arm. In an unleavened lump the children stood around her, their pale upturned faces unresponsive or frankly apprehensive. Sally wondered how far they would get.

Mike was not working below the waterfall where she had expected to find him, but she knew all she had to do was go on. This was where they had walked in the darkness and the rain, but by day it was new to her. Gone forever was the enchantment and mystery of this private place. The path was broad, safe. At intervals light had been let in and oaks and sycamores planted in the open spaces. Brightness was spreading over the water toward this eastern shore as the sun climbed. Sally felt eager and happy, light and buoyant. There was nothing she would have changed at that moment.

Mike was working on a footbridge a few yards up a beck which the track crossed by a shallow ford. Where the stream ran out into the lake there was a tiny triangular sandy beach, on either side of which the conifers had been felled, leaving grassy banks. Seeing Sally, Mike tossed down his mell and came to meet her, lively open pleasure on his face.

"So you finally woke up?" He scooped her into a

rough, one-armed hug, turning to walk with her, and it struck Sally that it was the sort of welcome a man would give to someone who was part of his life. That felt very good.

"I certainly did a bit more sleeping than the night before." They laughed. They would have laughed at anything.

Mike turned to face her, took her hands and held them wide as he studied her, smiling. "It's been a long, slow morning."

He was just finishing the rail of the bridge, and when that was done they turned their attention to the beck above it, its narrow, deep-cut course clogged in several places by mats of tangled branches, twigs and surface rubbish which winter spates had carried down. They worked away unhurriedly, talking or not as they felt like it. It was peaceful, wet, messy work with satisfying visible results, cool at first in the leafy shade, then surprisingly warm as the sun reached around into their sheltered bay.

From time to time people came by. All exchanged a greeting, most stopped to chat. Part of Mike's job was to "promote awareness" as he explained gravely to Sally after a long session with one earnest soul, who wished his awareness to extend to exhaustive details of walking routes, the history of local slate quarrying, the Grisedale Forest sculptures, and the possibility of seeing golden-eye.

"Is that another form of conjunctivitis?" Sally grumbled mildly, flat on her back on the bank where she had been lying half listening, pretending to feel impatient but knowing she wasn't really minding anything, while Mike dealt patiently with all the questions, which he knew mattered more than the answers anyway.

"Duck. He may spot them at the lower end of the lake. He'll certainly see mallard and dab-chicks—little grebe—if he's lucky."

"If he stops talking, more like." The sun glowed on her upturned face, warmed her bare arms. She felt as though she'd known Mike forever.

"How about some lunch, or is breakfast still too near for you?"

"Cheek. Come back to the cottage—oh, no, don't, Garth is scowling and tearing at the grass."

"Jackson? Oh, to hell with that. And I was dreaming of a nice cold beer, too."

"I could go and fetch something." She didn't really want to waste one moment away from him.

"You're staying here." He turned to the pickup as he spoke, the words thrown away, but Sally knew they were there to hold onto when this day was lost and gone.

Mike produced sausage rolls and apples and a pile of ham sandwiches. Sally saw a sudden unwanted picture of hands making them for him, his wife's hands, the wife they never mentioned and whom it was so important to keep shadowy and unreal. She was not ready yet for guilt to mar something that seemed good and clean and honest.

"Hope you like mustard. I'd slapped it on before I thought about it." Mike was propping up the flask against a rock as he spoke and Sally was glad he wouldn't see the absurd relief on her face. There was masses of stuff here, she now realized. He had made this lunch for them both. They were safe for a little longer in their fragile private enclave.

Prompted to interest by some of the questions the garrulous walker had asked, Sally added some of her own. What had he meant, for instance, about the pilgrims to Helvellyn? And the sculptures? In all Mike told her on that quiet afternoon she understood his love for this place. He was fascinated by its history and geology, its wildlife and ecology and the dangerous route its development was taking under the heavy hand of man. She saw his deep concern over the problems of balancing the modern demands of tourism against the survival of farmers and a rural way of life, but more importantly, to her, she read his passion for this patch of ground and his profound sense of belonging to it. In boyhood he had never been able to spend enough time here (she thought of her own love for Grianan, her feeling of being wrenched out of her shell when she had to leave it, her tears), but no one else in his family had shared his feelings. When his father died there had been no contest about ownership of the farm. His younger brother had gone back to Ireland, and their mother had gone with him.

"They used to come over fairly regularly, but mainly because the place gave them a cheap base for touring. They could never find much to do here." His face was somber; he seemed to mind this more than Sally would have expected. He must surely be used to it by now. "Anyway," he went on, pushing the thought away, "my mother has a fairly serious heart condition these days and probably won't leave home again. We'll have to go and see her in future."

"We." The word he had never used. The word Sally knew could only be ignored for a brief respite.

*   *   *

Waking knowing that someone was in the room, yet knowing in the same moment via some deep instinct that there was no reason to be afraid. Dimmest of grey light, the tall shape of Mike beside the bed.

"Thought you'd be sure to hear me in the kitchen." A clink as mugs went down on glass-covered pine. "Here, prop yourself up on this." He shoved a cushion behind the pillows, laughing at her as she blurrily hauled herself upright, fuddled with sleep and dazed with joyful surprise.

"So you decided not to lock the door after all?"

She hadn't realized she hadn't. What a helpful sub-conscious. "No need to up here, someone told me."

"Did they indeed? Wonder who that was." He set-tled comfortably on the bed against her hip, propping an arm across her, very much at ease. He loomed large and dark in the half light and she could feel the thud of her heart. But in spite of her delight at seeing him there, she took it for granted that as before they would only talk, intimate and absorbed and close. She be-lieved the ground rules had been laid down and she accepted them.

After the perfect hours yesterday, the peaceful work and leisurely talk, she had let Mike go home without her and had sat on for a while alone, savoring the contentment of the day in a mood of tranquil acquies-cence. Mike had been booked to give a talk to a Saga holiday group in Keswick, and knowing she wouldn't see him that evening she had wandered home as the warmth died from the day, at peace as she had not been for many months.

So now she was breathless with surprise when Mike suddenly took the mug out of her hands and put it down, slid his hands behind her shoulders and began to kiss her as though he meant it.

He laid her back eventually against the pillows, keeping his arms around her, and smiled at her in the growing light.

Sally gazed up at him, shaken, questioning, trying to find safe ground. "But why?" she whispered. "Why till now only one or two tiny butterflies of kisses, and now this?"

"The moment just comes, doesn't it?" His voice sounded light, teasing, but unnervingly loving.

Sally nodded, wordless. Nothing had ever felt so right. He bent his head to hers again. His moves, his pace; but it all felt so exactly what she needed. He was so sure, so much at ease, that it seemed at once incredibly exciting and the most natural thing in the world to be held and caressed by him. She felt her unsure, tight-clamped body melt and clamor as it had not done for far too long.

Mike knew. He knew, precisely, everything she was feeling. And he understood her sharp involuntary exclamation of loss as he withdrew his arms and stood up.

"It's all right, I'm here, I'm here. Damned boots, not the gear in which to go a-wooing. And I think we'll have those mugs out of the danger zone. Ungrateful woman, you didn't even finish your coffee . . ."

She waited, this trivia, which she knew was meant to reassure her, hardly reaching her, trying to hold on to the sensations he had aroused, dreading the return of doubt and tension, and, because she dreaded it, feeling the chill spread through her warm eager body. She wanted this to be so good for him—but Julian hadn't found it good enough.

"I've forgotten how," she gasped absurdly, out of her distress, panic tightening her stomach like cramp.

"Well, I haven't," Mike said cheerfully, sliding in beside her and wrapping her up against him with a sort of robust matter-of-factness that did her a lot of good. "We'll get rid of this for a start." And he stripped away her nightdress deftly, making her feel as light as a doll when he lifted her with one arm.

"There, that's better." And then he said no more, his hands beginning to move over her body, gently exploring or, as it seemed to Sally as she gradually relaxed, rediscovering what he had always known.

He said only, "So tight," as he reached at last the aching longing place.

"Not good?" she asked, in terror that she was, after all, closing against him.

"It's beautiful," he breathed, and again, "God, so beautiful," as he slid into her.

And later, "That bastard Justin, Julian, whatever he was called, must have been out of his mind . . ."

Words to lock away. But Sally knew she didn't need them. Her body had not forgotten what to do; but at the same time it had discovered a satisfaction she had never imagined.

"I'll never be able to think of this house in the same way again, that's for sure," Mike remarked as he swiftly dressed, sounding exuberant and looking remarkably full of energy. "Going by in the old pick-up, remembering this." He scooped up Sally's nightdress and dropped it on the bed. She put a hand on it but couldn't be bothered to move any farther.

"You look a very relaxed lady," he commented with amusement, gazing down at her. Then he stooped to take her face in his hands and kiss her lightly. "Stay there, have a little kip." He balled his fist, pushed it gently against her cheek. "And don't forget, you are a lovely, lovely woman."

She reached up both hands to capture his, held it for one moment against her face, eyes closed, feeling his lack of hurry, then delivered his hand back to him.

The day was warm, warm enough to take a rug and lie out on the sweet-smelling pale mown grass. In a glow of indolent euphoria Sally dozed and dreamed the hours away. Her body felt light, renewed, coordinated. More importantly, she felt sure of herself in some deep fundamental way that was new to her.

There could be no relationship. By his restraint, by what he very gently wasn't saying, Mike had made that clear and Sally respected him for it. She closed her mind to the first bite of anguish that something like this should exist, all of it—Mike, this place, the chemistry between them—and not be for her. It wasn't jealousy of his wife or even envy. It was loss, loss free of resentment or disappointment since nothing had been promised, nothing hoped for. Yet part of her wanted it to be this way. She knew she wasn't ready for serious involvement with anyone; she felt too vulnerable and fearful. Instantaneous and powerful though the feeling between them had been, there had all along been a strong sense of boundaries which would not be crossed. Mike wasn't free; she was fairly sure he had made love to her against his better judgment. The very absence of discussion about what they were doing, and of any attempt to justify it, was revealing in itself. They had simply found something marvelous, each sure of the other's reaction, and they wanted to keep it happy and uncomplicated if they could. Mike would not hurt her; instead he had given her a delight she had thought might never be there for her again, and this new confidence in herself. What more could she ask?

And how she shrank from doing harm in his life. She had asked no questions about it, been careful to make no references that would even touch upon it. She did not pretend she had not taken something which didn't belong to her, but she had allowed that to be Mike's decision. Aunt Janey certainly wouldn't approve, but Sally offered no propitiatory excuses to her image and felt no regret. This was something outside real life, outside time.

The hours, the days and the sequence of Mike's snatched visits blurred, never later to be disentangled in her mind. There was an early morning walk which took them right around the western shore of the lake; there was an hour at sunset high on the fell watching a flaming sky change behind the tumbled mass of the western hills; there was a rainy afternoon when she had not expected him and they made love with the squalls pelting and drumming against the window and grape-dark clouds making it seem that dusk had already come.

It was on this afternoon that Mike said, "It won't be quite so easy to see you for the next day or two. Weekend and all that."

His voice was brusque, unintentionally she knew. Time was no longer theirs.

"I'll go," she said, leaping over all the implications and options.

"I won't let you," he said instantly and fiercely, gripping her tightly, and she needed no clearer statement of how he felt. But when he released her, turning on his back and throwing an arm up behind his head, his face shuttered, she knew he was quite aware that his instinctive reaction could mean nothing.

"You understand, don't you," he said, in a tight voice after a pause. It wasn't a question. "I don't need to spell it out."

"We've both always known."

"I didn't want to be a bastard to you—especially after what you'd been through. But I have been, after all."

"No, you haven't. Because there's never been any expectation of anything more. Everything between us has been honest."

"I don't want to spoil this place for you. I'd hate to think you felt you couldn't come back because of what's happened between us. This is part of your life, a place you care about."

"I'll come back." Impossible to imagine.

"I'll look out for a red Renault coming along the lane."

Sally nodded, smiling, unable to speak.

"You've always been so discreet. You've never asked a single question. I'm so grateful to you for that." His voice was thick, emotion almost getting the better of him. "And I can't give you a damn thing."

"You know what you've given me," she said steadily.

"Is that what you feel? Is that what you'll take away with you?" She knew he had accepted that she must go, but that made it very near and real.

"Yes. You've put me together again." Time to return to lightness if they could.

He turned to her, seizing her roughly, crushing her to him. "You know what this has meant to me, don't you? I don't want you wondering later. I want you to be sure that it's been really important."

But when after a quick rough hug he released her, tossing back the duvet, leaping out of bed resolutely, all her good sense and discipline fled. Oh, no, not like this, she felt her whole self cry out in horrified dismay and loss. Not without loving once more, not like this, finally, for good . . .

"Mike—" She sat up, arms out, heard the threat of tears in her voice.

He leaned down to her, his face tight with pain. "Sally, come on, we mustn't get—we must be—" He couldn't find the words, but already his urgent appeal had reached her. He was right; they must keep it light. Anything else would deny the whole tone of their meeting, ephemeral, transient—one heavy-handed touch and it would be destroyed forever.

She hunted through her anguish for some words that would do no damage.

"You've even reconciled me to Aunt Ursula's silly house."

Banal, but he accepted it, letting it return them to ordinary things. "And what would she think if she could see you now?"

Before he went he took her hands for one silent moment vibrant with all the things they mustn't say, things foregone, things never claimed. It was too late now. Sally's hands clutched his and he made no effort to loosen her grip, allowing it to relax when she was ready.

She looked up at him, nodded. His eyes thanked her, read the ache of loss in hers and winced at it.

Then his steps going away. The house an empty drum again. Sally found she was struggling for breath against the hard tightness of chest and throat. Don't cry, she told herself. He'd hate it. This was just a gift of loving and laughter that fell into our hands, satisfying and complete. Gain not loss.

Chapter 5

At five-thirty Sally gave up trying to sleep and, feeling numb and hollow, got up and went mechanically through the chores of packing and tidying, refusing to let pain penetrate as she walked out of the cottage which had become such a different place for her now. She crept quietly along the lane, her whole being concentrated on getting away before there was any possible chance of seeing Mike as she passed the farm.

Would she ever be able to come back? If she did, would it seem in spite of what he had said, that she had come in the hope of seeing him? But he had been adamant that she must not lose this place because of him. But come and do what? Sit in the cottage, walk the fells, avoiding their shared places, alone, remembering?

The remorseless traffic of the A74, pelting the slush of a gray rainy day across her windscreen, pushing along too fast for the visibility, focused her mind, however disagreeably. Then it was just numb miles, automatic actions.

Only as she ran into Muirend some time mid-morning did practical considerations re-emerge, the inflexible Grianan rule for one—phone and see if anything's needed, don't waste wheels going up the glen. But she literally felt she couldn't stop, that if she did she would be unable to go on. As though these thoughts were turning in some isolated compartment of her brain, her hands and feet took no notice of them at all, just kept on driving. She was through Muirend already. How long since she had last driven up here? A weekend four years ago—that was disgraceful.

God, she hadn't even let them know she was coming today. Aunt Janey was not a person you just landed on to suit your own timetable. And what excuse was there not to have done so? She had known since yesterday afternoon that she couldn't stay at Edalmere. Where had the evening gone? She couldn't remember. And the cottage itself—had she turned off the heating, the immersion? She should at least have emptied the kitchen bin, left the key at the Jacksons'. She shook her head angrily, as if to dislodge the guilty reminders, feeling Grianan reaching forward with its expected standards, its work ethic, its paramount law of guests first, no matter what. Those eccentric, articulate guests, tough enough to withstand Janey's rigorous approach, as confident as privileged lives could make them—was she ready to cope with their assurance, their courteous demands so inflexibly made?

The road was climbing. This was a wider, higher landscape than the Lakeland one, its lines more sweeping, its beauty spare and challenging. Sally felt the old excitement rise in response, yet at the same time a resistance build to the moment of arriving. It was a long time since she had subjected herself to Grianan and its exigencies. In this mood of raw loneliness, the immediate loss of what she had found with Mike sharper now than the misery of Julian's rejection

and the débâcle of unraveling wedding plans and returning presents and facing the world as a single (unwanted) person again, Grianan seemed suddenly the
last place she wanted to be. There would be Janey's
discerning eyes to face, not only with all that fiasco
still to explain, but knowing that yesterday she, Sally,
had been in bed with the husband of their Edalmere
neighbor, whom Janey undoubtedly knew. Put like
that, the magical happiness with Mike, kept till now
so carefully separate and intact, was abruptly brought
into the light of everyday social reality.

Sally felt rattled and unready, needing more time
to prepare for this. But what was the alternative? She
had given up her job, sold her house and with them
lost a whole circle and lifestyle. She drove grimly on.

Then an unexpected thing happened. She turned
into the climbing drive between the gray boles of tow-
ering beeches, just-unfurling leaves not yet concealing
the fine tracery of the branches, and came out onto
the wide shelf where the square, stone house stared
out across the glen. Leaving everything in the car, she
crossed the gravel to the two semicircular stone steps
which her feet took with an automatic hop and jump.
The weight of the heavy door as she twisted the
square brass handle was utterly accustomed. And in
that instant the harried vulnerable present fell away.
The smell of childhood met and engulfed her. Boots
and washed stone, fires of birch and fir, real beeswax
mixed with turpentine, tweed, fifty-year-old carpet,
lilac, Aunt Janey's horrible cat.

And Sally knew that this was the only place where
she could possibly have come, to deal with the new
pain and the old. She stood in the slowly tocking quiet,
feeling her tense muscles relax. For this moment, be-

fore anyone knew she was here, she could luxuriate in the sensation of absolute belonging.

As though Grianan itself awoke her conscience she was suddenly glad that, although she would make no excuses for entering into the brief compelling affair with Mike, she need feel no guilt over the way she had behaved on parting. She hadn't wept, hadn't made things difficult for him. She had put down no markers for the future, asked for nothing. And she knew he would be grateful for that, grateful, probably, today to find that she had gone.

The door from the dining room opened. "Sally! *What* a lovely surprise! Maureen insisted she'd heard a car but of course I thought she just wanted me out of the kitchen as usual—"

Aunt Janey, brown face creased into her big grin, thick gray hair curling as bouncily as Sally's own, denim skirt stretched over solid hips, bare legs already tanned, broad feet in basket-like sandals. Sally felt an impulse to hug her, saw her aunt check her own impulse to do the same, and understood that hesitation with a piercing new clarity. She had rebuffed such gestures in the years when she had turned her back on the family, and Janey had been careful to respect her wishes.

"Hello, Aunt Janey." She felt wooden, uncertain, caught unexpectedly in a storm of conflicting emotions and associations.

"Darling, darling Sally. How wonderful it is to see you again."

"I should have phoned. I'm sorry."

"You're here, that's all that matters. I've been so looking forward to it." Her pleasure was warm and open, her eyes smiling, drinking in every detail of Sally's appearance.

Thank God she can be relied on not to say I look too tired and too thin, Sally thought, both of which were true. And she won't say how long it is since I was last here either.

"Coffee before we bring in your things? You must have set off very early."

Dawn light in the little room. Remembering the dawn when Mike had first come in . . .

"Pretty early." Sally found she had to clear her throat. "Yes, coffee would be good, thanks." And on a long sigh, "It's lovely to be back."

She meant it. The years when she had felt it a boring duty to give up part of her holidays to come up here—and the years when she hadn't bothered—her resentment at always being dragged in to help with some crisis or other, the present dread of having to explain about Julian, vanished. The love of the earlier years swept back. This was refuge; this was home.

Janey beamed at her in pleasure. "How good to hear you say that."

"I mean it," Sally said, and with a loving instinct too long buried, stepped forward quickly to wrap her arms around that sturdy body and kiss the cheek soft as an over-wintered apple. Janey responded with a vigor that squeezed the breath out of her niece.

"Oh, dear Sally," she said, and Sally was astonished to hear a huskiness in her voice. "Now" ("enough of this nonsense" rang in the single syllable, and Sally grinned, comfortable with that), "come along and we'll organize that coffee."

In the dining room a small, dark woman with a clear line of moustache and skin that looked permanently unwashed was banging down a tray of silver. "I knew fine I'd heard a car," she said by way of greeting.

"Yes, how very clever of you. Bring some coffee to the sitting room for us, would you, Maureen?"

"Well, Sally, and how are you? Are the phones not working down in England then?"

"Mellowing nicely with the years, I see," Sally remarked, laughing at her.

"Am I to make this coffee before I get my silver away?" Maureen demanded pettishly of Janey.

"Oh, don't be such a pain." Janey replied equably. "And fresh coffee, please, not what's left over from filling the flasks."

"Would I do that?" asked Maureen affrontedly, winking at Sally.

Sally laughed, her spirits lifting. Aunt Janey and Maureen locked in combat was part of the very air of Grianan.

"Given the slightest chance, you most certainly would," Aunt Janey was retorting. "And if you don't get those pigeons into the marinade soon they won't be fit to cook for dinner. And don't skimp the brandy like you did last time, either."

"If what I do's not good enough . . . " pitched at a receding mutter as Maureen flounced through the leather-lined service door.

All absolutely normal, yet Sally sensed something special about her welcome today. Not least because there was Janey stopping in the middle of the morning to drink coffee, *sitting down*, in her private sanctum, a small study with French windows opening onto a paved, sheltered angle where there were always cuttings taking root and pot plants hardening off amid a scuff of tools, twine, disintegrating trugs and mud-hardened, holey gloves.

The room itself, ferociously guarded even from guests who had been coming to Grianan since the days when Janey first let them in, was a cavern of piled clutter, redolent of Janey's thin black cigars, wood smoke and the huge gray Persian cat which rose in wrath to puff itself out to twice its size at the sight of an old enemy before bounding away over a row of budding geraniums. Here Janey read Dickens and Trollope and Louis L'Amour, drank gin-and-mixed and listened to Mahler and Wagner, watched rugby, wrote acid letters to tradesmen and kept her collection of Victorian cookery and household books.

"Now, is this coffee going to be drinkable?" she asked, before Maureen was well out of the room, adding with her gruff laugh when the door had banged, "I'm surprised she didn't tell me to make it myself. She must be pleased to see you, Sally."

"I don't know how she puts up with you."

"Can't think what you mean. No cook was ever better treated." Janey could control her eyes and mouth but not her dimples. "Now—" all of Sally's early life in that "now" of her Aunt Janey. She waited, biddable, consciously soothed by all these well-known things.

"About your room. Your old one is so tiny that I wondered if you would prefer a more grown-up one now. Then I thought how chilling it might be to find yourself moved without being asked. Then again I thought you might be exasperated to find yourself with Little Gray Rabbit *et al.* still around. Then I realized I simply didn't know what you'd like, so Connie got two rooms ready."

Sally was startled at how much Janey had told her there, and at how much the question had exercised her. She felt touched and grateful to think of her aunt anxiously tossing the decision back and forth. It was so unlike her to hesitate over such considerations. And Sally was even more startled to realize that Janey was actually prepared to give up a letting bedroom. Her return must have mattered to Janey, she thought with genuine surprise. Perhaps the invitation to come here for the summer hadn't been made solely to offer Sally a pause to sort herself out.

"Come and see what you think."

Janey had chosen for her the old west dressing room, a very popular room. White-paneled, with windows on two sides, with its elegant curved French bed and the kingwood *bureau* plat inlaid with olive and satinwood which was one of the special pieces in the house, it was indeed a grown-up room, and giving it to Sally would deprive Janey of a sizable slice of income throughout the summer.

"Don't say anything yet," Janey ordered as Sally turned to her helplessly. Back they went to the door on the main landing which opened onto a narrow staircase. Had it really always been that steep? Sally wondered in disbelief. But though the eye might have forgotten, her feet found it exactly as remembered. A vivid recollection came back of running lightly through the silent house, wafting up this narrow flight, heart knocking with excited guilt and relief to be safely back after a forbidden rendezvous with Jed.

At the top of the stairs long attic rooms on either side held the usual miscellany of broken lamps, rejected furniture, old files and cash books, washstands and chamber pots, iron bed-ends, trunks, cardboard boxes and Christmas decorations. Straight ahead opened a slit of a room high above the front door, its casement window wide, Janey style, to the cool damp morning. Sally's ideas on a desirable temperature might have changed, but the view clear across Drum-veyn to Ben Breac framed by that long window still made her catch her breath in delight. The pink cream-sprigged wallpaper was faded, the pattern of the coun-terpane almost invisible, but the Pooh-sticks rug was still there, washed almost white, the collection of carved animals on the shelf, the well-read books (less Beatrix Potter, which the Edalmere surfeit had put her off for life). Memories poured back—first evenings of school holidays, the dread that any detail would be changed, the relief when everything was exactly the same, the joy of gulping in the sweet glen air after the hours in the train, the wild, choking, almost unbear-able thankfulness to be here again, safe.

"I don't think I feel very grown-up after all," Sally said unsteadily, and Janey gave her a quick look then patted her arm with her hard-working, dirt-engrained hand. For two pins they might have embraced again.

"Then we'll fetch your things," was all her aunt said, but Sally knew she was pleased.

"I'll fetch them." Janey hadn't charged up the stairs in quite her remembered style, Sally had noted. "And then would you mind very much if I had a sleep?"

Sleep, at Grianan, in the *daytime*? But either Janey had grown more tolerant or Sally looked in worse case than she knew, for Janey only said, "Come down whenever you like. Just do whatever you want to do, little Sally, I mean it."

Sally would never have believed that she could pass out like that, at half past eleven in the morning, still dressed, simply collapsing on to the narrow white-painted bed and dragging her duvet over her and letting all the misery of the messy past and the new raw longing swirl away into oblivion.

Chapter 6

Sounds woke her. Car wheels on the gravel, car doors slamming, feet scrunching, an exasperated female voice, "Oh, Bracken, do get a move on, you've had all day to do that." Around her the house itself felt different, peopled, living.

Mike. Instant waking happiness to think of him, followed by the hammer-blow of fact. For a moment she lay folded in on herself, not ready yet to grapple with Grianan. If only it were an ordinary house where she could have time and peace. But then she would be face to face with Janey's honest eyes. Sally might think she had behaved well over Mike, walking away quietly when the moment came, but Janey would not see it in that light.

Well, a few more stolen moments of memories would do no harm. But they were a two-edged indulgence. Easy as it had been to persuade herself when she was with Mike that because there had been no false hopes there would be no pain, the reality of knowing she would never see him again, that he would never make love to her again, was going to take time to accept. But those few light-filled, floating days without doubt or reserve had been worth it; God, they had been worth it.

Presently she turned on her back and pulled herself up on her pillows, letting her eyes rove from one well-loved object to the next, consciously trying to divert her thoughts. Her room in her father's house had undergone several dramatic changes in her flouting adolescence, but this simple, narrow, childish room she had never touched. Why? she wondered now. Had it represented the only acceptable stability?

How far she had come from that passionate child's love for this place. What a wedge she had deliberately driven between Janey and herself over the years. That naïvely eager journey to Australia had done the damage, destroying the fantasies of an emotional reunion with her mother which would restore the bond between them (and put her ahead of everyone and everything else in her mother's affections, she was able to say honestly now). After that disaster she had been bitterly determined to establish her own independent life, to achieve a security which no one else's failure in love or understanding could damage. But she had seen it, she realized now for the first time, in rigidly material terms. She had worked hard at university, got a good degree and landed the excellent job at Sieber Research with a defiant, almost vengeful satisfaction, then had set about establishing for herself a settled, comfortable lifestyle which would have suited a fifty-year-old. Julian had been part of that world, the world of "good" jobs—and, come to that, good salaries, good cars, good houses and good prospects. She had thought that with him she would be safe, that nothing would ever change.

Groaning, she threw back the duvet. No good lying here and letting those well-worn thoughts take over yet again. Better to go down, face people. Though surely no one would expect her to plunge into work tonight.

Half past four. Guests coming in from their invigorating outdoor activities, changing their shoes, washing their hands, tidying their hair, hurrying down to sit around the table in the library and help themselves with polite greed to a huge tea of scones, pancakes, homemade jam, heather honey and Maureen's cakes. Then there would be the sound of baths being run all over the house. Boots and nailed walking shoes would be stuffed with newspaper and left in the boiler room, socks prickly with heather tips draped over radiators to stiffen overnight, dog bowls brought down to be filled, light-wool dresses zipped up and club/regimental/old-school ties adjusted, never-cleaned jewelry fastened around scraggy necks. Everyone would gather for drinks in the drawing room. . . .

Oh, Mike, I want you to be here so that I can laugh with you. How long would it be before that need faded? And how could it be so strong after so short a time with him?

Only Connie was about in the kitchen regions, big, slow-moving Connie who did the rooms in the mornings and sometimes stayed on for the afternoon to clean brass and silver.

"Well, it's grand to see you back," she said comfortably, "but whatever in the world have you been doing to yourself? You're thin as a rake, lass. I can see that we'll have to feed you up."

Bless you, Janey, for not saying it. But it occurred to Sally to wonder with a new perception what it cost her blunt, outspoken aunt to refrain from such natural expressions of concern.

"How are you, Connie? And the family?"

"Ach, we're all pretty much the same as we were, I suppose," Connie said peacefully. "There's treacle scones over there. I didn't put them all out for their tea. We've only the ten in tonight and they've more than enough to be going on with. You put the kettle on, love, my hands are black."

Sally lit the old popping gas ring that used to terrify her as a child and didn't fill her with much confidence now, and set the battered kettle rockily upon it. Janey's kitchen no one invaded. It was not at all the cosy gathering place one might have expected. It had an Aga, certainly, because much of Janey's French-style country cooking demanded long hours in slow ovens, but the rest of it was strictly functional. No rocking chairs or patchwork cushions here, no friendly chats or fly cuppies, no time frittered away dipping into the tabloids or slapping together a gash sandwich. Even Marchmain the cat was banned. The Environmental Health Officer might mutter about beetly storerooms and rotting skirting-boards and overflowing baskets of laundry dumped down in the silver pantry, but he was able to commend the big kitchen with visible relief.

Sally made tea and buttered the brown, still-warm scones, relishing the positive comfort of reaching for familiar things in familiar places, then perched in her old spot on the dresser while Connie's podgy gray fingers worked on unhurriedly through the pile of polish-smeared rat-tail spoons.

"So you're to be up for the whole summer. Quite like old times. Miss Buchanan'll be fine and pleased to have you here. She's not as young as she used to be—and that goes for the rest of us, too."

"Well, we'll see how it goes," Sally said temperately, conscious of a reluctance to be committed, a resistance to assumptions being made.

"Then back to England, will it be?" Connie asked with an automatic disparagement in her tone of which she was quite unconscious.

"Probably." But Sally couldn't imagine it. Already her life in Reading seemed utterly unreal. Except that Mike was in England. Oh, for God's sake, she warned herself angrily, don't start thinking like that.

She had just opened her jaws to take a bite of fat scone slathered with bramble jelly, when the door from the passage opened and a stranger walked quietly in.

He was slightly built, Sally's age or perhaps older, with a thin brown face and smooth dark hair to his collar. He was wearing a faded shirt and well-washed jeans which had been beautifully ironed but showed signs of rough usage. Her mouth still open, Sally looked at him with interest. He was definitely a new style of guest for Grianan. Then lowering the scone she said hastily, "Were you looking for tea? It's put out in the library."

"Not for me, I'm afraid," he said in a gentle and markedly upper-class English voice, a small, lopsided, friendly smile twisting his well-shaped mouth.

"Oh, my, that's a good one," crowed Connie. "You'll be telling me to have my tea in the library next. Piers is the gardener, have you no' met him yet?"

"How do you do?" He offered a slim hand, his dark eyes smiling without embarrassment. His lashes were long and soft and sooty black, his teeth very white and even. Wherever had he come from? As he turned to take the mug Connie had quickly filled for him, dirty hands or not, Sally was aware of the contained grace of his movements.

"Any tea in the pot?" Janey came stumping in. "Sally, you're up. Had a good sleep? I think we've got a rabbit in, Piers, a baby one by the look of the nibbles at the lettuce. We'll have to check the whole fence again, fearful waste of time. Oh, thanks, that's lovely. Goodness, Connie, you have got on. Are all the punters back?"

Janey had mud on the worn hem of her skirt, a dark ring around her thick calves where the earthy tops of her gumboots had rubbed, and the bright green feathery tips of early fennel in her hand sent out a potent wave of aniseed.

"All except the Ormondes," Connie replied. "The rest are in at their tea."

Marshaled. Counted. In the right place at the right time. Sally grinned privately.

"Sally, you'll remember the Ormondes. He's a High Court Judge; she stitches away without pause at that hideous Venetian needlework. I once accused her of only doing it here because she's always in exactly the same place every year but she told me she's covered seventeen chairs already. Seventeen chairs! Do you seriously suppose they have seventeen friends to sit on them?"

Janey's stubby hands swiftly buttering a scone for herself, the appalling things she said about the guests for her own entertainment and mostly without malice, the sight of Connie rubbing away at her spoons, Piers' intriguing and somehow unthreatening presence—all these added up to something Sally knew suddenly she could face after all. She felt calmed, sanguine. It would all lap around her and gradually the destructive threadbare anger over Julian would dissipate and be forgotten, and the newer, simpler pain of missing Mike would be easier to bear, and only the happiness he'd given her would remain.

Connie was bundling up her grimy cloths and carrying a tray of gleaming silver to the sink.

"We'll do those, Connie. You've stayed quite late enough and I'm very grateful. But your family will be clamoring to be fed."

"Do you want a hand with them, Aunt Janey?" Sally asked as Connie departed. She must be feeling better, she thought wryly; she certainly hadn't intended to make any such offer yet.

"Absolutely not, everything's under control. You're not to do a thing tonight, or until you want to. I mean it, no argument. Damn, oh damn, there's the rain on again and all the washing's out. Come on . . . "

Marchmain flew in as they flew out, Janey, Sally and Piers, leaping up the crooked stone steps through the gap in the beech hedge, laughing and swearing in the fierce downpour, bumping into each other as they gathered flapping sheets into hasty bundles, hurled them into baskets, dropped pegs, shouting, "Quick, quick!" at each other like idiots.

In the laundry with its dipping flagged floor and deep vats of sinks, its squad of flatirons on the hob in the cavern of the chimney and a huge towel press that looked like something which could have started the industrial revolution, they wiped the rain from their faces, folded anything ready to be ironed and hung the rest on the long pulleys, Piers neat-fingered, intent, quite at ease with such a job.

The telephone was ringing as they went along the draughty passage. The rain had lowered the temperature sharply and Sally shivered. Janey was incredibly stingy about the central heating and was unreasonably inclined to take a moral stand about it too. Mercifully it didn't get as far as Sally's little room anyway, so she was beyond the reach of Janey's heavy hand on the control switch and was allowed the indulgence of an electric heater. Perhaps now she was "grown-up" she would be allowed to keep it on for as long as she liked as well. Somehow she didn't see Janey dashing up and down to monitor it as readily as she used to. At least in this respect Aunt Ursula's domestic economy had been an improvement. Edalmere. The warm, busy, gadget-ridden kitchen. Mike's clean-cut profile, the light in his greeny-brown eyes when he was teasing her, the strange cocooned peace of being with him . . .

"Wretched child!" Aunt Janey at the telephone was exclaiming, and Sally noticed Piers' face soften in a sort of resigned affection, though she observed that he carefully did not share his amusement with her. She liked him for that.

"You're not feeling too well? And what precisely am I to understand by that?" Aunt Janey was demanding heatedly. "I suppose something more attractive than washing my pots has offered itself, though I find it hard to imagine what. A disco, perhaps? A trip to the cinema in Muirend? Oh, now you're feeling like death? Then do by all means die, but first I should be grateful if you would deliver the cream which you promised to bring up with you. You're not feeling up to that? Naturally not, but please remember, if I hear that you have moved one step outside that house tonight . . ."

Janey and her light touch with her minions. The

surprising thing was that they were rash enough to phone in the first place, Sally thought, laughter rising freely for the first time that day.

"These frightful people," growled Janey, banging down the receiver. "To think they are being allowed to overrun the planet. I do feel the Chinese have the right idea . . ."

"Do we need the cream for tonight?" Piers asked.

Sally noted the "we" with interest. Support, involvement?

"Apricot pancakes are fairly meaningless without it. And I've made the compote already. It's shrimp soup too, that needs a good dollop. Damn, damn, damn. Well, nothing for it, I shall have to go down and fetch it. Oh, *miserable* girl, she knows perfectly well it's Maureen's night off."

"Aunt Janey, I'll go." Solidarity or not, Sally noticed that Piers wasn't offering. He finished work at five, presumably. She wondered where he was living.

"No, Sally, I won't hear of it. You've only just arrived. You're not to do a thing this evening, I'm quite adamant about that. I shall have plenty of time to get everything done if I go straight away."

Taking the twisting road down to the village Sally played with surface exasperation. Bloody place, its demands always had to come first and Janey was always leaping from one crisis to another. But under the layers of reluctance and impatience, unmistakable cheerfulness was rising. Who had expected anything to be any different, anyway? And wouldn't it have been rather disappointing to find it was? Also, being hustled from one thing to the next without time to draw breath had to be the best therapy she could ask for.

She was prepared to look in the old place by the

garage wall where anything perishable brought up by the school bus was left in the weedy shade, but it seemed that late-night opening had reached Ellig. A yawning teenager in jeans and full makeup lolled beside an electronic till in a new glassed-in box of an office, waiting for customers to help themselves at self-service pumps. She handed over the cream without interest. One or two people were about, but Sally was conscious of an irrational desire not to be recognized. She had not prepared a face to meet the faces she might meet. In one of the mood swings of this long fraught day she felt actually alien, almost afraid that she would be greeted with hostility. She reminded herself that she had continued to appear here from time to time through the years; no one but she could know how far she had distanced herself emotionally. Or had Janey guessed?

Inevitably, when dinnertime came she did the potwash. More surprisingly, Piers not only appeared to help her but in a formal wordless ballet that looked pretty accustomed to Sally he fed Janey the necessary backup throughout the meal. No one waited in the dining room. In her unsavory butcher's apron Janey crashed in and out from time to time, slapping ashets and dishes of delectable food on the sideboard.

The guests helped themselves and cleared the plates with a "we're family" zeal, particularly if a rare newcomer were present. If something had to be carved Janey would sharpen her knife *in situ* with flashing steel and masculine showmanship and, spattered spectacles on the end of her nose, would perform with the skill taught her by Sally's grandfather when he gave up hope of a son. Occasionally the rite was delegated to a male guest, but only after a critical public assessment which few survived.

Tonight the haunch of roe *sauté* with juniper berries required no blade wielding and Janey's visits to the dining room were confined to appraising what people had on their plates (nervous guests had to resist the temptation to put their arms around them) and humphing at overeffusive compliments. She considered producing good food an everyday skill, not an art form. This could be a delicate tightrope to walk for those guests who came year after year to gormandize.

Crescendo to hot cheese soufflé—guests at this time of the year tended to belong to the savory-eating vintage—then companionable diminuendo of coffee and homemade peppermints in the drawing room, a long-retired general dealing shakily with the port and brandy, and in the kitchen the washing machine churning, Marchmain writhing backward and forward on the windowsill yelling greedy demands through the steamy glass, and food at last for the slaves.

By this stage Janey only ever wanted a plate of anything she could shovel in with a fork and tonight Sally felt the same. Two plates of roe and creamed potato and baby beans appeared from the bottom oven of the Aga when the tidying up was done.

"Doesn't Piers get food?" Sally asked, looking around for him.

"Not mine," Janey said with one of her snorts of laughter that made you forget she was the eldest of the three sisters and well into her sixties. "He's welcome to it, of course, but he's a vegetarian. It must be quite loathsome for him to help dish up cooked creatures. He's so good to help as he does."

"So who is he?" Sally asked as they carried their

plates through to the untidy chilly sitting room. "Where does he live? How did he turn up here?"

"He's Piers Hinchcliffe." A slight warning note there that Sally's questions, or her manner of asking them, had not been wholly acceptable.

"And?" Sally persisted nevertheless. Piers was too outlandish in this setting to be accepted without some editing.

"And he lives in the garden cottage. He came here looking for peace."

(As she had been. Dusk on the lakeshore, quiet voices flowing . . . Don't think about that.)

"Oh, come on Janey," she protested. "There must be more to tell than that."

"Oh dear, labels," said Aunt Janey, sounding quite cross. "Well, he's an organic gardener, with a special interest in companiate gardening if that means anything to you, and he doesn't like noise or anger or machines. He doesn't accept frameworks of time either, which means I live in a permanent state of guilt because I can't possibly repay him for all the hours he puts in."

"He doesn't drive?"

"It is a pest up here," Janey acknowledged.

"And I suppose he hates money too?" Sally immediately regretted the cynicism when Janey fixed her with a cold eye.

"You disappoint me."

Even now Sally felt a flush come to her cheeks at that long-remembered tart rebuke. Her standards and attitudes would need some overhauling here. How Janey would hate what had happened with Mike. She would feel Sally had abused the freedom to use the cottage. (But I did my best, I came away, I truly did my best.) Without realizing she was going to do it, Sally reached out a hand to touch Janey's muscular forearm, noticing as she did so how crêpey the brown skin had become.

It was an unprecedented form of apology between them but if Janey was surprised she didn't show it. Nor did she reject the gesture. "He's naïve about money," she amended, and Sally knew she was making the effort to meet her halfway. She also knew that, for her own part, the gesture had been made not so much in apology but out of a need not to feel alone.

In the pearl-clean early morning the garden cottage looked as simple and neat as a piece of cross-stitch, with its blue slate roof, its central door and two white-painted windows. A strip of gravel along its front wall separated it from mown grass dredged with dew, flanked by symmetrical mounds of rhododendrons covered with fat buds. That was all, and it satisfied Sally as deeply as it always had.

It wasn't like her to be out in the garden at this hour—unless she was on the way home. Memories of her flighty youth made her grin. She had gone to sleep readily enough the night before but had been harried by restless dreams. Waking to find it was first light, thoughts of that other early morning when Mike had first made love to her, and then of yesterday's bleak departure, had flooded unbearably back. She had felt she needed time to work through them before the day engulfed her.

She had gone to one of her favorite places, climbing the high stile over the deer fence which formed the outer boundary of Grianan and heading up the hill to a high jut of rock overhanging a small cliff. The varied

greens of the trees reaching away down the line of the
river had become gradually distinguishable as the light
grew and warmed. The white froth of wild cherry blos-
som, mixed with the pinky-fawn of copper-beeches in
new leaf, dominated the landscape below her. Here
she had been on Glen Ellig estate which lay at the
head of the glen, and here she used to come to meet
Jed, fifteen years ago.

Her mind barely paused on the memory, thoughts
of Mike consuming her. To find something so incredible and know that it was not for her was going to take
some getting used to. If he had been free. The vision
tortured her with its unattainable simplicity. But men
like Mike were never free. They were the natural family men, the providers and protectors.

Coming back slowly to the fence, noting the violets
out in the place where they always first appeared, she
had reminded herself that she was grateful for what
he had given her. He had made her feel wanted again,
whole, normal, functional. Couldn't she just learn to
accept it on that level, as some wonderful therapy,
given to her when the time was right?

"Would you like to come in for coffee?"

Sally jumped, gasping. The early morning world had
seemed so completely hers.

"I startled you, I'm sorry. I should have made a
little harmless noise. I've been out seeing if I could
spot marauding baby rabbits."

Piers, smiling, calm, kind, with that freshly laun-
dered look of his in clean jeans and another soft pale
shirt. "Come in. Talk a little." Was there a sympathetic perceptiveness in his smile or did she just want
to see that? Silently Sally followed him. Perhaps she

would be able to talk to him. She had a feeling that his air of enigmatic reserve might cloak a wide tolerance.

The cottage was an enormous surprise. Much as she had always loved its simple exterior she remembered the inside as dark, dingy and ugly, forever connected in her mind with a bad-tempered old gardener who used to shout at his wife.

Now it was bare, clean, light and beautiful, the internal walls removed, the shell taken back to the stone and newly repointed, the wood of doors, window frames, floor and fireplace stripped. There was a futon on the floor, Navajo rugs, stone jars of dried grasses, a long row of books against the wall and what looked like a flute case on the mantelpiece. No untidy objects, no sign of any clothes which she supposed must be in the cupboards flanking the fire, which had now been converted to a wood-burning stove.

"How beautiful," Sally exclaimed, transfixed with delight in the doorway. "I used to hate coming in here. How long have you been living in it?"

"Since last summer."

Almost a year. Had Janey told her about him? Perhaps in one of those letters she had barely had time to read in the preparations for the wedding. The non-wedding.

"Come and see the kitchen."

Earthenware on white shelves, old-fashioned sweet jars full of pulses and cereals and pasta, ropes of garlic and onions, bunches of herbs, a rack of spice jars.

They sat side by side on the futon with freshly brewed coffee in fine china mugs.

"Will Grianan help you?" Piers asked.

For a moment Sally floundered. The question leapt so many facts which he couldn't know and she couldn't explain. Then she saw that there was no need to explain. He had understood enough to ask the question, and Sally was absolutely sure that Aunt Janey would not have discussed her with him. He simply knew there had been hurt.

"I don't know," she answered him equally simply.

"It's a good place," was all he said.

Sally looked about her, at the pure lines and natural materials of the simple room, its door standing wide to the dew-silvered garden. "Has it helped you?" she asked in her turn.

"More than any place I've ever known."

"Janey didn't say why I'm here?"

"No. But she's delighted that you are."

"She said so?" Sally asked in surprise.

"No," he repeated, amused.

The room accepted their silence and their thoughts.

"Give it time," he said gently after a while.

"Yes, I know." It didn't matter what he knew or guessed; he was right.

Walking back to the house Sally felt as though some of his quietness had transferred itself to her. Yesterday's momentary feeling of being alien seemed extravagant and unreal. There was a place for her here. She went via Janey's azalea garden, pausing to stand with eyes closed to drink in the intoxicating morning draught of scents, then followed the long grassy path down to the house, bordered by beds already bright with primula, polyanthus, honesty, globe flowers and cushions of pink saxifrage.

Restored and comforted by it all, she even felt she could face the porridge pot, the waft of kippers, the pungent smell of elderly khaki knapsacks, the long-winded instructions that accompanied the ancient flasks waiting to be filled. ("Now, I'd better do the cork, I know just how it goes. I put this piece of greaseproof paper around it, you see, then it's perfectly secure. No one else ever gets it *quite* right. . . .")

Then the house emptying at last, with a final echo of the restrained impatience of partners harnessed together for fifty years, "Oh, Hector, you can't have lost the keys *again*. . . ."

It would do. It was a start.

Chapter 7

"Did you run into the Danahers at all while you were at Edalmere?"

Sally was sitting with Janey on the low stone wall beside the compost heap trimming a pile of rhubarb. A bright stem landing on the green fans revealed that she was not as ready for the question as she had believed. Reaching down to retrieve it she was careful not to let Janey see her face.

"I saw the children in the lane once or twice. And I ran into him working on the new path around the lake." She had already decided on that, with no idea of how impossible she would find it to say his name.

"Oh, good, I'd hoped you would meet." Janey didn't seem to have noticed anything odd in her voice. "Mike was so good to Ursula after Teddy died and when she was ill herself. He looked in every day. She was determined to stay there but it would have been impossible without someone nearby prepared to keep an eye on her."

"But didn't she have a nurse?" Sally was ashamed of how little she knew of the details of that swiftly ravening cancer. She saw that she had been allowed to be ignorant of its horror like a child, and like a child had accepted that. Even now, most of her mind had locked on to the thought of Mike, imagining him there in the house with minute clarity—his loose-limbed stride as he crossed the kitchen, the freckles on the back of the tanned hand he reached to the door handle, his voice calling a reassuring greeting . . . He had taken trouble over maddening, chattering Ursula, he would have been gentle with her. Sally felt the blood in her veins pulse at the vividness of these images.

"That was only when she came back from hospital the last time," Janey was saying, and Sally dragged her mind back with a wrenching effort. "Before that she really could manage." Reassuring herself. "But I should have gone down more often, made the time." Janey too.

"It was good of her neighbors to do it." Clumsy, and creakingly obvious to revert to him, but Sally couldn't help herself.

"It was always Mike. I don't think Isobel ever went along. Her preference is generally to head the other way along the lane." With a little huff of sardonic amusement.

Isobel. It had to come. The shadowy person whom Sally had permitted no name, no face, no form, had to take on an identity some time. And once that happened the rest could not be ignored: status, rights, possession. A first, base, sickening jealousy gripped her.

What had Janey said? There had been some implication there. Sally was too shaken to pin it down.

" . . . rather a romantic way to meet," Janey was continuing, bending with her big bottom inelegantly stuck out to gather up an armful of the slim pink stalks, indifferent to their juicy feet against her skirt.

The words, little as they told her, nevertheless scored themselves into Sally's brain, never to be eradicated.

" . . . he found her on a beach, it seems. In Malaysia. They were both traveling, wandering down the coast." *No,* that was something we shared. "She'd been with some chap who'd dumped her, leaving her with no cash and no ticket home. Mike of course stepped in. And that was that."

She was heading down the path ahead of Sally, speaking half over her shoulder. Sally longed for more, dreaded it like the drill swinging in toward a tooth.

"Mike Danaher's one of the world's great looker-afterers, of course. Such a competent person, such wide interests. Did he tell you about his painting? No, of course, he wouldn't, but he's very talented. He doesn't give it much time, sadly, but his stuff goes really well in the gallery in the old village school and at the Grisedale theater and so on. It's hard to imagine that side of him when you see him out there heaving boulders and swinging his ax—he's a qualified tree surgeon too, by the way. His son Michael loves the place, fortunately. He's always out and about with his father whenever he gets the chance . . . Now, we'll get this lot straight into the freezer—so good when it's young, far too nice to waste on jam. We'll keep back enough to make crumble for tonight, though. The first of the season's always a treat."

Sally had been greedy for any detail connected with Mike and she had paid the price. With piercing regret she knew that the perfect bubble of their loving privacy had burst. Real life with its probing touch had not let it float and sparkle for long.

* * *

Keeping occupied was the only thing that helped and that at least was easy at Grianan, however mundane the activities. She deliberately avoided the long solitary walks she used to indulge in because she knew she would not be able to keep her mind off fantasies of Mike writing, Mike telephoning, Mike even miraculously appearing. At times she felt sure he would never give up something so good—or, angry and hurting, she would put it in cruder terms—if he'd been prepared to knock her off practically on his own doorstep then surely he'd find a way to get in touch with her now, if he wanted to.

And that was the painful core of it all. She knew she mustn't fool herself. Their meeting, inevitably, had meant different things to each of them. For her there had been a stronger attraction than she had felt for any other man, reassurance and tenderness after the time alone, and delight and confidence in her own sexuality restored. For Mike it could be nothing more than a brief and finite affair, however genuine his feelings had been. What would please him best would be to know that it was that way for her too. And to know he'd left her happier than he found her. Well, I am, I am, she cried to him, but it had been such a little time to have together.

At least she didn't have to go through the harrowing business of looking for letters or waiting for the phone to ring. All she had to do was throw herself into the scrum of Grianan life: helping in the kitchen where Aunt Janey unswervingly pursued perfection and Maureen hissed and muttered as her short cuts were circumvented one by one; hurtling up and down the glen fetching eggs from here, honey from there, lend-

ing the fish kettle, delivering plants; or being trusted
with some piece of garden drudgery where she could
do no harm.

Anything was better, she would remind herself,
weeding gravel or ironing pillowslips or scraping the
scrambled-egg pan, than torturing herself over happiness glimpsed and gone.

"I suppose I really ought to sell the Edalmere cottage."

Shattering comment lightly tossed out by Janey one
wet afternoon when she could find no further excuse
for avoiding the bills and was sitting glumly at her
desk with her hair on end and her feet twisted around
the legs of her chair like a rebellious child.

"Sell it?" Sally felt literally winded, not only by the
unexpected suggestion but by discovering how far she
had been from accepting that she would never be
there with Mike again.

"Well, I hardly use it and to tell you the truth I
find the drive down a bit daunting these days. A little
capital would come in handy. We keep sticking on the
elastoplast when what this place needs is the knife."
She spoke abstractedly, statement in one hand, mash
of grubby invoices in the other. "This has to be the
purest fiction—they cannot seriously believe they did
all this?" she snorted, pushing up her spectacles with
the back of her thick wrist.

The roof, the wiring, the plumbing? Sally knew she
ought to be more interested and involved, but her
mind had flown to the little neglected cottage on its
sheltered grassy ledge above the trees, the white farmhouse looking out over the lake.

"But Janey, Edalmere—isn't it a good thing to keep

money in property?" She grabbed at the first practical thought that surfaced, trying to focus her mind. "Unless you urgently need a big injection of cash?"

Janey peered at her over the slipping spectacles. "I suppose so. And when you're here I may manage to get down more often. It's a perfect place to hole up and God knows I could do with a rest now and then." Sally couldn't ever remember her admitting it before. "But in the long term . . . I know you hate the house, and certainly Ursula's taste wasn't mine, but lots of people would think it delightful and it's in a very attractive location, particularly now Mike's doing all the work on the walks around the lake and so on. I can't believe this man, he's saying I haven't paid him since March, what does he think checks are, junk mail . . . ?"

Sally sank back into her chair, feeling as though she had swum a mile. Janey hadn't meant it seriously. It wasn't happening. But then she asked herself, frowning, why had she been so shaken? Did she seriously think that one day, when enough time had passed, she would be able to go back? Go coolly along the lane without listening for the sound of the pickup coming, pass the house without a flicker of feeling, walk the lake path without looking, longing, remembering?

Don't think.

"Janey, how would you like me to sort that lot out for you?"

"Oh, darling, would you? Honestly, would you? I hardly liked to ask, you do so much already."

"I might be better at that than at making meringues." Yesterday's disaster.

"I certainly hope so. Come along then, start now." Janey sounded gay and relieved, moving her chair to one side, sweeping a clear space on the desk with her forearm. Sally drew up a chair beside her. Engage the brain.

"So you're back in the glen."

She had known she would have to face this sooner or later. The scruffy but quite new-looking Daihatsu jeep cruised to a halt beside her as she walked out of the garage in Muirend, leaving Janey's hard-worked Astra estate to have four new tires put on—not Janey's idea.

"Hello, Jed."

The thick black hair and beard had a touch of gray in them now, the powerful shoulders were heavier, but the black eyes were as searching and fleering and truculent as ever. An intimidating character, Sally thought, yet taken aback to find an unmistakable response quiver in her as he swung down and slammed the door behind him without taking his eyes off her face. Fifteen years. That frisson of—whatever it had been—was just association, Sally assured herself hastily.

"So you haven't forgotten me then?" Had he realized? Still the same probing look from which it was so hard to drag one's eyes.

"Of course I remember you, Jed." Social, polite.

He laughed at her, neat white teeth appearing in a mouth whose smallness the beard disguised. "Aye, and I remember you. You're staying a bit longer than usual this time, I hear."

He sounded teasing but there was an edge to it, as ever. At sixteen it had made Sally feel defensive, yet still eager for his approval.

"How are the family? All well?"

Jed's smile widened. She saw he had no intention of letting her pretend they were mere acquaintances.

"Bloody wild, the lot of them," he replied, his eyes still examining her openly. "And their mother's the worst of all." Easy, refusing to be patronized.

"I hear you're the boss now on Glen Ellig?" He had been shepherd all those years ago; Connie had told her he was now farm manager.

Flash of white teeth again, though his eyes didn't smile. "Old Miss Hutchinson doesn't give me much trouble." He jerked his head at the vehicle behind him. Sally had been surprised to hear she was still alive, a reclusive and eccentric old soul who hadn't left her shabby run-down farm for twenty years or more.

"You must find the grieve's house a big improvement—a lot more room for the family."

The right sort of thing to say. Ursula-speak, Sally recognized, grinning inwardly.

But Jed was having none of it. "You're looking well. Ripening with age, as they say."

Just enough of an innuendo there to rouse again that flicker of physical response. Mike had reawakened her body, as she was all too well aware, but it was startling to find that Jed's knowing eyes could so easily stir it. His own body had thickened and matured; a filthy quilted gilet showed off the massive shoulders; his legs were like tree trunks in stained and faded jeans. His stance made the aggressive statement she remembered of old, challenging every male he met, displaying to every female.

"But you've given up those lonely walks to the head of the glen these days?" He was watching her as though he knew exactly how he made her feel, and the suggestive note in his voice ran a little cold brush of reluctant excitement across her skin.

"I have," she agreed, angry with herself, making a determined effort to keep her voice light, her eyes meeting his squarely. Whatever responses he had aroused, the longing was not for him.

"Is that a fact?" he asked lazily. "Well, then, I'd best be on my way." Casually, so that it was not clear that there was a connection, but making the first move to go so that he was in control.

"I think so," Sally agreed coolly, and she saw his grin widen as he turned to get into the jeep.

"Bonnie hair you always had," he called as he let in the clutch.

She remembered his huge hands, devoid of any finesse, burying themselves in it as he held her mouth to his.

"You bastard, Jed Maclachlan," she said under her breath as she walked fast into the town. She had thought there might be some brief awkwardness in meeting him for the first time; she hadn't imagined for a second that he would still show any interest in her. Proprietorial interest in a woman he had once possessed, she told herself caustically, or mere automatic reaction to any woman between puberty and menopause. But she couldn't pretend that it had had no effect.

Blended scents rose around Sally as she cut tough stems of thyme from the overgrown bushes at the more ragged end of the herb bed.

"Before the sun reaches them but after the dew has dried. Use a sharp knife. Don't crush the leaves or they'll lose their fragrance." Oh, give me a break, Aunt Janey. But the inner protest was good-humored.

"Are you going to dry them or freeze them?" Piers stood in the sunlight on the mossy path, a bundle of stakes under his arm.

"Ho, that's decision-making. Outside my job spec.," she told him, snipping industriously.

Piers laid down the stakes and, taking a knife from his back pocket, bent to help her. "Want some marjoram too?"

"Everything. I've been waiting for days to get all this no-rain, post-dew, pre-sun stuff just right."

"Not hankering yet for a bit of decision-making?"

"Nope."

"Do you ever miss your old job?"

Pause. Piers worked quietly on. Sally knew he wouldn't repeat the question. He respected everyone's right to reserve. The question itself had not been important anyway.

"It could be satisfying on occasion. Demanding even."

He waited patiently for a more informative answer, if she felt ready to give one.

"Demanding in the wrong way, though," she went on slowly, after an interval of snipping away companionably in the aromatic sunny warmth. "More stress and frustration than a sense of achievement, in general. I seemed to be forever pushing and shoving to get things organized against the clock. Schedules were always too tight and could be thrown into chaos by someone at a higher level changing his mind about a detail that seemed trivial to him. But I used to batter away at it all, never really questioning the end result. I was good at my job. I'd have gone on thinking it all mattered, I suppose, being promoted, getting pay rises."

Or I'd have given up work altogether and stayed at home and pressed buttons in my streamlined house, watched by the little red eyes of timers, my days ordered and segmented by beeps and pings.

"I didn't even see how artificial it was. I was leading a life considered normal, acceptable, praiseworthy even. Yet now—" She straightened, her hand crushing the purple-leaved sage she held, her eyes blind to the regimented stretch of hoed earth across the path with its thin green lines and mathematically regular potato drills, the pruned currant bushes against the wall, above which rose the lifting swells of the Drumveyn moor and the great curving ridge of Ben Breac. "Sometimes, now, I find I do miss the thought of a job stretching ahead of me. A career even," she said on a note of self-deprecation which Piers ignored. "I shall have to start thinking about what to do next, I suppose."

She realized that a month ago, less, she had been shutting her mind to it in terror, her self-confidence in tatters. Now the thought was there, ready to be turned over, tossed around, without urgency or threat.

"This is a good place for thinking," Piers said, laying their plunder in effortless order on the weathered gray trug. "Establishing values."

"I think you've established yours?" Sally suggested, smiling at him, ready to turn to another subject.

"You don't read much, do you?" he asked.

What did that have to do with anything, Sally wondered. "I'm out of the habit, I suppose."

"It might help." She felt, as she had felt before with him, that they had said to each other all the things that words had left out. She felt that without explanations he somehow comprehended everything about Julian and about Mike, without names, without places, without facts. He knew about rawness and need, and that was enough.

"There are thoughts one comes across," Piers went on in his understated way. "Meeting one's own feelings brilliantly phrased—and therefore shared. Come and look whenever you feel like it. You may find things that are right for you."

. . . the garden cottage on midsummer nights, moths dashing themselves against the glowing apricot shade of the single lamp, Piers cross-legged on the futon playing Andean folk songs on his flute, Sally stretched out beside him, taking comfort from the light asexual contact of his thigh, dreaming, pain held at bay.

Once he read poetry to her. But it was too soon, too apposite. She had fled from Piers' voice, which understood too clearly what it read. So on the next occasion he turned to Colette's astringent philosophy and verbal exactness, then to Patrick Leigh Fermor for beauty, and to Macaulay to lure her into cheerfully pounding out the rhythms with him.

The tendrils of this life, of the glen itself, were reaching out to her, as she was aware. She had assimilated the various changes, new houses fringing the village, cottages which she remembered inhabited now abandoned and roofless, the beautiful old humpbacked bridge flattened, the road straightened and widened in several places—which actually she thought rather an improvement but which Janey fulminated against as vandalism. There were more English voices to be heard, more retired people about, the school was threatened with closure and tree-guards ranked like the crosses in a war cemetery on Drumveyn, where Sir Charles Napier had been succeeded by a son much more conscious than his father had ever been of conservation issues.

On her lending and borrowing expeditions Sally met newcomers drawn willy-nilly into Janey's trading network, and renewed acquaintance with families who had known the Buchanans for three generations. (Janey had, after all, been moved and delighted that Sally had decided to use the Buchanan name herself.)

There were changes among them too. Over in the next glen to the west tragedy had struck Affran, where Lewis Galbraith had drunk himself to death and left debts which meant the estate had to be sold. It had been bought by a Dutch shooting syndicate who used one of the lodges, and its beautiful big house stood empty. The Galbraith daughter, Philippa, a near contemporary of Sally's, had apparently gone into the Air Force, which seemed a bit extreme.

At Baldarroch, droopy spineless Margot Thorne had been replaced by Julie, a rough-cut product of the LSE who had little time for glen socializing, but whom Sally rather liked. And at Drumveyn, across the glen, there was a new young Lady Napier who, according to Janey, had been hitchhiking up the glen and given a lift by her future mother-in-law. Not only given a lift but taken home to cook for the family. Now she was married to Archie and they had adopted two small girls. Pauly was a big, warm, friendly creature, always up to her eyes in some activity, but always with time to chat. The atmosphere of the formerly daunting house had been transformed and Sally, who had gone there with disagreeable memories of unrelaxed chil-

dren's parties and a cold and frightening downstairs
loo, was completely won over. All this was intriguing
and fun, and Sally felt that possibilities for renewed
contacts were waiting in the wings, when she was
ready to face them.

Meanwhile, the usual emergencies rolled over Grianan: blocked drains, a jackdaw coming down the chimney and flying about the dining room during dinner,
shedding droppings and soot, a herd of Glen Ellig
stirks getting into the garden to be driven out with
the spry and resourceful assistance of the guests. (Jed's
son Gordon came to collect them and rattled Sally
considerably by being a replica of his father as she
remembered him, and by giving her much the same
arrogant once-over with black insolent eyes.)

So the skin of the place began to grow over her;
her sense of rootlessness faded. No decisions need be
made yet. Julian had dropped out of her mind and
recent wounds were clean.

Then a letter came with a Kendal postmark. Not a
letter, as it proved, when her shaking hands had
ripped the envelope open, but a plain postcard which
said, "I'm still looking out for that red Renault."

Chapter 8

For one awful moment of doubt Sally stood rooted, not knowing how to greet him. It was as though she couldn't gauge the footing they had been on, or how far in the weeks since she had seen him her thoughts and feelings would have diverged from his.

She gazed at him helplessly, her body trembling with uncertainty. No uncertainty for Mike. He plunged forward beaming to seize her, lifting her off her feet, swinging her around exuberantly, head back to laugh into her face, then crushing her tightly in his arms.

"Hey, little anxious face, aren't you pleased to see me?"

"Oh, Mike." She tried to hide the surprising giveaway tears against his shoulder. But he wanted to see them, wanted everything about her, the laughter and the tears, telling and touch and above all her body loving and giving.

"I couldn't not see you again. You do understand that, don't you?" he asked later, his voice very quiet, almost constrained, his arm gathering her close against him, her head in the hollow of his shoulder. He meant, Sally knew, that he wanted her to understand on what terms, warning her that nothing in their situation had changed.

"It's all right. I know."

He gave a low exclamation which was close to a groan. "I don't want to hurt you," he said, lifting his head and twisting so that he could look into her face, his own tight with dislike of what he was saying. "God knows, Sally, the last thing in the world I want to do is hurt you."

She reached up to run her hands through the springy dark red hair, pressed closer to him, wanting to hold on to their drifting satisfied peace, not wanting to see in his eyes the self-condemnation of the man who knows this wish and these words are futile.

"I won't be hurt by you. Hoping is what hurts."

The sort of hurt he meant anyway. The rest she would have to cope with as best she could. It was her choice.

But they both knew exactly where they stood. They needed more of each; their discovery of each other had mattered too much to be given up so soon. They both felt incapable of relinquishing something so marvelous with so many things still to say, so much loving still to share. The outcome would not change and after this brief exchange they didn't discuss it.

Edalmere. The very name took on a different meaning on the snatched days of early summer when Sally would take off down the glen at dawn or as soon as dinner was over, turning thankfully off the motorway to take the roundabout route which climbed to Edal village, to come at last along the lane with hammering heart, wondering how soon Mike would be able to get away.

He was working much further around the lake now, on the western shore, and a key memory for Sally was of walking along the track in the fresh morning air, going from shade to dappled sunlight, the clean tree-and-lake smells in her nostrils, noting work he had done, pausing to look down the open views which had so altered this once closed-in and inaccessible shore, and going on with pleasure rising in her like champagne at the prospect of coming soon out of the trees and seeing him working there, the long active body, the concentrated energy, the smile on the bony brown face as he saw her.

Once or twice he took time off and they had a whole day on the fells together, going over to Haweswater or along High Rigg, but preferring the less frequented if less interesting ground to the east. They didn't cover a lot of miles on these expeditions; what they both wanted was solitude, being together in the landscape Mike loved. And in the evenings the lake was theirs, the walkers and birders and environmental-study groups gone, the car-park empty, the cormorants on their island for the night, the swans drifting on the dark water, the owls calling above the woods. Even the pretentious little cottage became a treasured place because it was theirs.

"It's so good to *talk*," Mike would say with satisfaction, in the languid contentment after loving. "I never really talk to anyone these days." It was the nearest he ever came to a comment on his relationship with Isobel. A crumb. Though Sally supposed it could not be perfect if he was here with her.

Little by little facts filtered in. Learning more of Mike's life, his day-to-day concerns, his interests and tastes and attitudes—and at this stage inevitably Sally thirsted for all this—brought with it other less desirable knowledge. The "we" of marriage could not be eliminated entirely. His son she knew was Michael;

now his daughter had become Kirsty, the name an unwanted clue to the identity of the "rabid Scot" he had once referred to. Sally wanted to hear about the children because they were part of him and he loved them—and also, with a grim honesty, because references to them kept matters in true perspective. Whatever fantasies might creep in, in spite of her most determined efforts, about Mike one day leaving Isobel, she could never for one moment pretend that he would leave his children. He was a responsible, loving man who would do all he could to protect and look after his family. By character and training he was a man who took charge, sorted things out, made things work. He would not walk away from a job. And that was part of his attraction.

She was also obliged to accept that he was a lively, talented and gregarious person and with that went the reluctant awareness that she was not going to be the only female who would find him attractive or whose company he would enjoy. The only small consolation, though it had its downside of leaving him open to these contacts which she could definitely have done without, was that Isobel rarely seemed to go anywhere with him. He went alone to conservation meetings, spoke to various groups on environmental subjects, but was also part of a wide circle of Lakeland painters, writers and musicians and it was here, Sally knew, that he found the stimulus and friendship closest to his heart.

The drive back to Grianan, battling up the hated A74, became something to be dreaded, something she had nightmares about. Once there, no matter how doggedly she tried to fill her mind and time with work, images of Mike—at home, with his family, somewhere around the lakeshore with Michael at weekends sharing the jobs she had done with him, spending his evenings in some intelligent, articulate, relaxed, likeminded group—were not easy to deal with.

It was hard, too, after their marvelous love-making not to let her mind go forward to thoughts of having his child. She had most scrupulously gone back on the Pill, but sometimes the primitive need to have some part of Mike which belonged to her tempted her to miss taking it.

She would find herself becoming obsessed with mental pictures which flayed her with their vividness—of the day Michael was born, was laid in Mike's arms, when Mike had first felt the light, warm weight of him, when he and Isobel had looked at each other, thankful, with love. There must have been love. No dodging. Whatever state their marriage was in now, and apart from her own presence in Mike's life there was no hint that anything was wrong with it at all, there must have been love. That moment was something she, Sally, could never have, giving him his first-born. It belonged to Isobel, along with all the other moments of the children's babyhood and growing up, illnesses, crises, achievements, fun. All the normal but astounding intimacy of marriage. And it was there still. Nothing Mike had ever said had suggested otherwise.

These thoughts mostly attacked her when she was exhausted after the drive home, the emotional high of the few greedily hoarded hours, too much loving and too little sleep. It was then that she would wish that "something would happen" to Isobel, something unspecified but final, simply and painlessly removing her from the face of the earth.

Then after a night's sleep, after the normality of

being with Janey and Piers, these nightmarish confused thoughts would retreat, leaving only the day-to-day bite of loss, which in its turn gave way to looking forward to the next opportunity for taking the road south.

The next worst thing to missing Mike was deceiving Janey. If she noticed that Sally returned from these "days off" at Edalmere more exhausted than when she left her aunt made no comment, but that didn't help the guilt. But Sally knew it was something she could never discuss with her; Janey would condemn such behavior out of hand and would never begin to understand the compulsion and the need.

Piers, perhaps, Sally could have told, but she realized that in some curious way there was no need to. He simply understood that she was in need of help and comfort, and gently he offered it, the impersonal solace of beauty, music and peace. Sometimes of words, since words were important to them both, gradually allowing Sally some small insights into his own life, realizing that at present it would be impossible for her to talk about hers.

Bit by bit she pieced together a background for him, a conventional—and rather grand—home, an existence at public school made tolerable by remaining largely underground, the absolute refusal to go up to university or to conform in any way to the life expected of him, then the solitary journeys to off-beat places, the dabblings with the more mystic forms of religion, the jobs on organic farms in California, Kerry and New Zealand. He didn't care for direct questions and Sally didn't ask them, each allowing the other their essential privacy.

She never enquired either how Mike managed to

spend as much time as he did with her when she was at Edalmere. It was from a disapproving comment of Janey's that she learned Isobel was always running up and down to see her mother, who lived alone near Jedburgh.

"One of those mothers who simply can't let go," Janey said. "I met her once. She used to come and visit Ursula to tell her what a frightful backwater Edalmere was and how she wished her daughter was living somewhere more civilized. I told her she should get to know Elsa Callander. They were made for each other."

Sally dreaded meeting Isobel in the lane or the village. Once she saw the estate car parked outside the shop and went on to Windermere, startled to find herself literally trembling as she drove.

"You're so discreet," Mike said, as he had said before. Now he sounded almost angry, hating to require it of her, helpless to put it right.

"It makes it easier for me as well," she pointed out gently.

"I know, but I feel so bloody guilty. To you, I mean. And you never complain."

"We both know what we're doing." How swiftly complaining or demanding would destroy what they had.

"You're very good." He sounded awkward, trapped in his frustration that this was something he couldn't tackle and sort out. "You never ask for anything I can't give you."

"I come here of my own choice. I could stay away."

"You'd better not," he retorted promptly and illogically, so that they were able to laugh and the moment of constraint passed.

* * *

Pain was unavoidable. Janey took the chance of a quiet spell at Grianan to go down to the cottage for two or three days off and phoned to see how the hotel was faring—or what Maureen was up to.

"You're sure she's making proper mayonnaise?"

"Janey, what on earth can you do about it if she's rushing down to the village to buy Hellmann's?"

"Come home at once!" Janey exploded with one of her gruff laughs.

"Unwind, let go. We're fine. How's the weather down there?" I hope it's pouring. Sorry, Aunt J, nothing personal, just petty envy eating into me that you're there and I'm not.

"Oh, I can't tell you how perfect it is. This garden's an absolute sun-trap, isn't it? I even went down to swim at the old jetty and found the Danahers there picnicking. Such fun."

Intolerable idyllic scene—the happy closed family unit opening to welcome Janey, the backdrop of lake and hills. It was their place, their home, fixed and unassailable. Knives and swords of jealousy.

And Janey home once more, chatting obliviously. "What a lot they've done to that old house. Mike took me along to see his studio in the barn. Shelves and shelves of books. He has such a range of interests and he's so knowledgeable. I could have listened to him for hours."

I want to be there, Sally thought in furious despair. I want to see that private place of his. She had taken the chance on one of her visits to the cottage to go in search of some of his work in the local galleries, and been moved almost to tears to discover the delicate exact water-colors of the landscape she had shared with him. She had not allowed herself to buy one, with a deep instinct that to own anything tangible that was part of him would be wrong and taking more than was permissible. She never let her mind even flirt with the idea of any long-term relationship. Fantasies were something else, a craving indulged when loneliness grew too stark, but recognized always, implacably, for what they were.

But there was great happiness in their brief times together that summer. Sally had never imagined she could feel so close to anyone, so effortlessly in touch with feeling and intention and reaction, so sure. And certainly she had never experienced such physical awareness, nerve ends alive to his lightest touch, senses floundering at the mere smell of his skin, her body flowing and opening to him.

"You're incredible," he would say, staring into her eyes to read there what his hands were doing to her. "It really is like touching a live wire."

It's love, she wanted to say, submerging with a gasp under the waves of sensation. But love was not a word they allowed themselves.

As the season built up and Grianan grew busier it grew harder to make the time to go down to see him. And the crowded summer roads made the journey longer and more frustrating. Janey was willing to let Sally take time off whenever she wanted it, delighted that she used Edalmere as a refuge as she did herself, but once school holidays had started Connie and Maureen both wanted more time at home and the house, of course, was full.

The retired couples of early summer, the ardent botanists and bird-watchers and walkers, gave way to fishing and shooting families, often second-generation

Grianan guests, whose needs were far more varied and demanding. Many of them Sally knew, and they welcomed her warmly, so that inevitably she found herself drawn more and more closely into the life of the house.

Janey always pretended that she couldn't bear the guests. She spoke as though only privation had made her open her doors to a horde of insufferable hooligans. They were given the dates she offered them and the rooms she decided they should have. She refused them sweet sherry, cigarettes, milk chocolate, white bread and tea after lunch, and not even the children were allowed tomato ketchup. She roared through the house if they ran the water cold and growled as ferociously as Marchmain if they dared to approach her when she was gardening.

On the other hand she gave them breakfast at any unearthly hour they asked for it, dreamed up delicious packed lunches for them, fed chilly fishermen gargantuan late suppers and held through thick and thin to her everything-home-made promise. Sally had known her go to bed exhausted at midnight, leaving bread to rise, get up a couple of hours later to knock it back, and then again to put it in the oven. Her bedroom, known as the Apple Room, was over the kitchen, "so that I can bang about whenever I feel like it," as she put it.

Apart from the immense and endless care she took over the guests, the truth was that she loved their company. They were her friends, for only people of the robust cut she preferred would have continued to come. One of the shared interests, as well as food, birds and gardens, was music, and one of Sally's most abiding images of Grianan in the years she had stayed away had been of summer evenings in the big drawing room, level golden light pouring in through the three long sash windows, her eyes on the outline of Ben Breac, etched more and more sharply against the sunset light, as a pure voice sang *lieder,* a violin drew out its sweetness, or Aunt Janey thundered away on the piano at the more dramatic music she favored.

It was all so dated, a scene that could have been enacted in this room at any time in the last hundred years, but innocent, good, *safe.* The deep-bosomed lady with the untidy chignon who had sung *lieder* was dead, but now Piers was here with his flute. The mood remained unchanged, and Sally could ache and dream under cover of its nostalgic sentimentality.

She knew that she was lucky to be in such a place, where not only could every moment be filled, but where mind and spirit were not starved. And where when the chance to vanish presented itself it could be seized.

For Mike it was not so easy. Sally couldn't warn him when she was free and sometimes her visits were hopelessly mistimed. Later than in Scotland, but all too soon, the children were on holiday and Michael spent every moment he could with his father. Cousins of Isobel's came to stay, Mike's brother was over from Ireland. Once when Sally snatched the chance to go down for two days she saw Mike only once, for one brief hour on a rainy evening. He was as loving and tender as ever but she was aware of the subtle pull away from her, whether of time or conscience she could not tell.

It was during the two empty days of that visit, hanging uncertainly about the cottage wondering if Mike would come, or walking up on the fell determined to do something positive, that she felt for the first time an intruder in his life, and ashamed.

She told him how she felt, and that she would stay away till the holidays were over. He said little, his face grim, holding her tightly, but he didn't attempt to make her change her mind.

In September she went back, and they had three days of intense, aware happiness. When they talked it was of immediate inconsequential things. They shared their pleasure in the beauty around them—milk-washed morning skies with the bite of autumn in the air, rowan berries bright against blue water, yellowing bracken, scattered splashes of color around the lake where a branch here and there had caught the first frosts. And they touched each other, however lightly or casually, all the time, though never acknowledging the underlying ache of that need.

Hiding from it till the last evening when, already trapped by what was going to happen as though a net had been flung over them from which there could be no escape, they made no move to go to Sally's little room but sat on at the kitchen table with the dusk, earlier every evening now, gathering about them.

"Have you decided what you want to do, when the season's over at Grianan?"

Simple, normal question, but opening the doors wide to real life, which they had so carefully held at bay for these three days.

"No. Though it's time to think about it, I suppose." Sally had some vague ideas, but even to sketch them out would have distanced her from him, from this shared secret place, this precious time which already she could feel slipping away from them.

"You wouldn't consider staying on there?"

"I'd probably go mad with boredom in the winter." And it was becoming increasingly difficult to face Janey's honest gaze.

"You'll stay in Scotland?"

Then Sally saw that Mike's hands were clamped around his glass as though they would crush it by main force. She knew that he was forcing himself to ask these questions, forcing himself to face the fact that she would move on, make a new life for herself, in which he would have no part. Her eyes fixed on those rigid hands. After that one second of icy realization nothing really needed to be said. She made herself look up and met Mike's eyes; she saw that he could not speak. She felt her own lips tremble and pressed them tightly together. She reached out to touch his taut hands but he did not relax them, and at once she took her hand away, terrified of appearing to make some claim.

"Mike, it's all right. I know."

He shook his head once, his face clamped shut against the overwhelming feelings, then, not looking at her, said tightly, "It's just that sometimes when I go back I wonder what the hell I'm doing. To you as well."

In those two short sentences he had taken them from the vague and unstated to the specific heart of the problem. A terrible chill washed through Sally. From easy established habit, coming here when she could, Mike spotting the car and appearing the moment he was free, falling into each other's arms, loving, walking, talking—it was over. They had reached the end. Sally felt wild inner protest rising in her but she knew there was no going back from the words that had been spoken.

She summoned up all her resolution. Mike would hate a scene, would hate even an attempt to tell him what it meant to her. And didn't need to be told. "It's all right," she said. The accepted meaningless words of human reassurance.

"I don't want to—cause any waves." Banal response, but she understood that he couldn't bear to discuss this, and that it would be the only apology and self-justification he could bring himself to offer. The muscles of his face were rigid with pain, his eyes full of appeal and compassion.

"I know," she said again. "Nor do I."

"Christ, you're even making this easy for me," he protested with a spurt of shamed anger. For one treacherous dazzling second of hope Sally thought he wanted her to fight it, not let this happen. But in the same instant she knew she was wrong. He wasn't that sort of man. He made his own decisions and put a high value on self-discipline and courage.

"We mustn't spoil what we've had." Sally heard her own voice sounding too practical, almost brisk, but she knew he would not misread her tone.

"You've got some guts," Mike exclaimed, pulling her toward him so that she shouldn't see how much this had moved him. That last embrace was almost clumsy, without tenderness. Sally could feel the nubbly wool of his sweater against her cheek as he held her head tight against him, his own head pressing down upon hers, his arms like iron bars offering no consolation in this last hurtling frightening moment. There suddenly seemed to Sally a thousand things she hadn't said to him, needed to say, couldn't remember, would never be able to say now.

"Look at me," he said abruptly, urgently, gripping

her arms, holding her away from him. His eyes bored into hers. "We feel exactly the same," he said fiercely, giving her a slight rough shake which she thought he was quite unaware of, as though to insist on her comprehension. "Remember that. Exactly the same."

She nodded, mouth trembling, praying that the tears he would hate wouldn't overtake her yet.

The whine of the gate, familiar signal of his arrival, the sound that could set her blood racing, sounded behind him for the last time. Sally sank down at the table letting her forehead rest on the cool glossy varnish, wrapped her arms around her head and held herself together as best she could.

Chapter 9

Sally took a last look around the little office before locking up. A proprietorial satisfied look. The white shelves against the blue-gray walls she had fought over so obstinately with the painter, the orderly stock, were still new enough to give her a buzz. But the rows with Linda were turning into a pain.

It was just after seven but scarcely dark yet. The eternal winter of blizzards and floods and blocked roads must surely be over at last. Perhaps Linda would stop using them as an excuse for not turning up and start pulling her weight now.

Sally crossed the almost deserted Muirend square, crammed with parked cars during the day, and dived down a narrow cobbled vennel leading to the river. This was the old part of the town, until the early years of the century a bustling center of mills and warehouses. Since then it had been mainly used for tradesmen's yards, a brewery depot, stores of one kind and another. Most of these had recently moved to a new industrial estate on the far side of the town, several of the old stone buildings had been converted into flats, and the area was now considered rather desirable.

Sally had been lucky, as she had been lucky to snap

up the office premises on the square at just the right moment, to find the flat in the ex-boathouse loft, with its big window across the end wall overlooking the weir. It still pleased her to run up the stone outside stair—must get something into those tubs as soon as the weather's warmer, Janey will find something—and open the blue door into the long room which was kitchen and living area in one.

It had been easier in a way to drive away from Edalmere and Mike the last time than it had been the first. Then, too, many questions had been left unanswered; they had quite simply needed more of each other. During the summer months of their affair Sally had quite deliberately ignored her conscience, letting it be Mike's decision to be unfaithful to his wife, and in what degree. She had clung to what they had found together, while accepting that nothing could lie ahead but parting.

She had realized since that this luxury of moral abnegation had only been possible because Mike had taken responsibility for them both. He had kept before them his real priorities, not in words, but in the pace and tone he imposed. There had never been any agonies of uncertainty. The hardest thing Sally had had to face had been the lack of words when the end came. When she had done what had to be done, gone quietly away for good, she had needed, illogically but passionately, his assurance that he understood and was pleased with her. She wanted to be able to tell him that she had almost at once taken a grip on her life. A grim resolution, whether inherent or dinned into her by Janey (always it was her influence that counted for Sally, not her father's), had enabled her to get herself moving and make this new start.

Once she had captured Janey to talk to her about it, not giving her undivided attention of course, but tidying and cutting back the first victims to autumn on the herbaceous border, she had been startled at the enthusiasm of her aunt's response.

"Of course you must do it. I'm delighted you want to. This was never meant to be more than a stop-gap, though I've loved every minute of having you here and you've been the most tremendous help. Unskilled, admittedly, but devoted," she added, protecting a hypericum from Sally's secateurs. "Spring for those, as I'm sure you must know."

"These all right then? It may take some time to get organized, though," Sally went on, snipping away more cautiously. "Premises to find, all the legwork to do of leasing or buying. And someone else may get in first."

"In Muirend? Not a chance. But to be honest, it's the last place I'd have expected you to want to start up a business. I shall be thrilled to have you so near, but it's not what I'd have foreseen."

"I suppose being up here again I've discovered it's where I want to live." The only place that gave her any sense of belonging.

"That's good." But Janey darted her a sharp look. "Are you truly over it all? I haven't liked to ask— always too damned busy for one thing."

For one blank astounded moment Sally misunderstood, then hastily called her face to order, wondering what it had betrayed. "Well, Grianan in the summer is hardly the place for soul-baring chats," she managed to say easily—she hoped. "But yes, I'm over it."

Over Julian and her damaged pride. It all seemed so faraway now, and from this perspective she could see how unsuited to each other they had been. Her quite different feelings for Mike had taught her that.

"I'm glad. It was a hard knock to take and you've been so good about it." It struck Sally that the escapes to Edalmere, which Janey had never questioned, had been read as necessary time alone to recover.

"I know you haven't even started looking for anywhere to live yet, but do regard this as base, won't you, Sally, for as long as you need to. Goodness, how silly of me, I don't really have to say it, do I?"

"Well, I'm glad you did," Sally said firmly, reaching out to pat the scratched hand wielding the pruning knife. "Anyway, it will probably all take ages. It may never come off at all. You won't be getting rid of me yet, Aunt J."

"I count myself fortunate," Janey responded brusquely, and though for a second Sally thought she was being ironic, she saw with amazement that her aunt was blinking rapidly and pursing up her mouth in a most unwonted manner. "I don't think that potentilla will appreciate your attentions," she added tartly. Sally saw that their conversation was over.

Piers had not approved. "You've got a job here," was all he would say when Sally outlined her plan with an enthusiasm rather consciously whipped up.

"A job? Howking tatties?" They were working along the last row as they talked. "Or running up and down the glen with a boot full of laundry or loo rolls? Getting my head bitten off in the kitchen when Aunt Janey's had another fall-out with Maureen? Making beds and dusting because Connie's child is off school again with his new computer game?"

"There are few human activities which can't be reduced to similar terms," Piers pointed out calmly. "Certainly not wasting reams of paper on producing more and more photocopying and more and more mailshots, or persuading every innumerate small-business owner that his simple cash-book would be better replaced by a system that will oblige him to pay someone to run it and bury him in printouts."

"You know nothing whatsoever about it. That is a truly retrogressive attitude. A computer will take his books up to audit level, do his wages at a touch, and his end-of-year returns, tell him exactly what his cash level is, work out his projections."

"Jargon," Piers snapped, straightening up to face her. "I thought you had more innate intelligence." He sounded really angry and more contemptuous than Sally had ever heard him and she didn't like it. "And have you considered Janey's position?"

"Of course I have. I'll be less than twenty miles away. Have you forgotten that?"

"She would prefer to have you here."

Sally was astonished. "Janey? Are you serious? She thought I needed somewhere to lie low for a while, that's all. She knows I can't look on working at Grianan as permanent or fulfilling—"

Piers, the gentle and tolerant, threw his fork on the ground, kicked it for good measure, and walked away.

Often during the hectic weeks of finding the office and flat and looking for an assistant Sally had been tempted to contact Mike in some way. She told herself that she just wanted him to know what she was planning, where she would be, that she was all right.

Wanted to say to him, look how brave I am, how

well I'm coping, a dour inner voice amended. Wanted to give him the chance to contact her when she was alone, away from Janey's eye. He could telephone her at the flat, which had not been possible when she was at Grianan. They could say the things they hadn't said on parting. They could meet in some impersonal half-way spot, have lunch, catch up on news, as people did.

Rubbish; pathetic, dishonest rubbish. Nothing had altered, and she could not be the one to make the move. And why should Mike? He had everything in life that he needed. There would be no aching void for him, no incessant current of thoughts, associations, memories, running through every moment, every action.

Stop whining. Just get on with what you have to do—which had meant examining freezing cold office premises where it always seemed to be dusk and she always madly wanted to go to the loo, had meant grappling with dry rot, wet rot, woodworm, prohibiting clauses in leases, too many stairs, being too near the piggery, too far from the main drag. There was the interminable sequence of solicitor, bank, valuation, offer, closing date, failure. Then when it all began to come together at last the appalling winter had added its quota of problems.

Grianan had closed at the end of October. Sally had never known it in its dormant phase. She had always been there during school holidays, and even at Christmas Janey had always opened up for a house party. Not so now, it seemed.

"Haven't opened at Christmas for about five years," Janey said. That long? "To be honest, I can't face the hassle these days. It used to be fun, though." She sounded almost wistful and, looking at her face set for once in heavy lines, Sally realized how she depended on her aunt's energy and ebullience. It occurred to her that most women of Janey's age would have stopped working years ago.

Their world at Grianan during those autumn weeks shrank to the small sitting room and the kitchen, which temporarily took on a more human face. Sally could have done without Marchmain's unforgiving presence but he evidently regarded that as his open season and stayed close to Janey. Meals became simpler and fairly arbitrary as they worked their way through surpluses. Piers almost always joined them. During the day he and Janey attacked together the heavy work in the garden, in the evenings they listened to music, read or played chess. Seeing their quiet accustomed sharing of this time—they would go for literally hours without exchanging a word—it struck Sally that they had spent last winter here together, in this contented quietness. Did they mind her presence? And what, she began to wonder, did she contribute to the general scene? But nothing in their manner or behavior gave the slightest hint that she wasn't wanted.

On the contrary, Janey often openly expressed her pleasure that Sally would be living in Muirend, and Sally realized with surprise how much her aunt had been dreading the possibility that she would return south. Only once did she ask about Sally's father.

"Does he mind your being here?"

"I doubt if he knows where I am," Sally retorted, automatically resorting to glib antagonism as soon as he was mentioned.

Janey checked her with a quick grip on her arm. "You are not a child any more, Sally."

Sally looked away from her, ashamed but still mutinous.

"Sally, darling, I know that in terms of human relationships he did everything wrong, but do you suppose he isn't intelligent enough to realize that?"

Sally made an effort to reply without emphasis. "I did tell him that I'd be here for the summer. And I shall let him know my new address as soon as I move."

"Good. And Rose—are you—do you write to her?"

This was clearly harder to ask, and as Sally turned to look at her she saw how afraid Janey was of intruding, and how much she cared about the answer. It was like a new facet of her suddenly catching the light. Janey, the eldest sister, who, it had always been taken for granted, loved this house, this place, and was happy to spend her life here, but who after all had never been given much choice, particularly as both her sisters had fled.

Ursula, shallow and materialistic, had wanted only a marriage which would take her out of Glen Ellig and into a larger world, would allow her luxurious holidays in fashionable places and heating permanently on at full blast. She had been fortunate in finding Teddy, for the marriage entered into for such self-interested reasons had actually worked out well. Even more surprising was the fact that in the end she had been content to settle down at Edalmere, a setting not so different from that of her bored girlhood.

Rose, the youngest, had been less hard-headed. Finding herself in a marriage for which Sally now saw she had lacked the intellectual guns, she had taken the easy way out and abandoned it. Neither of them, Sally realized, looking at it in a new adult context, had given Janey much in the way of support, contact or love.

"Oh, Janey, I should have talked to you about all that long ago," she exclaimed, contrite. "I shouldn't have left you wondering." And saddened by it?

"I realized it had been a disaster when you came back from Australia, but I saw so little of you afterward. It's always been impossible to talk properly in this wretched place and you were always up here when we were at our busiest. Still, I blame myself for not making the time and trying to help. Can you tell me about it now? What happened with Rose?"

"I was just in the way." It was suddenly terribly obvious and terribly simple.

Janey's face tightened in pain, but her voice was carefully neutral. "She would have found it hard, you know, to meet you on such different terms, separate from your father. He'd made her so miserable."

Mike had said something of the sort.

"I was too young to handle it, too brash. I went there wanting far too much, expecting far too much." She had intended to live out there, Sally remembered with a small shock.

"Tell me about it."

"She never wrote and told you herself?" Sally asked curiously. The sisters had been close when they were younger, she knew, and to the others Janey had been a protective mother-figure for most of their lives.

"She said so little I knew there was a great deal more to tell," Janey replied drily. "Not the best of correspondents, my sister Rose. Tell me about the house, Orford, how they live, the family. . . ."

So now the move from Grianan had been made, and Sally was here, settled in the boathouse flat, spring was finally on the way and business looked promising.

Certainly all the small stuff in the shop, the copying, faxing and typing services, as well as the sale of stationery, was building up with reassuring steadiness. Sally knew that to find something which even half-used her skills in a small place like Muirend had been a great stroke of good fortune, and securing the franchise for the software package had been another. She already had two consultancy jobs in the bag, setting up office systems for a motel and a plumbing firm—and tonight had some work to do on both. She had been surprised to find how much pleasure and satisfaction she was deriving from her new enterprise, which she had embarked on more out of a resolve to find independent occupation than in any expectation of actually enjoying it.

She had just turned up the gas heating (she still felt she was defying Aunt Janey every time she did so) and shoved a lasagne into the microwave, looking forward to a peaceful evening's work at home, when the telephone rang. Janey.

"Darling, I just thought I'd let you know in case you were thinking of going up to Grianan this weekend—I'm down at Edalmere, having a little break before we open again. But there's masses of stuff in the freezer and Piers will be there, so just do whatever you want." She sounded terse and Sally's conscience stirred uncomfortably. She hadn't been up to Grianan very often in the rush to open the shop.

"I was thinking of going up as a matter of fact," she said, "but it would be nicer to do it when you're there. In any case I want to do some raiding, pinch some plants for my tubs. I don't think I'll risk doing that without you."

Janey didn't laugh. "Ask Piers. Take anything you like."

That didn't sound like her. "Janey, are you all right?" Had she been overdoing things, preparing for opening?

"I'm fine, Sally, but I've just heard some appalling news—" Sally could hear her gathering control. What on earth was coming? Her mother? "I'm sorry, it's rather shaken me. The poor Danahers, such a dreadful thing has happened. . . ."

For one icy heart-stopping moment Sally remembered how she used to wish that something would happen to Isobel. Horrified guilt held her rigid with shock. "Janey, what's happened?" she whispered.

Did she not believe that anything could happen to Mike? Afterward she couldn't imagine why her terrified thoughts had not flown instantly to him. Was it because he seemed to her so strong, so invincible?

"Poor Isobel, it really is the most terrible thing. Mike collapsed a few weeks ago, an aneurysm of the brain. He was rushed to Newcastle and they operated at once and managed to save him but he's in a total coma. . . ."

Sally had sunk to the floor, her legs pithless, clutching the receiver in both hands, shaking, tears spilling down her face. "Janey, that's so awful. . . ." she whispered. "So awful," she repeated desperately, more loudly, feeling it was vital to make some response that would sound normal.

"Yes, it's a frightful tragedy. Everyone here is so distressed about it. Of course they've had time by now to get accustomed to it but I must admit it was a great shock to me." She sounded deeply upset; old, Sally thought in a sudden flash of fear. "Such a strong, fit young man, absolutely in the prime of his life, it just doesn't seem possible."

That active well-muscled body, so intimately known, the long limbs and lean back, the rangy stride. The keen perceptive eyes and teasing smile. The competence, the caring and protectiveness. It could not all be destroyed like this, in an instant. "Janey, it's dreadful. . . ."

"I'm sorry to tell you such sad news. I think rather selfishly I wanted to share it with someone. Isobel has been wonderful, everyone says. Such a nightmare for her, the children to look after and having to go back and forth to Newcastle all the time . . ."

I can't go to him, Sally thought blankly. I can't help him or care for him or even see him. I can't find out how he is. I can't talk about him or share this numbing shock with anyone. I am shut off from him. In those first stunned moments she felt herself crying out that whatever wrong she or Mike had done this was too terrible a price to pay.

She stayed there huddled on the floor for a long time, weeping, as though to move would bring more pain.

Part Two

Part Two

Chapter 10

Sally moved through the days in a blur of shock and disbelief. Driving, she would be blinded by tears and have to pull up; or would arrive somewhere without any recollection of how she had got there. She did her best to deal coherently with Linda, the shop, reps, suppliers and customers. She forced her brain to concentrate on explaining accounts packages and spread sheets to computer-illiterate clients and often drove away quite unable to gauge how much she had managed to make clear to them. Twice she had to go back and deal with queries, and knew it was her own fault.

Small shreds of comfort gradually surfaced in her thoughts. Janey had told her the news on the phone and not face to face, so nothing had been given away to her. For this was Mike's life, Mike's privacy, which must be protected. And she was living alone, so did not have to go through the continual torture of pretence. Also, no one need ever know. All that was asked of her was that she should get through this alone. Frail spars, but they were there, and they saved her from going under.

At first she was desperate to see Mike, just to be near him, to reassure herself that he was still alive. She wanted to forget good sense and civilized behavior, cut through all the problems of finding him, getting access to him, simply to be with him for a few seconds and touch his hand. Then as she learned more about his condition from Janey she realized how pointless and destructive that would be. Mike knew nothing and no one. He didn't know where he was or who he was or what had happened to him. In all probability he never would. How could she contemplate for a second saying or doing anything that would bring more pain on his family? On Isobel. Sally's thoughts turned to her constantly in those first days, appalled at what she must be going through, and it put her own situation into perspective.

Work was the only thing that helped. And blessedly she was now working for herself, back doing what she had been trained to do, once more using her skills and experience, at whatever pace she chose to set. That pace was already demanding but went into overdrive when the inevitable run-in came with Linda.

Sally had gone up to Braemar to see a potential client and had run into a spring storm going over the old Devil's Elbow, engulfed suddenly in a blinding white-out. She had crawled on and had had a frightening time trying to keep to the road in the expanse of car-parks below the ski lifts, and was tense and shaky as she ran thankfully out of the snow on the eastern side of the pass.

When she reached Braemar and located the house she found it locked and deserted. An obliging neighbor told her that Mrs. McGivern was in hospital and had been for two days. Sally had driven home with murder in her heart and had arrived at the shop to find Linda on the step locking the door.

"What on earth do you think you're doing? It's not

nearly five-thirty," Sally demanded furiously, in no mood for good management techniques.

"Near enough," Linda mumbled, not looking at her. "Anyway, everyone else shuts at five."

"And we stay open to provide a service for them." Sally could hear the danger note in her voice but Linda apparently couldn't, since she merely shrugged, unlocking the door again in a martyred way but clearly having no intention of going through it herself.

"I want a word with you," Sally said grimly, sweeping in past her and slamming down her briefcase containing the carefully prepared accounts package. "Mrs. McGivern wasn't there. You don't happen to know anything about that, I suppose?"

"Was that the one in Braemar? Oh yes, she phoned yesterday, or it could have been Monday. She had to go into hospital or something. Didn't I say?"

Sally stared at her, disbelieving fury boiling up. This idle creature, with her ridiculous spiked hair and her round, pink, stupid face, had let her go all that way, in those horrible conditions, for absolutely nothing, and didn't give a toss.

"You are the most useless creature it has ever been my misfortune to work with!" Sally exploded, ugly rage rising in her like a turgid tide. All the frustrations of the day and the unrelenting helplessness and grief over Mike broke over Linda's head. It was nasty, brief and terminal. Linda responded with the only weapon she had and walked out there and then.

Satisfying as it had briefly been in a cathartic way, it left Sally with an impossible workload. However, two of the women who typed for her at home agreed to do a few hours in the shop to help out, until Sally took on a school-leaver called Cheryl who had just finished her Highers and been offered a place at Dundee in the autumn. She was not an original thinker, but she was cheerful and willing, a boon after Linda, and might last the summer.

Sally now had a computer in the flat and regularly took work home, pushing on into the small hours almost every night, shutting out the unendurable. She rarely went to Grianan, knowing she couldn't talk about Mike but not sure she could be with Janey without revealing too much. She knew Janey was hurt at her almost complete disappearance, and Piers disappointed in her on Janey's behalf. The affection and sense of homecoming of last summer seemed far away now. The reassuring discovery that Aunt Janey's love, rock-solid, had survived the years of neglect and noncommunication had helped then, but were impossible to tap into as a source of comfort for her present pain. And Piers' eyes were too discerning, his gentle patience too liable to draw out unwary confidences.

For the same reason she broke off the tenuous links that had begun to form with people like Julie Thorne and Pauly Napier, knowing she couldn't reach out to them without her rigid control breaking down.

All she could manage was to go doggedly on from day to day, schooling herself to separate thoughts of Mike from the rest of her life. That was the key. Brutal as it was to put it into words, the total destruction of Mike's world could have no effect whatsoever on hers. She had already been prepared to go on with her life without him; that had not altered in real terms.

But no matter how hard she tried there was, behind everything she thought and did, the image of him lying white and still, recognizing nothing, understanding nothing, strength and vigor stripped away. Remembering his stories about his knock-about youth, the physical feats, the challenges, the outrageous escapades, and remembering too the other side of him, the lover of natural beauty, the craftsman, the man who could paint those delicate water-colors of birds and trees, she would be drenched in tears for him. Now he was helpless, fed and cleaned and bundled about by busy hands—he who had been essentially one of those who make the world work, who construct, invent, repair and control. And one of those who look after others.

"Sally? Hi!"

An unknown female voice on the phone, young, warm and eager. A hint of Selly rather than Sally. Someone she had met in Australia? Though it hadn't been a time notable for friendships formed. It was perhaps revealing that her mind went to people met casually at Sunday barbies, on the beach, or on those trips she had made more to escape the overpowering Brumby family atmosphere than to explore a country where she had never felt at ease. She must have buried the thoughts of that family pretty deep.

"Hello? Is that Sally Buchanan?"

"Speaking." Someone who knew she had dropped Maynard. But they would have to know that to find this number.

"Oh, great! This is Nona." Nowner. Well, not quite. The voice still sounded excited, as though sure it was giving her a wonderful surprise. "D'you remember me?" Less certain.

Nona—offhand, independent-minded ten-year-old glowering at Sally from under an untidy flop of dark hair, patronizingly fit, skinny, brown, queen of her own little outdoor sporty world . . . The eldest of

Sally's mother's second brood, the one who had never for one moment relented.

"Nona! Where are you?" An infusion of telephone warmth as Sally's brain raced, half intrigued and half apprehensive, around the possible answers.

A laugh. "In Purth. Purth, Scotland, that is." No mistaking how much she had enjoyed saying that.

"Goodness," Sally said blankly. Less than an hour away.

"Thought I'd give you a surprise," the voice was rattling on. "I came across with a couple of friends and we've been touring around England, but they've gone over to Europe for a while and so I came on up to Scotland to see if I could see you. I phoned Aunt Janey and she gave me your number."

Aunt Janey! What a cheek! Then Sally pulled herself together hastily. Nona had just as much right to call Janey aunt as she had herself, though the thought had never struck her before. The word she had been rejecting forced itself into her consciousness—and not before time, she thought with shame. This eager friendly voice belonged not only to Janey's niece but to her, Sally's, sister.

"Nona, I can't believe it. I had no idea you were coming over."

"Oh, well, I told Mum not to say anything in her letters. See how everything worked out, you know."

The voice was definitely more hesitant now, a little rising inflection in the last words making them a question which Sally couldn't miss.

"But you're going to come and stay, aren't you? Have you got wheels? How are you traveling?"

"Well, I don't want to mess you about. I can stay at the hostel here, but it'd be cool to have a chat."

"Of course you can't stay at the hostel. I'll come and fetch you. Where are you phoning from?"

"The bus station. The next bus to Muirend leaves in seven minutes." They laughed at what this said, a tiny first step toward each other.

"I'll come straight away."

"I can be there in the time it would take you to get here, can't I?"

"Not quite. I'd come straight down the A9, the bus will have its own ideas."

"Still, it's not worth you coming. So where do I get off?"

"Where the bus ends up. I'll be waiting."

"Right, see you."

Finishing off what she was doing on the computer, reducing to order the paperwork which was spread all over the flat, checking on supplies then walking up to the square, Sally found she was not resentful but interested, her mind jogged into new channels.

Her eyebrows climbed into her hair as Nona appeared on the steps of the bus. The skinny scowling child had turned into a beauty. Dark hair sleeked smoothly back, white shirt knotted across brown midriff, slim thighs encased in brilliantly patterned shorts, wide smile flashing in a deeply tanned face—she looked stunning, and Sally wasn't surprised to see a trio of workmen in grimy overalls grin and wave goodbye, or the bus driver milk the service of getting her pack out of the luggage hold as long as he could.

"Hey, isn't this fantastic?" Nona cried, beaming.

In spite of the casual clothes, the battered sneakers on her feet, she had an air of elegance, her body fine-boned, the glossy hair pulled back into a French plait which swung to her shoulder blades, exposing a long, slender neck.

"Yes, it is," Sally said, laughing involuntarily, and she meant it.

"This is neat." Nona was fascinated by the echoing alley-ways down which Sally led her and the secluded little courtyard by the river.

"Ex-boathouse," Sally explained. "The dock below has been covered over to make a garage. The flat's up these steps."

Nona loved it all. "What a *place*," she exclaimed, roaming the long room, standing at the window to gaze down at the pool below the weir where the first yellow leaves drifted against the bank, then exclaiming again in delight as she realized that the blue shapes beyond the fields on the other side were hill not cloud.

"I was lucky to find it." And had hardly given herself time to enjoy it, Sally realized as she spoke. All summer she had used it as a mere shell in which to work, sleep and eat. She had done nothing to it since she moved in, and in spite of her tidying today it had more the air of a workroom than a home.

"OK if I look?" Nona nodded at the doors which led to the tiny bathroom and bedroom at the back.

"Help yourself."

"It's a really great place," she pronounced, coming back. "But listen, you don't have to put me up, you know. I can count to one."

With an air of being at home which Sally found oddly acceptable Nona leaned on the worktop beside her, pulling off grapes one by one and leaving the stalks and little blobs of green jelly behind. (Sally heard Aunt Janey's voice and grinned.)

"You're staying," she said. Part of her was still

tempted to let Nona go—her arrival was so sudden, the flat really not big enough for two—but at a deeper level she knew there was no question of evading this. It mattered; and she and this startling new Nona had things to say to each other.

"Well, I'll have the couch."

"We'll argue later. Food first—though the pickings may be a bit thin. We'll have to stock up properly tomorrow." As in much else, Sally had been subsisting on the minimum.

"I'll stand you a pub supper."

About to object, Sally realized how out of the habit she was of doing something so obvious and normal. She had never been in a pub or restaurant the whole time she had been living in Muirend, and hardly knew what was on offer. They tried a hotel half a mile down the river and enjoyed the garden even if Janey would have snorted at the food. They ate overcooked scampi and undercooked chips and drank Chardonnay, and Sally tried to relate the resentful child she remembered to this cheerful, laid-back girl.

Nona must be twenty-three or twenty-four now. Sally realized that she didn't even know when her birthday was. She knew from her mother's letters, which understandably tended to be a catalogue of the achievements of her young, that Nona had qualified as a physiotherapist, had worked briefly in a hospital in Melbourne and then moved to a private practice.

"You can make a bomb going private," Nona explained. "That's why I was able to come over. I'd always wanted to see England, well Scotland, or the UK I suppose I should say, mainly because of Mum of course. And I wanted to get to know Aunt Janey."

"You must have given her a surprise when you phoned out of the blue."

"She took it pretty well." Nona laughed at some memory she evidently enjoyed.

"You weren't sure you'd contact me, though?" It was better said, and surprisingly easy to be direct with her.

Nona's dark eyes met Sally's honestly. "Oh, I was sure I wanted to come, all right. I just didn't know how you'd react."

I did that, Sally thought with shame, I with my patronizing arrogance and open criticism. Sally had behaved that way because she had felt uncertain and unwanted, but that wasn't how it would have seemed to them. What had Bill Brumby thought of her? she wondered with sudden sharp embarrassment.

"I'm glad you phoned," she told Nona, and meant it. A second chance—and a reprieve from loneliness. "Tomorrow we'll go and see Janey."

"To tell you the truth she sounds a bit alarming." The word gained power from her accent, which though not particularly strong was still unfamiliar to Sally's ear.

"She can be. She's a dear though, really. Not that she'd like to hear me say so."

"Wasn't she a bit on the heavy side with Mum and Aunt Ursula? When they were growing up, I mean? Vetting their boyfriends and all that?"

It was unexpected and fascinating to find this new angle opening up, discovering her mother via Nona. They opened another bottle of wine when they got back to the flat and talked for hours.

When Sally was finally stretched out on the sofa— which she had insisted on taking because she was the shorter by three inches, but really preferred since a night never passed without the dark weight of sadness breaking her sleep and she knew she would need her resources of work, coffee and pacing—she realized that she hadn't thought about Mike all evening. It was good, but agonizing too, pushing him further into a shadow world where all contact must gradually and irretrievably be lost.

Their time together now had no existence outside her own brain and memory. She had made herself get used to that fact. Even if he recovered, though she knew from Janey that a total recovery could never be hoped for, Mike would never know that they had met. He had been in hospital for eight months now and had undergone eleven operations. He still didn't know who he was or who Isobel was. By this stage Sally had reached the limit of her capacity to suffer for him. It didn't hurt any less, but there were no new thoughts to think. The real and continuing nightmare was Isobel's. Sally could only be thankful that she herself had never been a source of pain to her; that Isobel had never known of her existence.

Sally took Nona up to Grianan the next morning. It was a mellow September day, the heather just turning to its first glowing rust, shining rows of black plastic bags bulging with hay in the fields, uncut barley still ripening, the road almost empty of summer caravans, sacks shrouding half the bed-and-breakfast signs.

Nona looked and asked, wound down her window and breathed in the clean air, thrilled to be seeing at last this glen where her mother had been born, and making Sally realize that for months she had been closing her eyes to the beauty of one of the loveliest, least-troubled spots on earth. And Nona's gasp of delight as they pulled up at the door of Grianan reminded her that the well-proportioned stone house, with its huge sash windows staring across the tree-sheltered lawn to the shapely mass of Ben Breac, was after all rather splendid.

Not surprisingly, Nona had no problems with Aunt Janey's forthright manner. She had a good deal of that directness herself, less the gruffness. What did startle Sally was Janey's warm delight in the appearance of this new niece. She felt a small sting of jealousy, followed by a most salutary new idea. Was it possible that independent, busy, positive Janey could sometimes be lonely?

Piers also, to Sally's secret indignation, was visibly bowled over by Nona. Watching his open pleasure, his smiling eyes, Sally was uncomfortably reminded that she had not mended fences with him after he had spoken his mind about her leaving Janey, nearly a year ago now. He knew nothing about Mike, though he had certainly guessed there was some man in her life last summer, and as far as he was concerned she had simply gone off to do her own thing when Janey needed help, and had buried herself determinedly in her own concerns ever since.

Maureen had had help in the kitchen this season, leaving Janey free to trundle around doing the jobs Sally had taken on, but it had been a real sacrifice for her aunt to do less cooking and Sally gathered that the plan hadn't worked out too well, which perhaps wasn't surprising.

Today, however, culinary shortcomings and kitchen warfare were dismissed with one or two pithy comments which made Nona blink, then grin appreciatively. The three of them set off to tour the house and, presently, Sally was aware of an odd feeling of being excluded as her mother's girlhood memories were recounted by Nona and edited by Janey with obvious enjoyment. Well, Sally reminded herself, she had been too young to be told any of this before her mother left. These were things you chatted and laughed about with a grown-up daughter, and when she had been old enough she had seen to it that they never reached the chatting stage. She minded quite surprisingly for a few minutes till she took hold of herself and began to listen. No point in missing out a second time—and Janey's frank pleasure in a youth suddenly returned to her and shared was irresistible.

They had lunch, Piers joining them, in the little paved corner outside the sitting room, basking in the yellow sunlight which had burned off the early haze. They strolled afterward in the garden blazing with great clumps of monbretia and michaelmas daisies and potentillas of every shade still in full flower. But was it really Aunt Janey setting this lazy pace? Sally found herself wondering more than once. Her aunt didn't even get her hands dirty, did no more than pull out an occasional bit of groundsel and dead-head a rose or two.

She left them quite soon, carrying a handful of herbs to get her *canard en daube* started, which she said would need at least four hours in the slow oven. Sally suspected that she chose dishes that would take a long time so that she could indulge herself in preparing them while Maureen and her assistant were off for the afternoon.

Sally led Nona through the wild end of the garden and took her up the hill to her favorite rocky viewpoint.

"God, you were lucky, growing up here," Nona sighed, gazing down the farmed and wooded glen, then letting her eyes follow the soaring bare skyline of the hills to its head. "This air, so soft, and smelling so gorgeous. And the colors, that amazing velvety green. No wonder you couldn't stand Orford."

"Did it show?" Sally asked guiltily, knowing the answer.

"Oh, well, it was a bit of a disaster, wasn't it?"

"Did you all hate me for turning up like that?"

"Hate you?" Nona turned in surprised protest. "Oh no, it wasn't like that at all. We were dying to meet you, big sister and all that, but then when you arrived we were scared to death of you. You seemed so grown up, and so ultra Pommie, you know." Again that rising inflection which made the words sound almost an appeal.

"So snooty, you mean?"

"Well, we could see you thought it was all pretty crude. And Mum always seemed to be ratty while you were there. I don't think she's ever forgiven herself."

Perceptions, Sally thought, with a wry sense of defeat and loss. Did one never learn that everyone looks at everything from his or her own angle?

"I was looking for all the wrong things." It was good, and surprisingly easy, to talk about it at last, perched there on the rock slab with the light wind bringing the sound of a tractor working far below them—Jed Maclachlan?—and the sun warm on their faces.

"I was so envious," Nona confessed.

"Of me?" Of what? They had seemed so invincibly secure, so united.

"Of the way you looked. That incredible hair, and your clothes. You made me feel such a mess."

"I don't think you have too much to worry about now," Sally commented with a little spurt of laughter, looking at the perfect profile, the shining hair, the evenly tanned skin that made her look so exotic.

"Oh, well, I suppose I can pass in a crowd," Nona acknowledged, grinning, and Sally was astonished at how close she felt to her after less than one day.

"You could stay up here, you know, if you wanted to," she suggested, as they paused on the way down to cram their mouths with blaeberries. "Janey would love to have you." The house would be full, but there was her own little room.

"That's an idea," Nona said, with a little sidelong questioning look. "I felt guilty about moving you out last night."

"Nona, you're perfectly welcome to stay at the flat."

Nona still hesitated, then said shyly, "I'd really love to be with you—sort of get to know you, if you really don't mind."

Sally stood up to face her, frowning, wanting there to be no doubt about this. "There's room for us both." Twenty-four hours ago the thought of someone intruding on her busy space would have been unthinkable. Now Sally wanted to give Nona the best she could offer. And deep down she knew that Nona had something to give in her turn which she most desperately needed.

She was right. Having Nona around lifted her out of her trough of lonely grief. And it was time. She had come to terms with the fact that Mike had gone. She had worked through the grim period of thinking it would have been better if he had died, and then the

shame that she could have believed this. She knew
that she must make the best of her own life and not
go on clinging to something that couldn't exist, had
never existed in reality. Now she had help.

Chapter 11

Having Nona around was like being plugged into a powerful regenerative current. In a matter of days she seemed to know half the population of Muirend and be involved in a dozen different activities. Much as she loved Grianan, Glen Ellig was too quiet and too remote for her. She needed people of her own age around, and endless new interests.

She went to play squash and volleyball and work out in the gym at the new leisure center which Sally had never so much as seen. She bought a mountain bike and disappeared helmeted and lycra-clad to explore Glen Maraich and Glen Ellig. At six in the morning when Sally was rattling away at the computer, having been unable to sleep and already on her fifth cup of coffee, Nona would be pushing up the steep hill above the town and taking a ten-mile run around the farms and lanes. She met the assistant pro from the Muirend golf club at a disco and in no time at all was having free lessons on the driving range. The mountain bike was soon joined in the garage by someone's cayak, then by a pair of second-hand skis she'd won in a raffle.

Bodies in sleeping bags appeared regularly on the floor of the flat, and other multinational birds of passage who couldn't be accommodated there were dispatched to Grianan and welcomed by Janey with a warmth Sally found surprising but which Nona took entirely for granted.

Not only did the flat silt up with the most stupendous mess but Sally's time was encroached upon just as thoroughly. At first she tolerated it because she knew it was good for her to be hauled out of absorption in her own affairs and because she felt she owed Nona something, but soon she began to like it.

There was no time to dwell on sad thoughts and she was freed at last from the mental and emotional deadlock over Mike. She saw, with gratitude, that she had been given the chance to make amends for past failures. The easy, warm, two-way relationship with Nona brought her not only nearer to her mother but to the whole family, including Nona's father, that silent background figure she had always so sweepingly discounted. How insufferable she must have seemed to him, she realized now, horrified when she looked back objectively at the way she had behaved and saw for the first time the remarkable restraint he'd shown. At nineteen she had been quite old enough and intelligent enough to have been fairer to him. Now Nona's chatter of home revealed him as generous, hard-working, easygoing and above all devoted to their mother. Sally saw that in her desperate insecurity she had closed her mind to their happiness together as though willing the relationship not to exist, far less be successful where that of her mother and her own father had failed.

The paperwork went back to the office. Apart from the fact that there was no longer room for it in the flat, Sally no longer needed to spend her evenings and weekends immersing herself in it, and the mere fact of another presence close by seemed to have cured the dreaded insomnia. Now she didn't need the work as a prop, and didn't need to spend her time out of shop hours on it anyway. She had efficient help at last. Nona came to work for her.

"Are you quite sure it's your scene?"

"You mean I'm not capable of doing it and that dozy Cheryl is?" (Cheryl had decided to "have a year out"—euphemism for failing her Highers, going on the dole and loafing around Muirend with her mates for the foreseeable future.)

"I meant you'd find it boring."

"Oh, what? I'm never bored. And it's not all running the copier—you do have the odd customer coming in and out, don't you? That should keep me awake."

Sally laughed, with a lively vision of the shop thronged with a new cross-section of customers, whose interest would not lie principally in A5 duplicate books or lever-arch files.

Most weekends found them heading for Grianan, often with extra passengers in the car. Nona couldn't get enough of the place and Sally had to deal with a most unworthy reaction of possessiveness on seeing her plunge enthusiastically into whatever job was in progress. When she herself had come back here eighteen months ago she had been so uptight. Nona simply dived in, eager to learn everything, laughing at her mistakes, full of energy, dauntingly fit, capable and adaptable. No problems in that extrovert, confident life.

Sally was to find that she was wrong again.

There wasn't a great deal of time for serious conversation as they rushed headlong through the days, though there was plenty of the companionable chat and laughter which she had been missing so badly. But occasionally they would find themselves with the flat to themselves for the evening and would open a bottle of wine and cook up something special. (Nona had been astounded and rather awed by Janey's approach to food, but she had taken to it as wholeheartedly as she would have embarked on some new sport.) After exchanging a lot of extravagant compliments on what they'd produced, they would sit talking for hours, as dusk gathered to darkness above the inky pool and the overhanging trees seemed to crowd closer.

Sally told Nona about Mike, but only that there had been a married man in her life a year ago, and that they had stopped seeing each other because of his wife and family. She could not, *could not,* put into words what had happened to him. And she didn't say she had met him at Edalmere, which of course Janey often talked about to Nona.

One evening when a gusty wind battered rain against the big panes and they had drawn the curtains for the first time, with that mixed enjoyment in the sense of coziness it gave and reluctance to admit that winter was near, Nona told Sally about the married man in her own life.

"It's one of the reasons I came over. The main reason really. It's got to be his decision."

The hedge of thorns—wife, children, house, finances, habit—and caring enough not to want to do harm. "Oh, Nona, that's so hard. I do know. But I had no idea, I'd really never guessed. What's he like, what does he do? Can you tell me about him, if you'd like to?"

"Oh, he's a great guy. Really great." Her voice softened and Sally caught her breath. Lovely as Nona was, she had never seen that gentleness in her face before and she found it moving and somehow precious, as though she had gained more of her in that glimpse of tenderness. And who would blame any man for loving her?

"Tell me about him—if it would help."

"Sometimes I feel quite desperate to. I know it doesn't do any good, but you know, I feel as though if I can't talk about him he doesn't exist."

The knife turning.

"Well, let's see," Nona said, settling herself more comfortably where she was sitting cross-legged on the cushioned window seat, and sounding more cheerful already. "He's called Ray, Ray Tamerlaine, and he's forty-two and you can bet Mum's going mad about that for starters." Sally recognized that the affectionate exasperation was a step back from more difficult revelations and let her take her time. "But when I'm with him it feels *right*, I never even think about the age thing, it just doesn't exist. And he's really young anyway, not immature or anything, I don't mean, just kind of young in his ways, you know."

Words were not Nona's field.

"Well, I'm not sure that 'Mum' can complain." The inverted commas couldn't quite be eradicated. Sally thought of her still as "Mummy," which was absurd, and "my mother" was impossibly possessive. "After all, my father's about that much older than she is."

"Straight up?" Nona looked at her in amazement. "She kept that very quiet."

"Mind you, that didn't work out, did it? Perhaps that's what she's worrying about?"

It was good to giggle together, and easier afterward for Nona to go on. "Ray really is special. He's one of the Port Phillip sea pilots, and to do that you have to have all kinds of skills and experience—and courage and all that."

"Sea pilot? What does he do exactly?"

"Coming into Melbourne Harbor from the Bass Strait through the narrows at Port Phillip there's this thing called the Rip. A sort of boil where the river and the tide meet and there isn't room for them both. The pilots have to go about five k's out to sea to get the ships lined up to bring them through this tiny passage. There's been a pilot station there for about a hundred and fifty years or something. You can't be a pilot unless you've been at sea, been a captain—"

Her love song. All her admiration and love for this man shone in her eyes.

"—things have been pretty bad with his wife for quite a while, not that she's got someone else, I mean, I only wish she had, it's just rowing and that. She likes doing different things—you know—but there are these great kids, two boys, and Ray's mad about them—"

Oh, little sister, I know, I know. . . .

Sally would have thought Nona altogether too robust and down-to-earth for Piers' taste, but from the first moment he openly adored her and she watched them together with a strange pang of loss. She had valued Piers' kindness and friendship in her first months back at Grianan and somewhere along the way she had lost them. She would hear Nona gabbling away to him and the two of them laughing as they worked together and wonder bleakly what they found to talk about. To Sally's knowledge Nona never opened a book; her whole life was extrovert, physical. Then she realized that what she was feeling was that they had no right to get on so well, and she was relieved to find that she could laugh at herself.

Janey equally delighted in Nona.

"It's so *good* to see you together," she would say to Sally with some of her old vigor. "Knits back together something that has been horribly unraveled over the years."

Sally was glad she had this new pleasure, for Janey had grown noticeably more impatient and short-tempered lately. She obviously did far too much, but who could stop her? She had lost weight and her skin no longer had that healthy outdoor look. She did less work in the garden, which probably explained it, and without that and cooking her life seemed to lack zest. Certainly she moved more slowly, had more trouble hauling herself out of a deep chair, snapped with less humor at her underlings and had even begun to allow things like baker's bread and frozen prawns into the house.

When Grianan closed in the autumn Janey went to Edalmere for a couple of weeks, an unheard-of length of time for her to be away.

Walking with Nona into the kitchen at Grianan on the evening her aunt returned, Sally felt a sick churning inside, knowing Janey would certainly have heard news of Mike. She was totally unprepared for what came, once the greetings were over and Janey had brought to the table the partridge *à la Catalane* she and Piers had prepared.

"By the way, Sally, I heard some wonderful news at Edalmere. Mike Danaher's out of hospital at last."

Sally stared at her in shock, delight mixed with the feeling of having received a dizzying blow.

"The family are absolutely overjoyed, of course," Janey was saying. "Now come and sit down, all of you, and don't let this get cold."

Dazed, Sally found herself in her chair. Why did the queasy knot in her stomach feel as though it had received a kick from a heavy boot? This was the best news there could be.

"Is this your neighbor at the cottage?" Nona was asking. "The one with the subarachnoid hemorrhage?"

Thank God for Nona with her brisk professional interest, Sally thought, trying to concentrate on helping herself to partridge, passing the potatoes. But she knew why the sensation of being winded had followed instantly on her joy to know Mike was at home. He belonged once more, completely and irrevocably, to Isobel and his family. As he clawed his way back to normal life he would learn everything in his world again, but he would never learn that Sally had been in it. But that was best for him; anything that meant he was making progress was wonderful.

"Subarachnoid?" Piers was asking. "Spiders?"

"The membrane is so fine it's like a spider's web. If a clot forms it presses on it and breaks through. One of my friends' fathers had one. He'd had headaches for ages and he began to vomit a lot, then he suddenly collapsed."

"That happened to Mike, the collapse, violent pain. I'm not sure what symptoms there had been beforehand," Janey said. "They operated I don't know how many times. They think he'll be nearly normal again eventually."

Nearly normal. Mike. The tight knot now seemed

to be in Sally's throat but she knew she should make some attempt to say something. "How long would it take someone to recover?" she asked Nona. Her voice sounded quavery, but all their voices were subdued, concerned, and no one noticed.

"It varies a lot," Nona replied. "Only about a third of patients survive, as far as I can remember. About fifteen percent are left with a permanent disability. One of the problems seems to be how well they cope with fitting back into ordinary life. My friend's father did all kinds of bizarre things."

"Yes, apparently Isobel is going through all that, poor girl." Janey looked distressed and suddenly much older, Sally thought. "Mike doesn't know what ordinary things in the house are for, opens cupboards and pulls everything out. Goes to wash in the middle of the night and gets back into the wrong bed. Shouts and swears."

Sally was shaking, knotting her hands under the table, fighting to hide her horror. She wanted to get up and shout herself, reject these searing images, silence Janey, shock the conventional concern off their faces. But a deep fierce source of courage somewhere made her control the wish to refuse this agony of knowledge; it was all she could do for him.

"—used to pee in the bath and the basin," Nona was saying, and Sally braced herself more resolutely. "But they wouldn't have let your friend go home if he was still too disinhibited. Especially not with children there. He'll be back in the family to relearn social controls. In fact children help a lot because they take things for granted and offer normal interaction."

"Isobel says that every day he has to be told where he is all over again, and her name and the children's names. Yet he remembered at once how to use the telephone—only the poor soul doesn't know who he's phoning."

It all felt so unreal, sitting there in the familiar kitchen, hearing the sympathetic voices flowing around her, performing like someone in a play the small business of cutting off a tender piece of partridge breast, putting the forkful in her mouth.

Poor soul. The hard body, the long hands with all their technical skill and strength which could also produce those delicate paintings, the tough exterior cloaking humor, tenderness and the essential goodness which she had respected enough to walk out of his life. Poor soul.

"—often patients can recall things they learned in childhood but all recent memory has gone. Or certain areas of memory will come back intact and not others. There was a case I heard about somewhere, a surgeon who was in a coma for a week, ill for a month, then the whole of his medical knowledge returned complete. He's in practice again now."

Worse almost than the images which tortured Sally after this conversation was the report Janey brought back after a later visit to Edalmere. It seemed that the aggressive, uncontrolled phase had lapsed into apathy and inertia. Mike now slept for most of the time, and sat in a chair in his studio for every waking hour. She could not check her tears at this desolate picture.

"Darling, I know, isn't it the saddest thing you ever heard?" Janey herself scrubbed roughly at her eyes with an earthy rag of handkerchief. "It breaks my heart to think of him in there as I pass. And he's so often on his own, that's the awful thing."

"On his own?" Sally heard her voice rise in horrified appeal that this couldn't be true. "How can he possibly be left alone?" she made herself ask on a note of more practical concern.

"Well, I'm quite sure he shouldn't be." Janey looked tight-lipped as she rammed a carrot along her chopping board with her thumb to fall in even slices under her rapidly rising and falling knife. "Isobel goes to see her mother a lot."

"She always did, didn't she?" Sally ventured after a tiny pause. She couldn't bear to leave it there.

"Yes, well." The knife blade swept the mound of carrot slices in one angry gesture onto the softened onion in a giant pan. Janey didn't take readily to cooking for four.

Sally hesitated. There was something here Janey wasn't saying. But whereas she had allowed herself to give in to the torturing need to hear more, anything, about Mike—there had been love between them, surely she had that right—to ask about Isobel was a different matter, and to make any kind of judgment on how she dealt with all she had to face would be unforgivable.

Though Janey's face wore a look of grim disapproval as she stirred her vegetables, Sally asked no more. Later she went out alone, going past her favorite rocky lookout, way up the steep face of the hill through the drab drenched heather, across a dead area of bone-white stems where it had been burned off, and up to the sparse grass and rock of the ridge. She went fast, oblivious of the sullen clouds, the pattern of black plantation and bleached fields carved by rain-dark dikes widening below her, trying to assimilate this new picture which hurt so much. Mike sitting hour

by hour, unmoving, alone. Mike who no longer knew
they had ever met.

There came sudden, disturbing realization. She could
go back. The thought spun her to a startled halt. She
had for so long thought of Edalmere as barred to her;
first because she and Mike couldn't go on seeing each
other without doing harm, then because she couldn't
bear to be there and shut off from him.

Now she saw that it wouldn't matter if she went
there or not; no one knew or guessed that she had
any interest in him. She could be near him, perhaps
glimpse him. At the very least she would be able to
give time to thoughts of him. If memories hurt too
much then she could come away. No one would know
about that either.

For the saddest of reasons she could go back with
complete impunity.

Chapter 12

There was grass growing down the middle of the lane, brushing the bottom of the car as it lurched into potholes. Mike used to scrape that hump, fill those holes. Who was doing his job now?

Sally met no one. Edal Bank looked deserted, no vehicles outside, no lights, no children's bicycles, no smoke from the chimney. Did she imagine its air of dereliction or was it just the tattiness of autumn, the drifts of leaves, the dead clumps which needed cutting back in the flower beds, the shaggy lawn. Just the distance of that neglected garden away, in the equally lifeless studio, was Mike sitting alone, trapped and lost in helpless confusion?

She drove steadily past, her mouth dry, her jaw clenched. Not till she reached the cottage did the terrible trembling overtake her, so that when she got out of the car she had to stand for a moment holding on to the door, taking deep breaths to steady herself. She had expected, did expect, nothing. She had only wanted to be near him, know that he was still there. If she could stand it. She wasn't sure now that she could.

The squawk of the unoiled gate was louder than ever, bringing memories surging. The kitchen felt stifling and airless. It was a year since she had been here.

Feeling as exposed to pain as if a skin had been flayed away she made herself walk through the house, into every room, braving whatever associations they would face her with. She was thankful to find that even in her little bedroom, soulless in the gray light of a November afternoon, the resolution she had worked so hard to build during the last year did not fail her. And anyway, she reminded herself sharply, what was this sort of pain compared to the tragedy which had torn Mike's life apart?

Though she felt at first that she was stepping on eggshells and there was a perpetual gnawing unease somewhere in her stomach which she identified as fear, fear of this hurting so much that she wouldn't be able to handle it, she did eventually find a certain relief and even comfort to be back. She could relive all that had happened, in silence, alone, damaging no one, depriving no one.

She could walk in the familiar places, could close her eyes and breathe in again the scent of those lost marvelous days, listen to the voices. But she couldn't turn into the ready arms, her hand would never again be taken in that firm warm grasp, nor her body be aroused and satisfied in their perfect loving. There were a lot of tears. But no one saw them, and she accepted them, knowing once they were over that she had been right to come. She was no longer shut off from the happiness she had found here, and more importantly she didn't feel so utterly excluded from what was happening to Mike.

For the first time she saw Isobel. The sound of the car coming along the track behind her as she walked to the village threw her into an instant flurry of remembering, momentary expectancy, then fury that she could be so absurd. Of course it couldn't be Mike.

The woman at the wheel acknowledged her with a lift of her hand, but to Sally's relief didn't stop. Bad enough that even in that brief glimpse an image had been stamped into her brain which she knew she would never be free of—a small-featured face with clear pale skin and light eyes, and a soft mass of curling, red-gold hair. Anonymity gone; the shadowy figure suddenly real and sharp—and pretty. Thank God I hadn't known that, Sally thought, stepping back into the track and walking on oppressed by fresh guilt. The cold white light of reality had abruptly replaced the golden glow of memory. She, Sally, had had an affair with this woman's husband, tenuous and temporary as it had been. And now it was not even a memory for Mike. It was between him and this woman that permanence existed, and commitment, a commitment all the greater because he was disabled.

It was Isobel who had gone through the hell of those months when he lay in a coma, driving endlessly back and forth to the hospital, sitting for hours by his bed when he was unaware of her presence, and at the same time looking after house and children. It was she who had gone through the hell of his return, the agony of dealing with his uncontrolled behavior, of watching her strong competent husband reduced to impotence, adrift in his own chaotic world. It was she who would care for him, leading him back along the slow road to a recovery whose extent no one could yet predict.

Their marriage was impregnable now, and walking blindly on Sally made herself face the facts. There would be solace for Mike in the familiar contact of his wife's body. That was something purely physical,

separate from the struggles of his impaired brain.
Could he make love? Was that act so fundamental
that it could never be forgotten? Did he have the same
desire? Was he capable of the actual exertion? After
the first helpless stab of jealous longing she was glad
to find that she hoped so, wanting that sweet and simple comfort to be there for him, since he had lost
so much.

She discovered that the need which had brought her
here, to assure herself of Mike's existence and to learn
all she could of his present state, was easily satisfied.
What had happened to the Danaher family was a topic
of great interest and sympathy locally.

"Gets out into the garden now. Doesn't do anything, like, just stands and stares, but it's better than
nothing, isn't it?"

Ann Jackson, overturning Sally's image of Mike im-
prisoned all day long in his chair in the studio. Just
to think of him outside, looking about him at the lake
and woods and fells he loved so much, was intensely
moving.

More unsettling was Elsa Callander's version when
she invited herself for coffee and held forth on the
subject with complacent authority, as though she alone
could understand Mike's condition. "He's perfectly capable of carrying on a conversation. Nothing compli-
cated, naturally, but that doesn't matter. Of course
he'll never be normal again, you can't expect that, can
you, but sometimes you'd hardly think there's anything wrong with him at all. Isobel is ridiculously over-
protective. When I called Mike was pathetically
pleased to see me. He says the same thing over and
over again but one can put up with that and I was
careful to keep everything very simple for him. And

goodness, it's early days yet, we can't expect miracles, can we? He should meet people, that's what I say, do him good, get back to normal. He's supposed to re-learn everything, Isobel said so herself, and what bet-ter way to do that than with supportive friends, especially as Isobel has to leave him such a lot. Her mother, you know, apparently she's not at all well."

This self-satisfied speech left Sally with such a wel-ter of helpless resentment and disturbing new informa-tion to sort out that she took off up the path through the wood as soon as her unwelcome visitor left. How she had longed to blaze out at the woman for her insensitivity, frustrated almost beyond endurance by the need to give no hint of personal involvement. And how desperately jealous she had felt that Elsa Cal-lander could call on the Danahers, could see Mike, had as it seemed some stake in him simply because she was a neighbor, while she, Sally, was forever shut out and obliged to deal alone with her grief.

These were not all the unsettling thoughts stirred up by Elsa. Sally was unlucky enough to be caught by her the next day on her way back from the village. As she was passing the bungalows at the foot of the lake a bossy voice hailed her and Elsa appeared around the end of her greenhouse carrying a plastic bowl.

"Where's that useless dog of mine, didn't utter a cheep. You perfectly futile creature, what on earth do you think I keep you for?"

The spaniel, now that she was there, produced an apathetic sound somewhere between a bark and a wail of terror and dodged an exasperated kick with a size eight green gumboot.

"Come along in, you haven't seen my little pad, have you?"

That Sally would not be bludgeoned into.

Foiled, Elsa came to the fence to chat. "Take some curly kale for your supper," she ordered bossily, thrusting forward her bowl. "It's doing tremendously well this year. Full of iron, frightfully good for you."

Frightful was the word. Not even Aunt Janey would win on curly kale.

"You really should eat plenty of—oh—"

She looked past Sally, discarding her like a piece of dropped litter, her attention riveted on a car coming down the lane. She nodded with an awkward duck of her head as Isobel Danaher drove by.

"That's not right, is it?" she said, her eyes following the car, speaking as though she had forgotten who Sally was, but impelled to voice her reaction.

"What do you mean?" Sally asked, frowning.

"Oh, well!" The slightly bulging eyes swung back to her, a look of eager satisfaction lighting them. "It's hardly right, is it? I mean, it can't be safe for *him*, being left alone like that. He could leave something switched on, burn the house down, anything. She hates the place, that's the whole trouble, always has. And now with him in that state, well, I suppose you can hardly blame her, but she should get someone in, any of us would sit with him. Up and down to Jedburgh all the time. That's where her mother lives, you know. Spends more time there than here, I sometimes think."

"But where are the children?"

"Oh, packed off to boarding school."

Why for people like Elsa must it always be "packed off"?

"She'd always insisted on that, though Mike wasn't keen, put it off as long as he could. Young Michael loves the place, of course, but there's nothing for them here, is there? And nothing for Isobel, no one could call her a country girl."

Sally wanted to get away, but in a horrible way wanted to hear more. Filled with a sense of distaste and unease she started to move on. The dog, supposing it would be expected to do something, followed along the fence, letting out a few half-hearted yaps, obliterating what Elsa was saying. Sally took her chance, said goodbye and walked hastily on. Behind her she could hear furious shouts of, "Oh, do shut up, you idiot!"

Why had that conversation about Isobel filled her with such a sense of foreboding, an instinct that here were things she did not wish to know? Certainly the news that the children were now away at school had made her sad on Mike's behalf, but that was assuming he would miss them. She didn't know that. Nor did she know what life in that house was now like, the day-to-day actuality of it. Perhaps it had been necessary to protect the children from things too hard for them to bear.

She was deep in these thoughts as she came level with Edal Bank when a movement caught her eye. She felt her limbs, her breath, the blood in her veins, check for one dizzy moment. Across the garden a tall pale figure was just going in at the studio door.

Seared on her clutching brain in that petrified instant was a picture to rack her in the months ahead. Ghost-pale; that was the prevailing impression. Bony skull with cropped gray hair; gray-blue shirt and pale jeans hanging off clothes-hanger shoulders and skele-

ton frame. His movements were laborious and slow,
or was it just that time for Sally had gone into a lower
gear as she tried to take a step forward and felt her
feet rooted to the ground, as she tried to call out and
could make no sound?

But should she call? Doubt gripped her. Would
Mike know her? Would it startle him to see her, harm
him? But he was there, he was there.

And then she realized that a car was coming along
the lane behind her, releasing her from the nightmarish slow-motion sensation. The moment vanished, the
one precious chance snatched away. Mike, who was
inaccessible to her, only to her, had gone with shuffling feet and sagging shoulders through the door of
the studio.

Garth Jackson was pulling up beside her. "Afternoon. I'm just fetching some plants from the garden
your auntie said I could take when she was up the
last time."

Plants. Sally swung around, feeling, in her shock and
sense of bitter loss, ready to strike him. A storm of
tears was rising in her, her chest a tight band of pain.

"Van's a bit of a mess. Better not offer you a lift, I
dare say. I'll just get along, then, see you up there . . ."
He had noticed nothing, great oaf of a man. His filthy
van ground away and Sally sank down where she was
on the bank, wound her arms tightly around her knees
and dropped her head on them, fighting one more
desperate lonely battle for control.

Unbearable as it was at the time, this incident did
put things finally into perspective for her. She had
seen with her own eyes that Mike had survived. The
days of thinking it would have been better if he had
died were long past. Now she knew that beyond all

doubt or hope he was cut off from her not only by his condition but by family, friends, neighbors. He would be cared for, would make a recovery of sorts, adjust to a new level of living. Nothing would ever put Sally or their brief shared happiness back into his memory or knowledge as he struggled back to some kind of normality. Even longing to see him had been an intrusion on her part, and she would not intrude any further on this sad family.

Chapter 13

"Hey, Sally, how would you like the flat to yourself again?" Nona came bounding up the stone steps and burst in dramatically.

"I wouldn't," Sally said blankly, arrested with one hand on the tap, the other holding the kettle under it to be filled. She might have muttered periodically at the chaos of sharing with Nona, the number of vagrants they succored, the plundered cupboards and fridge, but emphatically, without debate or question, she knew she didn't want her to go.

"Ah, that's nice, I thought you'd be over the moon." Nona let an armful of shopping slither onto the worktop, from where most of it continued to the floor, and gave Sally a quick hug. "But listen to this, it's great—"

She couldn't guess at Sally's hollow feeling of apprehension as she answered tartly, "OK, but there's no need to cover the floor in yogurt while you're telling me." Mothers say that sort of thing, she reminded herself, trying to calm down as she stopped to rescue the carton whose lid had split in the cascade. But then mothers must feel this sudden kicked emptiness and pluck at any handy side-issue to put off hearing the bad news—then rally to push dismay aside and show interest.

"Are you going home? Have you heard from Ray?"

The glow faded momentarily. "I wish. No, no point in going home yet, worse luck. Don't bother with all that stuff, Sal, I'll do it in a sec. Just listen, this is really cool, you're going to love it."

Am I? Sally wondered bleakly. If she wasn't going home where would it be—Kenya, Cairo or Karachi? Nona would take off sometime, that had always been clear, but God, she would miss her.

"I've found this great flat, in that new block behind the hospital. There's a couple of us going to share. How d'you like that for a plan? You won't have to trip over my junk any more, or my friends—"

"Here in town?" The relief was enormous. "But Nona, isn't it mad to pay rent when you can stay here? You know I love having you." Sally heard that turning into panicky appeal and tried again. "Of course, I understand if you need more elbow room, and you probably want to be with friends of your own—"

I do sound like a mother, she realized blankly. But the attempt to be objective didn't fool Nona and she laughed affectionately. "Come on, Sally, we've had a great time and I'm going to miss it as well, but this place was never meant for two unless they're married to each other, you know that."

"And you need your own space?"

"Oh, well, you know, party once in a while, have mates around for a few tinnies, give the blokes a chance . . ."

"Well, put like that." Sally knew Nona often hammed the accent to cloak something serious.

"It's been terrific, though. You know I've loved it here, don't you—being with you, I mean."

Getting to know a sister. Yes, it had been terrific. They smiled at each other across the heap of shopping.

"Well, at least you'll still be in Muirend. I thought for one horrible moment you were buzzing off again."

"No, I won't be buzzing off yet." Nona gave her an odd quick look, frowning, then evidently decided not to say whatever it was. Had she found some man here? Sally wondered. Given up hope of Ray? Or had she had some news from him?

But if that was the case Nona clearly didn't want to talk about it. "Come on," she said briskly, "I've got the key. Want to come and have a look?"

Thank goodness she'll still be here to help with the shop, Sally thought as they drove through the town, for she herself was involved more and more in the consultancy side of the business, the part she found most interesting and rewarding.

The flat was a series of tiny rectangles with neutral emulsion slapped on thin walls and synthetic rubber-backed speckled carpet everywhere. Its only attractive feature was a balcony looking south down the course of the river. Nona appeared to be entirely satisfied with it.

"So who are you sharing with?"

"One of the nurses from the hospital, Kerri. We saw her in the pub the other night?" Sally remembered a long-legged smiling Jamaican girl with a lucrative bent for liar dice. "And Pat, he'll be instructing at the dry ski slope from the beginning of the month."

"Any ideas for furniture?"

"Aunt Janey?"

Janey rose to the challenge with a zest Sally was

glad to see. She had been so much less energetic lately, starting jobs in the garden and abandoning them impatiently.

"Oh, I'm bored with all that," she would exclaim, throwing down her fork and walking off. Sally hadn't thought the word existed in her vocabulary. She was definitely looking her age, and perhaps it was hardly surprising that she wanted to spend more time indoors, tucked up in her sitting room with Marchmain shedding hairs all over her, reading Hornblower or *The Secret Garden* and other favorites not looked at for years, or leaning back, eyes closed, to be borne away on tumultuous waves of German grand opera.

But for Nona she roused herself to stump about the house waving the stick she now used at dreadful old servants' cupboards and listing lamps, exclaiming, "Take it, take it, for God's sake, save me burning it."

The friendship Sally had tentatively envisaged for herself with Pauly Napier had become a reality for Nona, and Drumveyn also proved a rich source of plunder, including a battered but handsome wing chair which Sally wouldn't have minded having in the boathouse flat.

The flat. Walking into its silence was chilling indeed for the first couple of evenings on her own. Of course she missed the superficial things, the easy gossip, the laughter, the chatting over a glass of wine as they got supper ready, the mild squabbling over their different music, the off-loading of the day's events. But at a deeper level Sally knew she didn't really like living alone, and that was now the long-term prospect ahead of her. Long-forgotten memories of the lonely time after Julian had gone back to his wife came pushing back, surfacing even in her dreams. And there was nothing to shield her from thoughts of Mike. But at least she didn't have to deal now with three-in-the-morning mistress fantasies about his marriage breaking up or Isobel running off with another man. He was removed from her now by a disaster too large and final to leave room for any such delusions. Appalling though the present facts were, they forced acceptance.

Though she missed Nona acutely, Sally eventually accepted her departure. She had come closer to Nona than to any member of the family since Janey in childhood, and that wasn't going to vanish. Perhaps they would never have the day-to-day intimacy and fun again but Nona would always be there, her sister, loved and valued.

And for the present, to Sally's relief, she was still very much in evidence.

"I thought you'd be very involved in the new set-up," Sally admitted one evening when Nona had come around bringing with her a Drumveyn pheasant which she then braised beautifully with celery and cream.

"Waste all this effort on that mob?" But Nona knew what Sally meant.

"I've missed you," Sally told her.

"Me too. If you had more room I'd still be here, believe me. Mind you, when I first came I didn't think I'd stay all that long."

"Nor did I, I must admit."

Again Sally caught that quick glance, the check, and had the odd feeling there was something she was missing. This time she was going to pursue it but the phone rang and the moment passed.

"There's even a chance it may be for me these

days," she remarked as she reached for it, and Nona laughed.

It was one of the bonuses of being solo again—the endless telephone calls had reduced to a trickle, gone were the strewn contents of smelly rucksacks, silent the incessant pounding of the washing machine. Sally could enjoy the return of peace and order, and also the discovery that she had come a long way from the loneliness of her first weeks here. Then she had had to work at a makeshift contentment, now she felt her life was on an even keel, with the business up and running and more absorbing all the time, the worst of the raw distress over Mike behind her.

The thought of him was always somewhere in the background of her mind, there was no escaping that, and every so often some association or reminder would stir a sharp impotent grief, but for the most part it was just something that had to be lived with, like the necessity of coming to terms with a death.

To Sally's surprise Janey was often at the new flat, quite at home with a dozen people around her un-wrapping pizzas for lunch at four o'clock, with sport at full roar on the television and beer the only drink on offer.

Even Piers, in spite of his preference for simplicity, beauty and natural materials, didn't seem to mind these philistine surroundings. He had never come to the boathouse, and Sally had to accept that he had never relented about her leaving Grianan, which he had seen as some kind of desertion. The consoling ease and peace she had found with him seemed very remote now.

The pique she felt at this loss was soon obliterated by a surprising new development.

A couple of weeks after Nona moved out, Sally had had a busy day, with a trip down to Dunkeld to introduce the owner of an antique shop to the mysteries of her new computer. She had found an intelligent, friendly girl, apprehensive about her lack of skills, but eager to learn and grateful for help. This was the best part of the job, the direct involvement with a new cherished undertaking, the knowledge that she could be of help, the creation of a bond between instructor and pupil, or expert and beginner, and driving away afterward knowing a link had been formed, a new contact made. The day had been fun, broken up by a long gossipy lunch, and in spite of treacherous black ice on the A9 Sally drove home in good spirits.

The temperature hadn't risen above freezing all day, and as she got out of the car to open the garage doors, the stone buildings around her little courtyard seemed to put out a deeper chill of their own, while cold lingered tangible as a shroud over the mist-hung river.

She had just had time for a scalding hot shower and was looking forward to the prospect of food when a heavy knock at the door startled her. More of Nona's chums to direct to the other end of town?

Dark and bulky against the frost glitter on slate roofs lit by the courtyard light, menacing in the first uncertain moment before she recognized him, stood Jed Maclachlan.

"Goodness," Sally said feebly, completely thrown.

"Going to invite me in, then?" He sounded pleased with himself, as much at ease as if he turned up there twice a week.

Would it ever be possible to see him without this

disquieting clench of the gut? Sally wondered helplessly, acutely aware of the old familiar mixture of
guilt, wariness and excitement at the sight of that massive frame and challenging stance. And this time there
was shock, too, to see him standing so calmly on her
doorstep as of right, when in all the months since she
had come north he had made no move to do more
than wave a greeting in passing or exchange a few
casual words.

Who was she trying to convince? Even in the brief-
est of those encounters his eyes had followed her, intent and mocking. As though he had been biding his
time, the thought came disconcertingly.

"Jed, what on earth are you doing here?"

"You're surely not expecting me to stand out here
while I tell you? Enough to freeze the balls off a brass
monkey, a night like yon."

Mutely Sally moved aside. She couldn't keep him
standing there, it was true—and icy air was pouring
into the flat at the same time—yet it was outrageous
to be pressured into letting him in. But she had glibly
discounted one element in the mixed emotions at
seeing him there—pleasure. Whether because of the
passionate feelings he had once roused in her, or because of some fundamental attraction which would
never change, pleasure there certainly was. Her brain
could tot up all his blatant faults but she could never
dislike him.

"So, nice little place." His speculative eyes combed
the room. As always, there was a flick of disparagement in his voice, reminding Sally that he had never
fully approved of anything she said or did or owned
or was. Then it had mattered to her; it sure as hell

wasn't going to get to her now, she decided with conviction.

"What can I do for you, Jed?" she asked briskly. "Don't tell me you want to computerize the Ellig farm accounts?"

But the follow-up hadn't been quick enough. She saw the gleam of white teeth in the dark beard. "What can you do for me? Don't you remember?" he asked softly.

The warning bells could hardly have rung louder.

He tramped with his big man's confident stride down the room and settled himself in the center of the sofa, one arm along its back, thick knees in moleskin breeches apart, huge booted feet out-turned. There was one cool clinical moment as Sally gazed at him and decided she was going to let this happen. The reasons didn't matter; they were no one's affair but her own. She made coffee, offered food, but of course he had already eaten. She shrugged goodbye to the moussaka she had been about to get out of the freezer when his knock came. Who cared?

They talked for hours. That too had always been part of the scene. Jed had implied then, as he did now, that it was a change for him to find a female who had anything to talk about. At sixteen, with all her eager adolescent ideas to be aired, and her conditioned acceptance of their different status and education, Sally hadn't questioned it. Now she winced to think of her patronizing confidence, amazed that he had been prepared to put up with it. But though she was far from that heedless confidence now, he could still make her feel that she gave him something he couldn't find elsewhere. Try as she might to dismiss it as part of his chat-up line, it could still work its charm. She liked him being there, his physical presence in the quiet room, his flamboyant looks, his pungent turn of phrase, the never-quite-absent frisson of challenge and uncertainty that he brought. And she savored an awareness of the stark night outside, frost-rimed stone, dark water slipping soundlessly by beneath the reaching ice, and the two of them secure in their enclave of light and comfort and seclusion, pulses beating in live warm bodies, senses alive, and that feeling between them that is the security of not being strangers.

They caught up piecemeal on the years, not referring yet to what had lain between them. Sally told him about Julian (but not Mike). They talked of Grianan and Janey, of Jed's job at Glen Ellig and his family. Here they were suddenly in deeper water than Sally had expected. He held forth passionately about the fights he had with Gordon, clearly too like his father for his own good, and about his defiant fleering daughters who, in spite of his forceful disgust at their behavior, he obviously adored. And with savage bitterness he talked about Moira, his wife, "drinking and whoring like there's no tomorrow."

"Is she still living with you at Ellig?" Sally had heard a few lurid rumors this summer.

"Just," he growled. "Got some fancy man in Aberfeldy but the bugger's out of a job, isn't he? She's better off with me and the bitch knows it."

"Do you want her to stay?"

"Christ, someone's got to put the tea on the table. Those daft girls won't do it. And Garry and Scott are still at school. Go down on the school bus every day, anyway."

Sally saw with a new perception the dilemma of a man like Jed. Man's work and woman's work; the clear divide. Easy to dismiss it as outrageously sexist, hopelessly outdated. But could anyone see a man like him cleaning a loo, wielding an iron? He saw himself as the provider, and after a long day's work in cold and rain and mud and snow he didn't expect to come in and peel the tatties. So he would put up with years of quarreling and nagging because he was trapped by his own culture and environment, just as Moira was. Who could blame either of them if they looked for something else?

"You took your time getting rid of that pal of yours, sister or whatever she is," Jed remarked, as though he'd read her thoughts.

"Yes, she's my sister," Sally replied crisply, reminded again that he could never accept anything about her life without somehow wanting to put it down. Resenting the class she belonged to, as she used to point out when she had had enough of it and wanted to wind him up.

"Aye, well, whatever. Nice bit of gear anyway."

Sally prayed he hadn't seen the leap of jealousy he had played for and aroused.

Jed grinned evilly. "Always plenty of blokes sniffing around when she was here, eh? Wouldn't mind having a go myself."

"You could try," Sally said politely, but she knew she hadn't fooled him.

"Yes, well, she's a wee bit young for me," he said, leaving the rest open.

"I think I'd agree there," Sally commented, letting her eyes travel critically over the thickening body, the gray threads in the splendid black hair.

"Just have to make do with second best then," he said. His eyes laughed at her, and she laughed too.

"You bastard, Jed. You haven't changed."

"You have though." With a sudden movement he was on his feet and reaching for her, plucking her out of her chair as though she weighed no more than a child. "You're a woman, and a bloody lovely one." His voice had roughened in a way she remembered; his grip on her arms as he held her a couple of inches away from his was heedless, ungentle. "Things have happened to you and you've got tougher, but by Christ you're still as sexy as ever. You got under my skin all those years ago and you've stayed there, you wee bugger."

Basic language perhaps, but with his eyes intent on hers, his deep voice husky, power pouring out of his hands, it could still do its work.

"Still full of simple charm, I see." But she couldn't make her voice casual.

She had one glimpse of the familiar wolfish grin as he bent his head and his lips came down on hers. She had always been able to recall his kisses, not surprisingly, perhaps, as they had been the first that had meant anything to her, but they had not been like this then. Her lonely needful body, woken by Mike to such delight, denied all touch for so long, stormed back to life.

She thought he was startled, because he wrapped her tight and close and held her for several moments, with a tenderness she by no means remembered from him. She knew that pounding through both of them was the question of whether or not he would stay. For her part Sally felt a reckless incapacity to decide, or to care much how the die fell.

He stood her off from him, and for once his expression was bleakly serious as he scrutinized her face.

They gazed at each other for a moment, like duelists for whom this is no longer a practice bout, then quietly he reached for the big coat which he had slung over a chair and turned toward the door. They didn't speak, but at the time Sally hardly noticed. Their thoughts clamored in the still room. They didn't say goodnight. Nor did Jed say, "I'll be back." Not in words, not aloud.

Part Three

Chapter 14

"There are two things to be said about Jed as a lover—he doesn't drink and he's clean."

"And he's good with his hands," Nona suggested.

"Well, that too," Sally agreed primly. "He's not made a bad job of this at all."

"That'd be right," Nona commented ironically. They were cleaning up the bathroom where Jed had been doing some tiling, a job left half finished by the previous occupants.

"He still gives me the creeps though," she added a moment later, not for the first time.

"Jed's OK," Sally said quietly.

"Well, he must have something going for him."

"Yup." They exchanged a little grin and left it there.

The truth was Sally hardly knew herself why she had let the affair develop. For three months now Jed had been coming to the boathouse flat. After his first visit there had been silence for about ten days, but she hadn't wasted much time speculating about when he would reappear or even whether she wanted him to. He would be back.

When he came he didn't waste time either. As Sally opened the door to him he reached a bear-like arm to scoop her up, lifting her off her feet and driving her back against the wall, using just enough of his great weight, or marginally more, to pin her there, his face unsmiling and intent. Sally held still, her eyes meeting his. She knew he was giving her a choice, to be made there and then. She didn't push him away.

"You want it, don't you?" he said, not teasing, and with no coarse overtone. Asking. Sally let her eyes answer with equal unequivocal plainness and felt his body harden against hers. His hands pushed up into her hair, gripping her skull tight. His dark eyes were lightless as a peat bog.

Sally wanted it. Whether at that moment she wanted him she couldn't have said. That seemed a separate issue still. Certainly nothing about Jed repelled her; the associations of the past were good and there was that essential rightness of feel, of smell, even of the uncompromising pressure of his body holding hers captive against the wall.

He was a splendid lover. Fifteen years ago she hadn't known how splendid. No frills, but she didn't expect any. No nonsense about soft lights, soft music, leisurely undressing. He clamped that iron arm around her and walked her to the bedroom, remarking only, "Thank Christ you've got a decent-sized bed," as he threw back the duvet with a rough gesture and began to strip off his clothes with concentration and speed.

"Straight to business as ever, I see," Sally commented mock-drily, then found herself suddenly elated, laughing as she pulled her sweatshirt over her head, uncomplicated anticipation filling her.

Jed didn't answer. That too she remembered. The decision taken, his mind was now unswervingly focused. She didn't mind. She didn't think he would fail her. In spite of the absence of words, she wasn't afraid he would go at her like a bull at a gate. Jed knew all about awakening a woman's body. Those years ago Sally hadn't known this wasn't always the case, had questioned nothing. Now she guessed he took the trouble because it would enhance his own pleasure, but the motive didn't matter.

His ham-like hands, not light, knew what they were doing. All she had to do was give herself up to them. His body was magnificent still and, as intoxicating as ever, there swept back the remembered sensation of her own helplessness and weightlessness at the mercy of his enormous strength. She had no reservations; it was glorious. And after loving the familiar pattern was still acceptable. Again, Jed didn't speak; words were not part of this act for him and indeed, she thought, would have angered him. But he didn't turn away. He rolled on to his back and pulled her against him, cupping a big hand around her head to settle it in the hollow of his shoulder, drawing her arm across the barrel of his chest where he liked to feel it, his own massive arm curving her in to his side. Then he slept, going out like a light. Sally drowsed and floated, pressed against his warmth and solidity, secure, relaxed and sated, amused at this replication of long-ago loving, wondering if he would wake just as before.

He did, after about ten minutes of profound oblivious sleep, and now he was ready to talk, to smoke, which she detested and had to put up with, and to lie there for hours if he had the time, sometimes making love again, and even again. The only difference was that since it was now available he also wanted tea by the gallon, which she was expected to get out of bed and make. She had the sense not to start any arguments about taking turns.

For a week or two he turned up constantly, obsessed with her, and she felt much the same about him, postponing appointments, bunking off from the shop and leaving everything to Nona, diving eagerly down the freezing lanes which led to the river, boot heels ringing on cold stone, to cosy sexy afternoons in the quiet flat that often stretched to two or three in the morning.

Jed never stayed for the whole night. His inhibitions and his fear of people talking were much deeper rooted than Sally's. It suited her quite well that he should go, except for the disagreeable moment when the drowsy nest was wrenched apart, shattering the mood of closeness and repletion. But sometimes she would tease him about it.

"You're here all hours of the day and night. What difference can three A.M. onward make?"

He would only mutter at her, cursing as he dragged on his clothes. She decided that, to him, staying all night with her would be taking a definite step, acknowledging an established relationship, a commitment even. And she suspected that he wanted to be able to deny any such thing to Moira, now embroiled with a second-hand car dealer in Calvine.

Also, to be fair, although she was indifferent to general glen opinion, her renewed involvement with Jed was something Sally was very anxious Aunt Janey shouldn't hear about. In relation to her aunt, Sally felt as guilty about the relationship as she had when she was sixteen, and she found herself at Grianan less and less that winter. Also, as before, she had a slight feeling of intruding on Janey and Piers—or was she looking for an extra reason to justify her absence?

But she had needed something like this affair. Oh, how she had needed it, the ecstatic surrender of the body, the simple and delicious oblivion, the solace of touch. Even just having "someone" in her life again. In a curious way it brought Mike closer, Mike as he had been, and when the fact of what had happened to him hit her again the loneliness was not so devastating.

Sally knew that she wasn't ready yet to embark on the uncertain seas of an affair with a stranger. But with Jed, deep under the conflict in outlook and attitudes, there was familiarity and trust. They differed over every detail of ordinary life—food, drink, music, television, mealtimes. They had furious rows and got frustrated with each other, Jed stamping out in a rage and Sally relieved to see him go, but there was also a lot of laughter, a lot of telling. The old attraction was still there and each was sure of it in the other. For Sally, knowing that Jed fancied her was a boost her ego sorely needed just then. And after the rows he always came back, and she always knew he would.

Sometimes he would potter away at jobs in the flat, like the bathroom tiling, or work on Sally's car with a flow of derogatory comments about the way she neglected it. She understood this; it was something he could offer her. He never arrived with a bottle of wine under his arm or took her out for a meal, that was not his style, but assuming the traditional practical male role was, and equally placing her in the subordinate female one.

He only seriously bored her when he got on to the subject of his family and its endless battles. He could get carried away far beyond the reach of lightness or humor, but Sally understood that having someone to talk it out to was a rare release for him. It didn't sound as though anyone did much listening in that wild fighting household at Ellig.

By and large she wanted him there. He filled a gap, would bring her no pain she couldn't deal with, and there were a lot of good times in those months. With his big laugh and chancy temper, his dark good looks and large appetites, he tore to shreds her too ordered, too self-indulgent solitude.

Nona's opinion of him never changed and there was an odd piquancy for Sally in having a younger sister disapproving of her. Mostly she held her tongue, for which Sally was grateful, but one evening when they were together in the shop putting through a backlog of copying and sending faxes, Nona seized the chance to say her piece, though the attack came from a quarter where Sally least expected it.

Sally had been talking idly about going down to Edinburgh to do some decent shopping and throwing out dates in a half-hearted way because she couldn't get up much enthusiasm for the plan, when Nona cut across her ramblings, saying sharply, "Never mind Edinburgh, isn't it about time you went up to Grianan? You haven't been there for weeks."

"So?" Sally demanded smartly, instantly on the defensive, knowing why she had been evading it.

Nona's eyebrows went up. "Wow, touched a nerve or what? Well, I suppose that's a good sign."

"What are you talking about?" Sally said crossly. "Anyway, you're hardly ever at Grianan yourself, you're skiing in Aviemore every weekend."

"Not quite."

"Well, when were you last there?" Sally asked, noisily tapping a sheaf of papers straight on the top of the copier.

"Two days ago."

Something in her tone arrested Sally. She turned quickly with the block of paper upright in her hands to find Nona watching her, the faxes abandoned.

"I didn't know that," she said less truculently, wondering with a strange little quiver of unease what was coming.

"Aunt Janey misses you."

"Did she say so?"

"Bloody hell, Sally," Nona exploded. "Don't nitpick. That's not the point and you know it."

"Sorry," Sally mumbled, ashamed of the prevarication. "I do keep meaning to go."

"Then go."

Sally stared at her in surprise, Nona's tone was uncompromising, her eyes hostile. For a moment Sally felt like making a fight of it; Nona had no right to tell her what to do. But she had, she was family, and Sally knew that she had stayed away from Janey for far too long.

The shock of seeing her was a moment that stayed with Sally forever, with its violent jumble of disbelief, compassion and guilt, and beneath them the first glimpse of a fearful yawning emptiness ahead. It's only been six weeks, seven at the most, her brain computed desperately, as though by insisting on this tiny stretch of time she could deny what she saw. Janey's skin seemed to sag from the diminished flesh, her eyes looked out from dark hollows, her hair was thin and flat, her movements heavy.

"Janey, darling Janey." Sally clung to her, shaking

with realization, torn with shame for her blindness, her absence, and terrified of what the answers must be to any questions she could ask.

"I didn't want to worry you. You've had enough unhappiness, enough to cope with."

No denial. That shook Sally to the depths. Janey's body felt unfamiliar, smelt wrong in some indefinable but not distasteful way. Just not her, not tanned, robust, healthy, outdoor Aunt Janey, with earth on her hands, sun and wind on her skin, redolent of herbs and potting compost and wood smoke and baking.

"I should have known, I should have seen—"

"Nonsense, why should you?"

Nona had. And so, it came to Sally suddenly, had Piers.

Later, she went to find him. Gardens and greenhouse were deserted, but she finally ran him to earth stripped to the waist in the biting March air, his arm thrust down the drain outside the old laundry. A part of Sally's brain noted how beautifully made his body was, the smooth olive skin at the moment faintly tinged with blue.

"You've despised me for staying away."

"Yes." A handful of dank blackened beech leaves, silted gray and stinking foully, landed by her boot toe.

"I truly didn't know."

"I don't see how you couldn't have." His voice was thin and unforgiving.

She squatted down beside him, tears stinging her eyes. "I don't see either. But it's true. Janey's always been—" She couldn't find the words. A grown-up, invincible, invulnerable. My rock, my strength. So utterly familiar that I never properly looked at her, never saw her.

Piers strained further down the pipe, his face concentrated, shutting her out. There was a gurgle far below and he withdrew his filthy stinking arm, shivering as he pushed himself to his feet. With his other hand he plucked his sweater and jacket from where he had tossed them over a bush. "Better get cleaned up," he said, and walked away.

Sally turned slowly after him as though weighted down by this new appalling sadness, aching at least for his tolerance even if she had forfeited his sympathy.

Nona too said, though more kindly, "I just don't see how you didn't realize. Janey wouldn't let us say a word to you till they decided to operate, but if everyone else knew why didn't you?"

"Absorbed in my own affairs," Sally said with the flatness of guilt. She'd thought she was learning not to be, thought she'd behaved well over parting from Mike, been generous in accepting Nona, gave as well as took with Jed. Pitiful. Nugatory. She had learned nothing and had failed the person who mattered most in the world.

It was such a short time to be given. As the first days of sun and thaw released the grip of winter in liquid sound and dazzling brilliance, all their hearts and minds concentrated on Janey. Not to the neglect of all else; that was not part of her ethic, and very sharp and clear the rules returned to Sally now, humbling her by their validity. She was ready of course to abandon Jed. Her mind was wholly directed to what was happening at Grianan, but was there also an element, she wondered uncomfortably, craven and belated, of making some propitiatory sacrifice?

Did Janey guess that? Perhaps she did; certainly she still had the power to take Sally by surprise.

"I don't want you rushing up here every other minute, you know," she told her tartly. "I may be dying but you're not. Life as usual."

"I haven't neglected anything," Sally protested, swallowing down the hard lump of what Janey had said, forcing her mind to think of the business, which was what she thought was in her aunt's mind.

"Really." A sardonic chuckle in the best Janey manner. "I'm not sure Jed Maclachlan would agree with you."

Sally felt her mouth open, a sight Janey evidently found rewarding, as her chuckle became a husky laugh. "Oh, little Sally, did you honestly suppose that in this glen such a liaison could be kept secret?"

"But I—" What? Had thought Muirend too far away; had thought Janey too bound up in Grianan to pay any attention to what she was doing?

"I have to admit it worried me considerably more," Janey went on calmly, "when you were fifteen. You were due back at school by the time I found out or there would certainly have been some old-fashioned ructions."

"You knew?" Sally asked dazedly.

"Not soon enough, by all accounts." Janey sounded for a moment her old vigorous self. "I just had to hope you'd be the same shape by next holidays—and employ some diversionary tactics, as you may recall."

Sally began to laugh. Wily old devil. Even her longing to see Jed again had not been proof against that offer of skiing in Kitzbühel.

"I decided it might all be a bit spartan in the winter anyway," she confessed, remembering her swift weighing up of the alternatives.

"How very prosaic," Janey chided, but her eyes were twinkling.

With a sudden surge of love for her, of admiration for her handling of such a potentially explosive situation, and anguish at the frightening changes rushing upon them, Sally went to hug her. They clung tightly, in silence.

"Not sure I can cope with too much of that," Janey remarked when they released each other, batting a hand across her eyes, but with the other giving Sally a little pat to soften the words.

Sally knew what she meant.

It was weird to see Jed with permission, as it were. Not that Janey approved, of course. "He'll be trouble if you get too involved," she warned, "though that's entirely up to you. There is something undeniably engaging about him but he'll never pull himself clear of that layabout family of his—and deep down he doesn't want to."

Sometimes Sally agreed with her, sometimes she wasn't sure. Moira seemed to have vanished for good this time, Gordon was fed up with all the hassle and was working on a farm near Crianlarich. Bonnie, the elder daughter, was pregnant and living with a long-distance lorry driver, while the younger children were doing much as they pleased and supposedly keeping house for their father.

Jed, too, had known that Aunt Janey had cancer. Not that he ever pronounced the word; the glen taboo still held firm. When Sally told him he was incredulous that she hadn't realized and almost as reproachful as Nona and Piers. Somehow it was the final straw. Racked by shame, dismayed at the enormity of what lay in wait, Sally burst into a storm of tears.

"Oh, here now, lassie." Jed's comfort was instant and encompassing. "Come here to me, don't upset yourself like that. Your auntie'll be with us for a while yet. You can see her often—you could bide up at Grianan, come to that. The snow's over now, you could easy enough get up and down the glen to your work."

But Sally knew that Janey disliked the idea of them all closing in on her, and realizing that brought home all the more acutely the loneliness of what her aunt faced, the awesomeness of the step she must take alone.

In only one matter did Janey directly ask for help. "I'm not one of those sifting and sorting people," she remarked one day, looking ruefully round her cluttered sitting room. "Can you bear to have this lot to deal with when I've gone? I don't care what happens to it, just do whatever's easiest, but I'd rather like everything to go on looking the same meanwhile."

"Janey, of course you mustn't touch a thing," Sally cried, horrified at the idea for her aunt's sake but at the same time filled with a cowardly dread of having to live with visible reminders of what was coming.

"Hoped you'd say that," Janey grunted. "But there is one thing slightly on my mind which I should see to myself. I ought to go to Edalmere and sort out what's left of Ursula's belongings. I've put it off and put it off but I really can't do that any more. But I wondered, would you come with me?"

"Of course I will." Rush of piercing, stinging associations.

"Dreadful bore, I know, but I'm not sure I can tackle it alone. Guilt chiefly, I suppose, not liking her as much as I should have done. But God, she was silly, the silliest person I ever knew." It was good to see the glint of sardonic humor. "And Sally, no planning now. Just do whatever you like with the cottage afterward. It will be yours."

Strange circumstances in which to return to the place where Mike lived out his shadowy existence. Two seas of grief meeting, like the Rip Nona talked about where Ray brought the big ships in through the boil and surge. At that time of intense feeling the comparison didn't seem extravagant.

Chapter 15

Apprehension, shot through with an irresistible nostalgia, clutched at Sally as she drove south, and she felt the tremble of nervous dread in her hands as she passed through Edal village and the road climbed to the lake. Once in the lane each yard seemed to crawl by, each stone and blade of grass separately visible. Yet when she pulled up outside the cottage it seemed to have been over in seconds, meeting no one, seeing no one; emptiness, normality.

With what felt like a physical effort she wrenched her mind back to Janey. What must this feel like for her, coming back to this place which was so tied up with family memories, knowing she was here to tick off last-time things? And had the journey tired her, would the house, unused all winter, be damp and unwelcoming?

Janey clumped stiffly into the kitchen, surveying it with a resigned chuck of her head. "Poor old Ursula," where it was always "darling Rose," "she really was perfectly potty. Perhaps we could give this lot to the Beatrix Potter Society, or whatever it calls itself. Some of the china stuff is quite valuable. But you must do exactly as you like—change it, keep it, sell it. Same with Grianan." She swung round on Sally with a sudden fierceness which betrayed how much more that mattered. "Do you hear me? No idiotic business of trying to work out what Janey would have liked or Janey would have minded."

Sally nodded, the muscles of her face tightening. "Except that to think what Janey would like can be a useful yardstick."

"Oh ho, pretty speech. Useful when it suits you," Janey mocked, darting a glinting look at her niece from under wild untended brows. But Sally knew she was pleased. "Come on, let's settle in and do something about food."

"I'll do—" Sally broke off as the glint became a glare "—some of that," she amended meekly, and Janey snorted, grinning.

"Do you know, I'm quite looking forward to this. When were we last on our own together? Must be years."

It was a time that would always be precious to Sally. She felt that only by the merest chance had she salvaged it. The terror that Janey could have slipped away while she was obliviously unaware was enough to wake her sweating in the night. Yet the happiness of being with her, the feeling of closeness—though by a shared preference they kept to a light tone on the whole—was scored through by the poignancy of the job they had come here to do, the sifting and sorting which Janey could not face in her own life. Working their way through the crowded shelves and cupboards, Sally was all too aware that soon she would be doing this for her. Their minds open to memories, their hands momentarily caressed objects which led their thoughts back to other hands, other people, other days. Bad enough to pack away finally the life that

Ursula and Teddy had shared in this house, but almost unbearable for Sally to know that much of Janey was being relegated to the past at the same time. And beneath the immediate sadness of these visual and tactile associations lay her own private pain at being back in this landscape which other memories made so significant for her.

Sometimes she would feel frantic to get away from the claustrophobic cottage, from a too relentless consciousness of farewell and endings. Sometimes too she felt that Janey might prefer to be alone with the photographs and letters and mementoes left in place till now. Then, walking on the fell or wandering around the lake path, Sally would be seized with a sense of wasting irreplaceable time with Janey and would race back, pushing her own memories aside to wait their turn.

It was impossible to shut them out entirely. There was always milk to fetch, shopping to do. Always the lakeside track and the silent house. Always the thudding heart and steps that became self-conscious as she passed its windows, hope and questions flurrying up.

On a gusty morning of flittering sunlight and colors that deepened and faded as the clouds bowled along before a crisp wind, on her way back from the village she saw Mike. She didn't realize it was Mike at first, just catching sight of a tall figure standing across the lane from Edal Bank, on the edge of the cleared space between the trees that gave a view across the lake. But then, as though her brain had recognized him before her eyes gave it the message, she felt her knees begin to quiver, her feet stumble on stones that suddenly seemed larger and rougher, as with her eyes fixed on that still figure she walked automatically on.

Her throat was dry and she folded her lips tightly to stop them trembling.

How could she even for an instant have mistaken that lean height, those long limbs? It was Mike, Mike in familiar cords which now sagged off him, and big loose oatmeal sweater, standing with a curious passivity gazing out over the lake. Would he move? Would he turn to go in before she reached him? Would someone come out, call him in? It did not seem possible that she might be about to speak to him. Must she nod and pass with a greeting, a stranger to him?

He had seen her now, was watching her approach, peering at her intently and curiously, and it was odd how striking this small absence of customary adult good manners was.

"Hello, Mike." Sally found that her voice sounded unused, creaky, those two simple words venturing the huge questions that crashed around her brain.

"Hello there." He sounded friendly, pleased, utterly normal, and for one heart stopping moment Sally thought that he knew her. Then she looked into his face and saw only a sort of general willing affability there. He was not so pitifully gaunt as when she had last glimpsed him. In fact his face was unexpectedly fleshy and, she saw with a shock, almost unlined, as though all trace of the experiences of his forty or so years had been wiped from it. The shape of his head, the strong cheekbones, the hazel eyes, the thick curly hair though gray now, still made him good-looking, but the keenness, the humor, the look of easy authority had gone. Sally had always disliked the joking phrase, "no one at home," and now its full cruel meaning hit her like a blow. That was exactly how his eyes looked; bland, blank and vulnerable in their naïve friendliness.

"Mike—" Words stuck like marbles in her throat. "Mike, it's Sally. Do you—?"

She checked herself, appalled. How could her first question to him be, "Do you remember?" Yet what else was there to say? How could she even ask him how he was?

But he was looking even more intently into her face, stooping to peer at her, social niceties lost in the urgent struggle to piece things together in his brain, a struggle which Sally realized he must go through every moment of every day.

"Yes . . ." he was saying, "yes . . . I know who you are. *Wait* a minute now . . ." He spoke differently, slowly, in a sort of relaxed sing-song as though there were all the time in the world. As for him there was, time stretching empty, unmeasured, without demands or divisions or horizons. "You used to help with the bridges. Yes, that's right. You built the bridges."

Shred of recollection, connecting her with that first visit. Stunned, Sally gazed at him, her face tight, hardly believing what she had heard and terrified of rushing in and destroying this fragile link. "That's right," she said quietly, her voice unsteady. "I stayed at the cottage." She gestured along the lane.

"*That's* right," he said again, still in that slow voice, but this time with evident satisfaction. "I remember you. The cottage along the lake. I haven't been in the place for years."

"We used to go out to shoot foxes," Sally offered carefully.

"Foxes, that's right, I remember that." She knew

instantly that he didn't. He was using the line she had
fed him. "And you stayed at the cottage."

She had said that too, but here she was certain that,
however confusedly, he had made the connection. She
gained a tiny insight into how, gropingly, he patched
together fragments of memory.

"So where are you living now?" he asked.

"At Grianan, in Glen Ellig, with Aunt Janey."

"Oh, yes, Glen Ellig, that's right." Nothing. Then,
amazingly, "You were in Australia."

"That's right, I was." Sally could hardly get the
words out. She held herself rigid, hands twined in the
plastic loops of the carrier bag with the milk and
bread. She wanted to throw her arms around him,
hold him safe from the appalling thing that had overtaken him. "We used to swap traveler's tales."

"That's right, we did." He laughed a little, apparently pleased that he was getting things right, but obviously not remembering. "Good days, weren't they?"
Meaningless, just something he had learned to say to
people. "So you were in Australia? Where did we
meet?"

"We met here," Sally said gently, her voice only
just under control. "I was staying at the cottage along
the lake." Using his own phrase.

"The cottage, that's right." He nodded, but frowning a little now. "So where are you living now?"

"In Glen Ellig."

He nodded again, but looked troubled. "I've been
ill you know," he said. "Gone a bit cuckoo, they tell
me. Can't remember anything."

"Mike." It was a whisper. The crude phrase was not
one he would ever have used. Anguish engulfed Sally.
She looked away from him, across the dark ripple pat-

tern of the water under the driving wind, to the thick encircling trees and the clean sweep of fell above. She got her voice under control and turned to him. "You're getting better all the time, though, aren't you?"

"Oh, I'm a lot better than I was," he said instantly. "Couldn't remember this place at all, you know, when I first came out of hospital. Didn't know where I was. Didn't know Isobel or the children."

"You'll keep on getting better," Sally said, more pleading than reassuring.

"Oh, I'll be just about back to normal. Almost completely normal." Words he had been taught. "And when do you go back to Australia?"

Returning to the one sure point he had established, or mere inconsequential grasping at anything that took him away from a subject he didn't like?

"I was just there for a visit, a few years ago."

"A few years ago?" Meaningless overemphatic surprise as though he had heard people make this sort of response. "So where are you living now?"

This seemed to be something he needed to establish to place her if he could in some context to which he could relate. Glen Ellig meant nothing so his brain returned again and again to the question, struggling to make a connection.

"I'm staying just now at the cottage," Sally said, again pointing along the track through the trees.

"You must come and see us," he said warmly. A social reflex back in place. "Isobel would love to see you."

Sally walked on, torn to pieces by the fluctuating promise and checks of this exchange. Beyond her wildest hope had been the moment when Mike had volunteered the remark that she had helped him with the bridges. He had said that, hadn't he? she asked herself anxiously. It hadn't come from any information she had fed him? But no, he had volunteered it at once, perhaps before his brain became clogged with conscious effort to remember more about her. Perhaps his brain tired. His remark about Isobel indicated that as they talked he had lost track completely of who Sally was. His conversation had been like a patchwork of instinctive reactions, the independent function of his floundering brain, stitched together with things re-imposed, retaught. "You must come and see us." That was what people said. But then the agony of that flat, "I've gone cuckoo," itself a dated phrase lodged in his vocabulary perhaps in childhood.

Harried by pity, a searing sense of loss, yet a hope more vivid than she had allowed herself for months, Sally knew she couldn't face Janey yet. Leaving the shopping bag at the bottom of the drive she went on along the lake, past the path to the fell, and ducked and wove her way to the secret place below the water-fall, a place so intimately connected with that first meeting with Mike that she had not had the courage to go back to it since they had parted. There she crouched for a long time, letting the emotions come as they would; and the tears.

"It's hard to believe, isn't it, that any woman could even think of being unfaithful, with her husband in such a state, poor man. But Isobel's always had a hard streak in her, I've said so often enough, and this just goes to show."

They hadn't been able to stop her this time, Elsa Callander, her eyes gleaming with satisfaction, her eager voice gobbling out the gossip like some self-righteous turkey cock dressed by House of Fraser.

"Of course she still looks after him, he's always clean and so on, and frankly he doesn't know which day of the week it is and probably never will, so in a way I suppose it doesn't matter, but it's the principle of the thing, isn't it? I mean, all this pretence of going to see her mother, up and down to Jedburgh two and three times a week, the children kept away from him, left for hours and hours on his own."

An outraged instinct to protect Mike made Sally want to leap up and shout her into silence. How dared she write him off so callously, how dared she invade his privacy in such a way? Yet in spite of her furious anger, her brain seized on the implications of this gossip. Had Isobel really found someone else? Was she truly abandoning Mike, not just for hours alone, which surely was not only callous but potentially dangerous, but for good?

"It's none of our business," Janey was protesting, but her voice so lacked its usual firmness that Sally's attention was caught. In fact it was surprising that Janey had let this frightful woman rant on as long as she had, and looking at her aunt more carefully Sally saw how this visit had drained her and was annoyed with herself for allowing it. They had spent the morning packing up dozens of china and wood and plaster and fur and felt figures of Squirrel Nutkin and Co., and Janey should have been resting now, not pinned down under the bombardment of Elsa Callander's uncharitable innuendoes.

"Well, we're all neighbors," Elsa was pointing out affrontedly. "The poor man ought to be having therapy, companionship. I offered, naturally, but Isobel was quite rude about it. But fancy doing that, when he's quite helpless, it doesn't bear thinking about, does it? He may be a vegetable, I mean, it's hard to know if he *feels* anything any more, isn't it? But still, there's a certain level of civilized behavior—"

"I'm sorry," Sally broke in, trying to keep her voice polite and ordinary. "I think Aunt Janey's rather tired. We had a busy morning."

"Oh, don't mind me," Elsa cried gaily, not moving. "I can see you've been packing up. Could give you a hand, you know." Her eyes raked the boxes, the bare shelves. "I hope you don't mind my asking, only naturally it would affect everyone here, but are you by any chance thinking of selling? Only one never knows quite who might—"

Aunt Janey gave her one look of unconcealed loathing, leaned back in her chair and shut her eyes.

"I really must ask you to go," Sally said to Elsa, getting up quickly, not prepared to wrap up the request in conciliatory phrases.

She didn't seem to hear. "Now you must both come and see me before you go. Not tomorrow because it's Senior Citizens' afternoon and I really feel I should support it, the dear old things depend on my being there, but Thursday would be ideal, shall we say four?"

She was so imperviously encased in her arrogance and stupidity that Sally knew she would be congratulating herself as she went down the drive on her kindness in rescuing them from their solitude and boredom.

Sally went in and knelt beside Janey's chair, conscious of the little flutter of fear which was becoming all too familiar to see her slumped there so wearily.

This mattered most. The tentative speculation stirred by Elsa's gossiping words would wait.

Janey opened one eye. "Dreadful woman. How about some fresh tea to wash the taste of her out of our mouths?"

It was so good to hear her evil chuckle that Sally leaned to wrap her arms around her and crush her close.

"Terribly sad though," Janey remarked, when the tea was made, "this business of the Danahers. One wonders what the outcome will be. It's easy to condemn Isobel, but what must it have been like for her, the whole fabric of her marriage torn apart in a few moments? And who can judge what harm is being done to Mike? All these press-button reactions from people like Elsa Callander—how can any of us know how something like that would affect him?"

She sounded thoughtful, concerned, not asking for comment, and thankfully Sally offered none.

The new development, with all its startling implications, had begun to sink in. Or the possibility of it, for how far could Elsa be trusted? What, truly, was left of the Mike she had known in the man she had talked to yesterday? What spark, what humor, what remnants of the qualities that had made up his strong personality? And who was she to judge Isobel, who had had to face the nightmare of caring for this wreck of a husband? What kind of relationship could exist between them now? What kind of hell was it to share the house, their bed, with his physical likeness become an empty shell?

Would Isobel leave him? Had she really found someone else, or were the trips to Jedburgh simply to find comfort in her mother's company, in her own old home? If she did decide, for whatever reason, that she couldn't stay with him, what would become of Mike? When he recovered would he understand what happened? How much would he be capable of feeling? And how much did he miss the children? Did he understand that they had been sent away because of him?

And how much would he remember about Sally herself as his recovery progressed? Would more details of their meeting and their times together, their loving, filter back? It had crossed Sally's mind that perhaps after their conversation yesterday he might have gone in and told Isobel about it. But who would he have said Sally was? Then she had realized that probably by the time he reached the house all awareness of their meeting would have vanished, and that was achingly sad too.

In the few days Janey and Sally spent at Edalmere there were other glimpses of Mike, scraping the wound raw over and over again. Worst was passing the house, compulsively drawn to look at its silent face, and seeing him standing at the window, a still gray shape. He would raise an arm as Sally waved and the image stayed with her hauntingly, the robot movement, obedient, without comprehension.

Back at Grianan, where Sally now spent almost as much time as at the flat, she did her best to accept that he was finally gone. At no point would their lives ever touch. No one, including Mike himself, knew that any relationship had ever existed between them. There was no way she could ever, on any pretext, find a way into the unhappy circle of those who were part of his life.

This had to be faced, accepted, then set aside. Janey now occupied all their thoughts. For Nona and Sally the shop had become a mere job, confined strictly to opening hours. They didn't neglect it but it was no longer their first priority.

Sally still saw Jed. Coming back from Edalmere after that harrowing visit with Janey it had been the greatest uncomplicated solace to go into his arms, be swept up into the intensity of sex, and afterwards to plummet into sleep without conscience or doubts, free for a while of the whole tragic tangle.

Out of bed, things with Jed weren't so good. Sally was beginning to realize, as Janey had warned, that the tirades about his family which always ended up focusing on Moira weren't so much about venting anger as an obsessive circling around something that wasn't going to go away. Moira was turning up more frequently at Glen Ellig, apparently having trouble with her lover (or lovers, Sally couldn't always keep track), and there were blistering scenes, ending with doors beaten down, smashed furniture and dramatic walk outs. One wondered in what state Miss Hutchinson's executors would find the grieve's house when she died.

Jed would appear at the boathouse after these dramas vowing that Moira was never going to set foot in the place again, and it was about now that he began to hint that perhaps Sally might like to move in with him.

When he first suggested it she even for an instant considered it—a measure of how bereft and directionless her life felt without Mike in it. It held the simple attraction of not being alone, of a permanent relationship, even the vain thought that Jed might improve if she lived with him. But at once, fortunately for her self-esteem, there rose up before her eyes the actuality of the dark, ugly, battered house, mince and tatties every day at five-thirty, muddy oily stinking overalls, quarrelling voices, cans of beer, Radio One, cigarette smoke and fag ends everywhere.

She also knew, shuddering to think that even for thirty seconds her own need had made her contemplate the idea, that Jed, whether he realized it or not, was using her as a weapon in the engrossing battle with Moira. And that, finally, put the whole thing into perspective for Sally. She and Jed had needed each other, even helped each other, but the old hold he had had over her had at last worn thin and was finally broken.

Janey underwent a second operation at the end of May, and though they all knew it could only be a temporary remission as before, she did seem better once she had recovered from the immediate trauma, and her humor and mental liveliness were soon back in place.

It was now that Sally received a great shock and a great lesson, the last gift Janey was to give her. She had been up the hill behind the house one evening and was coming down into the garden from the high grassy "drying green" when she saw a sight that shook her through and through.

Janey still used the old apple room above the kitchen in spite of the narrow twisting stair up to it. As Sally came down the slope the light was on, the curtains open and she could see right into the room. It had always satisfied her deeply, associated as it was with fat downy comfort and childhood cuddles and security. In a way it was very unJaney, since she had simply lifted everything straight out of her mother's old room and transferred it there without changing anything. It was all very feminine, pale peach and cream, but of course it was completely Janey not to have bothered about colors so long as things were still usable. Sally looked in now with pleasure at the soft lamplight, the big bed with its high tattered satin head-board, its plump pillows, its ragged flounces and mounded, faded, pink eiderdown quilt. She looked in expecting a comforting familiar picture of Janey with her spectacles on the end of her nose devouring her ninth or tenth Sharpe novel—hurrying to finish them, Sally thought, with the unbearable stab of foreboding which was never far away in these fleeting days.

Instead she saw two lovers, entwined, close, at peace. With a shock that drove the breath out of her lungs in an incredulous gasp, she saw Janey, head back, eyes closed, her arm about Piers, whose dark head was curved down, quiet on her breast. Sally saw in that one stunned second the darkness of his skin against Janey's, the accustomed ease of their bodies, the fine texture of old linen, the round mark Janey's head had rubbed on the faded-to-white buttoned satin behind her. And she saw unmistakable serene contain-ment in the softly lit scene.

Astounded, floundering, she found she was groping for a revulsion which seemed somehow obligatory. It didn't come, for which she would for ever be thankful. Instead, wondering, tentative at first but quite definite, there came a sense of the fitness of what she had seen, followed by an amused tender delight.

Still punch drunk by this revelation, Sally turned away and went along the face of the slope and down into the vegetable garden where the long beds had been dug over but, except for one small corner, not planted this year.

Janey and Piers. So simple, so astounding but so obvious. Many things fell neatly into place and with the satisfying sense of things made clear a great delight filled Sally that Janey had had this, had had her lover to bring her happiness. It thrilled her to realize that the contented accord she had so often observed between Janey and Piers had had its roots in this wonderful intimacy.

No wonder Piers had been so protective of Janey, so angered by Sally's neglect and blindness. But how marvelous for her, Sally thought, wandering on with an instinctive wish not to intrude upon them by so much as entering the house, how marvelous to have Piers' gentleness and perceptiveness lavished upon her.

Lucky Janey, she thought, between laughter and tears. Oh, lucky Janey.

Chapter 16

There was no question of Grianan opening at Easter and Sally found that her mind blanked out in cowardly fear any thoughts of its future beyond that point. She and Janey had written to tell the guests. The closest friends among them Janey insisted on telling herself, her brown marbled Swan fountain pen, which she had used as long as Sally could remember, sweeping firmly across the pages. Sally dealt with the rest, a task that left her drained and depressed. To write over and over again, "as Aunt Janey has terminal cancer," which was what Janey wanted her to say, was like a blow descending repeatedly on the same spot.

The replies poured in, nearly all of them, after distressed and shocked reactions to Janey's illness, going on to say what Grianan had meant to them through the years. For the first time Sally saw Janey's prosaic acceptance of what was coming rocked as she read those loving testimonials to her care and hard work.

"How can I not see them all again?" she demanded passionately, crushing a handful of pages untidily to her bosom.

"All those boring old nuisances?" Sally teased her, but very affectionately, going to her and folding her aunt's rough, much whiter head against her while Janey sniffed noisily.

"I know what I'll do, I'll have a party for the nuisances," she announced with resolution, pushing Sally away. "After all, I can't go without gloating once more to Hugo over my *nudiflorum*—it's going to do better than ever this year. And maddening as the Pettifers are they've pretty well grown into the woodwork by now. Then there's poor old Esmond; who on earth is going to take him on, with his herbal tea seven times a day and his hand-washed silk vests—?"

The project grew at breathless speed and ran away with them. From thinking casually that they could manage a few old fogies for a dinner party then shunt them off to the Cluny Arms in Kirkton, Piers, Nona and Sally began to panic about a houseful of guests who clearly had every intention of staying the night if not the weekend, and were all equally confident of right of tenure to "their" rooms.

But that wasn't all. It was becoming obvious that Janey's network for the trading of honey and cream, butter and eggs, fish and game, plants and logs, could not be ignored. Its members were the friends of her girlhood, their parents friends of Sally's grandparents. Janey had done little socializing outside Grianan for many years but such friendships were solid and unchanging.

"Maureen and Connie can't possibly cope with this lot, even with all of us to help them," Piers pointed out, as they sifted through piles of eager replies and did horrified sums.

"Janey mustn't do a thing anyway." On that they were united. It was an absolute condition of having the party at all. But though they all made a big thing of insisting on it Sally knew, with chill dismay, that Janey wasn't really arguing.

One thing was plain, everyone who intended to come intended to help. "We shan't expect a thing, we'll make our own beds, do the washing up, be no trouble at all," the letters promised. "Don't do masses of cooking, we'll all bring stuff," people like Pauly Napier from Drumveyn and Penny Forsyth from Alltmore told them firmly.

"We're not short of resources anyway," Sally remarked after a tricky conversation with Lady Hay of Sillerton, who had made up her mind that they should have her frightful old butler Dewes to "run things" for them.

"If we've got all these ex-ambassadors and judges and generals' wives and things fighting about who's going to clean the loos, then let them get on with it, I say," was Nona's reaction.

It was clearly the answer and suddenly it all became as Janey had intended, the reason for the whole enterprise tacitly and thankfully ignored in shared activity.

The only person seriously objecting was Marchmain, who had been under the impression that the house was at last his. He did a lot of stalking about in a marked manner, spitting at Sally, whom he particularly disliked, and swearing and growling even at Janey. When the house began to fill on a Friday evening in June he decamped in fury to the garden cottage, which Sally thought an excellent decision.

It was a weekend with feelings treacherously near the surface. There was the tremendously buoyant mood, almost tangible throughout the house, of a group gathered in a place they cared about because of their love for one valued person, a love they were ready to show and share. And beneath that there was the unbelieving grief, publicly hidden, which would pluck at people unawares, sending them abruptly out of rooms in the middle of a conversation, or driving them to the garden to stand with their backs to the house gazing out over the patterned midsummer greens of the glen to Ben Breac's shapely peak, remembering.

The weather was mostly kind to them. It must have been, for afterwards Sally could scarcely remember what it had been like. What she did remember was the extreme efficiency of her elderly male shirt-sleeved pot-washing team; the mountains of wonderful food which appeared on the long tables which Jed and Piers had set up in the library and dining room; the laughter over a large-scale dog-fight on the lawn into which half a dozen people dived without hesitation to wrench the furious snarling animals apart by their tails; and the extraordinary sensation of being part of what every person in the room was feeling as they sat in the absolute stillness of the drawing room and listened for the last time to the sentimental familiar music in the long-drawn-out summer dusk.

Even more poignant was the image of Aunt Janey, the still center to whom all turned, on whom everything revolved; Janey passive, allowing herself to be looked after. Sally could hardly bear, and knew she was not alone, to make the comparison with the days when her aunt was the driving force behind the whole show, stumping rapidly about house and garden, ordering, bullying, reprimanding, giving, making, laughing, doing.

There was a terrible bright gaiety about the thanks

and goodbyes, a universal abruptness about the way
one car after another took off down the drive.

Janey went into hospital again in early July. This time
they didn't operate. She came home after a couple of
days and two weeks later she died.

Piers left, mute, rigid, his thin face taut and twisted
with pain. Gazing into that hurting face, the eyes
guarding their grief so tenaciously, Sally knew she
couldn't ask if he would come back. To her he had
never relented. He felt that she had failed in love for
Janey. Sometimes she suspected that he felt she failed
in love in general. She longed to say something to let
him see that she knew the truth of his relationship
with Janey and was glad of it, but of course it was
impossible to refer to it in any way. Equally impossible
at this point to attempt to break through to some understanding between the two of them. It would be
pure selfishness on her part to try, Sally knew, intrusive and unforgivable. But Janey had given Piers the
Garden Cottage and Sally didn't want any disapproval
he felt for her personally to interfere with what her
aunt had wanted.

"Piers, you do know that if you want to use the
cottage—" A clumsy beginning since it was now his.
She tried again. "I mean, please don't feel that if you
live in it you have to be involved here—" Worse still,
hopelessly open to misinterpretation.

The deeds had been carefully drawn up giving separate access and rights to water, leaving Sally's options
open to sell Grianan if she wished. That hadn't been
discussed but she knew that realistically Janey had expected it to happen.

Piers hadn't answered, had simply shaken his head.

He looked beaten and stunned, withdrawn deep into that ferocious reserve of his. Sally wanted to ask where he would go, what he would do, but knew such questions would not be acceptable.

Then Nona, her arms tight around Sally, her cheek wet against hers. "You're sure you'll be all right?"

"I'll be all right."

"I hate leaving you, I feel pulled apart, but I've got to go back. I can't wait any longer, but I just couldn't go till . . ."

"I know." Sally hugged her. "I'm only thankful that you stayed this long. I couldn't have got through it without you, you know that. And it meant so much to Janey too, having you here. Not just for yourself but because you were her link with mother."

Janey had refused utterly to let them tell Rose in time for her to come. They both understood that she had known she didn't have the reserves of strength left to deal with such a reunion. But she had come very close to Nona in those last weeks.

"You'll write, won't you?" Nona didn't mean write to her when she had gone.

"I've already written." In the raw aching time after Janey's death Sally had found it surprisingly easy to express many things to her mother which had long needed to be said. "I wrote to father, too. I thought he'd like to know about Janey." But she hadn't written in time for him to come to the funeral.

"Hey, that's *good*," Nona said warmly, hoping as Sally knew that this would forge a new link. Nona had worried about Sally being alone but she didn't want to delay going home any longer. She had at last confessed that Ray Tamerlaine had written to her over two months ago, telling her that he and his wife were now living apart and filing for divorce, and asking Nona to come back. Sally wished so much that Janey could have known about this generously kept secret, this loving sacrifice which filled her with gratitude and respect for Nona every time she thought on it.

"It's only miles, remember," Nona said now, "only hours. We'll never be really separate again." It was true, and it made a big difference.

"You've got to look after yourself."

"I am looking after myself."

"Oh aye, I can see that." Jed sounded more disgusted than concerned.

He had found her walking up the drive as darkness fell, August dark, creeping forward measurably evening by evening. Sally had been wandering by the river. She hadn't intended to go so far and her feet in old canvas shoes were soaked, her hair and sweatshirt misted with fine rain, her hands icy.

Chuntering away Jed dumped her into his jeep, drove up to the unlocked, unlit house and pushed her ahead of him into the kitchen, the muttering increasing as he found the Aga cold and mean draughts swirling in from the open door to the stone passage. He put the kettle on the gas cooker, yanked down the roller towel from behind the door and threw it at her with orders to dry her hair and get her sweatshirt off, then fetched a jacket from the row of hooks by the back door and hustled her into it.

"It'll be no bloody help to anybody if you catch your death of cold," he nagged away, picking up the towel Sally had thrown on the table and giving her head an extra harsh rub. "And how the hell do you ever get this lot dry anyway?"

"Jed, I'm fine," Sally protested, rocking on her feet under his ministrations and trying to push the heavy hands away. You must give me time, she wanted to plead, time for grieving. But she knew it would upset him.

"So what are you going to do about this place, tell me that?"

Sally knew this change of attack was part of his anxiety for her and she smiled gratefully at his broad back as the kettle began to whistle and he strode to quell it.

"I'll decide sooner or later."

"You canna' just let everything go to rack and ruin while you're doing it."

"I'm not going to. Oh, Jed, that's lovely." She took the steaming mug he thrust toward her with a smile of thanks. "Don't worry about me, I'll sort everything out in time."

"And that place in the Lake District, your other auntie's house, what's to become of it?"

"I suppose it will have to be sold." Janey had left Nona and the others respectable sums, the cottage to Piers. Sally had everything else. To keep Grianan she would have to throw all she had at it, the shop, the boathouse flat, the Edalmere cottage. She wasn't ready to do that yet, for how could she decide about Grianan? She couldn't envisage running it in the old manner and Janey still seemed too close for her to consider any other. But it would be impossible to keep it otherwise.

She knew that she was ducking the necessity of getting rid of the cottage on Edalmere, her only link with Mike. To destroy that, to deprive herself of the chance of being near him, of catching a glimpse of him now and then—the thought set up an instant resistance. She couldn't put out of her mind the amazing moment, brief and tantalizing as it had been, when he had known who she was. The stunned joy of remembering it never lessened. He could only get better; other memories might return for him. Though good sense might make her see that she had no place in his present existence, instinct balked at the idea of cutting off all possible contact with him.

She and Jed lit the fire in the small sitting room and sat for hours, talking but not touching, in this room which still spoke of Janey in every crowded inch but which Sally had not been able to bring herself to alter in any detail. Sex with Jed would have been unimaginable here, and she knew he felt the same. And although the big house lay around them, empty, her own, they made no move to find a more acceptable place. Sally knew then, without a word being said, that there would be no more loving between them, and she couldn't escape a momentary ache of loss for that straightforward pleasure.

"You'll take care of yourself now?" Jed repeated as she went out with him to the jeep, speaking with a sort of bullying insistence which said he didn't believe she would and was worried about it. It was as close as he could come to voicing loving concern.

"Don't worry, I won't go to pieces." Sally promised, reaching up to wrap her arms around his solid pillar of a neck, consciously luxuriating in his big hug as he crushingly responded.

"You could have fooled me, wandering about like that after dark soaked to the skin," he grumbled. "Now I'm there, mind, if there's anything you're needing."

Sally knew he meant it. He was her nearest neighbor at Grianan and would do for her what he had done for Janey. He would be on hand in any emergency, help with jobs she couldn't tackle alone and "give an eye" to the place when she was down in Muirend. But there would be no more love making. They had moved on. She shivered, wrapping her arms around her body, and turned to run into the empty, chilly house.

It was odd how easily Jed became distanced from her, almost as though nothing had ever happened between them, on Sally's part the adolescent infatuation finally worked through, on Jed's his real life taking over. Moira turned up one day at the end of harvest and after a stupendous row which could almost be heard in the village announced that she was staying. The rest of the family had already come straggling home. Bonnie was there with her baby, Gordon working for his father again with hardly more than one shouting match a day. None of them could do without each other. Sally knew she had never really figured in the equation.

However, as she had assured Jed, she wasn't going to pieces, or anything like it. The desolation of Janey's going had to be got through and there were no short cuts to that. She missed Nona very much and minded about Piers' departure more even than she had expected, yet she found in herself a strength which surprised her, an absence of desperation, even an absence of loneliness. It was as though Janey's courage, Nona's selflessness, the depths of Piers' grief all helped her.

Grianan must wait. She didn't strip it or shroud it in dust-sheets. It looked as it always had, as though it was waiting only for the gruff laugh, the heavy tread, the rich smell of glorious food, the pounding piano, to spring back to busy life. Marchmain waited too, poor cat. He had refused to stay with Connie or Maureen and had come obstinately home each time he was taken away. In spite of their dire prophecies of pining, starvation or death in battle the pampered creature fended for himself admirably. Sally wasn't altogether surprised; Marchmain was a ruthless survivor if ever there was one.

It took her a while to find someone to replace Nona in the shop and she was very busy, which helped. Small businesses seemed to be starting up everywhere. Most collapsed and premises stood empty with ominous regularity but nothing could deter fresh optimists from leaping in in their turn. It was profitable for Sally, though there was a ghoulish feel to it sometimes and she often found herself giving warnings against her own interests. No one ever took any notice of them.

She was discovering that something else had changed since Janey's death, becoming subtly aware of a new attitude from the friends in the glen who had poured to the party and the funeral. Sally, as the only Buchanan left at Grianan, had inherited them, as it were, and in their different ways they let her know that they were there for her when she was ready to turn to them. She didn't need them yet. Like the decision about Grianan itself, she had to have time. But knowing that this easy, undemanding friendship was on offer was definitely consoling. Another bequest from Janey.

As the weeks slipped by and the awful emptiness at waking, the feeling of living in a house whose roof had been torn off, gradually became less frightening,

Sally realized that she had another new source of strength to tap into. Through Nona she had regained a family. She had turned her back on it so determinedly after the disastrous visit to Australia that for years she had had no sense of it existing for her. Now they were suddenly there, part of her life; it was as simple as that. Not only Nona's frequent glowing postcards—presumably less daunting than getting down to a letter (only then she would have so much to say that she would write smaller and smaller, going around and around the edges, squashing the address into a tiny balloon)—but letters from their mother brought them all close.

Writing first about Janey and Grianan, free in her grief to allow herself at last nostalgia without apology, Rose had moved on with growing ease to talk of the matters which lay unresolved between them—how she had felt about leaving Sally's father, about leaving Sally, how she had blamed herself for her inability to welcome her when she had come to Orford. For Sally it was like being released from an emotional straitjacket and she let her mother know it.

Rose wrote too about Nona and Ray, and there was something very special for Sally about finding herself accepted naturally in the big sister role, consulted, her views accepted, able to do her share even at this distance in reconciling her mother to Nona's moving in with Ray, which she had lost no time in doing.

Less easy, much less warm, was the letter Sally's father eventually wrote. It crackled with the stress he had felt in producing it but he too used Janey's death to open doors between them. It was strange to find him remembering Grianan with affection. Somehow Sally had shut him out of all memories there, but of course he had been there often with Rose in the early days of their marriage and with Sally when she was small. Now she found she was able to dredge up deep-buried recollections of him—absorbedly fishing as she and her mother came along the river bank carrying the picnic, absorbedly reading in the library, unlit pipe clenched in his teeth, always with that excluding concentration, that intense self-sufficiency.

He didn't bare his soul to Sally in his careful letter, didn't refer to her mother or to the clashes that had driven Sally from home, but he did say, "Although we have drifted apart in recent years, never, never feel that you cannot turn to me for anything you need. I suppose I've always taken it for granted that you would know that, but thinking over what I should say to you in this letter it occurred to me that perhaps it has to be stated. I often feel a need to know more of your life than the bare bones of major events or new addresses. But work, as you will recall, can always protect me from doing anything even slightly difficult. . . ."

The wry twist of self-mockery dispelled the chill of his words and Sally understood, with her first adult appreciation of her father, how hard it was for him to make contact with another human being.

So although from day to day she was terribly alone, there was none of the sensation of her life being on hold which she had experienced when Julian, behaving so well, had gone back to his wife. She knew she could cope better now. Love, friendship and support were on offer. She had a base.

Part Four

Part Four

Chapter 17

A fierce northwesterly drove down the lake, funneled by the hills, whipping up white crests on the waves, breaking in douches of spray against the jetty where Sally sat with her arms wrapped around her knees, her face up to the wind and the wet. If she slitted her eyes and looked only at the racing water, after a moment or two there was a feeling of the whole jetty tugging free and surging slowly forward. It was exhilarating, and gave her a strange sense of solitary defiance.

She had come often to Edalmere in the months since Janey died and the others had gone away. She had never expected to be able to do so, had never consciously planned it, but weekends in the flat were restless and long and Grianan was a house peopled by ghosts.

Coming here tentatively, needing a different scene but not ready to face people, she had wondered if Mike, having once recognized her, would remember more, perhaps talk about her. Isobel had enough to deal with. But from Ann Jackson and Elsa, from comments made in the village and her own observation, Sally had learned how completely each moment vanished for Mike as it passed. His immediate memory didn't exist. Each time he saw Sally he had no idea they had met since his illness and the conversation was always precisely the same. She knew she was gone from his brain the moment she walked away.

It was a miracle to be able to speak to him, be close enough to touch him, though she never did so, and let her eyes drink in those physical details which hadn't changed. The distressing image she had taken away after the visit with Janey, of the still figure at the window staring hopelessly out, dogged her less. Mike was often out of doors now, sitting in the garden or standing at the edge of the lake, and he looked fitter, his skin brown and freckled, more flesh on the long bones. Just to catch a glimpse of him filled Sally with thankfulness to know he had survived, though it hurt to see the terrible locked-in loneliness of his fight back to some tenable level of living.

Eagerly as she noted each tiny sign of progress, he was still far from the Mike she had known. His face had a strange new blandness, his movements were heavy, his humor and energy and natural authority gone. He lived in an introverted world of groping uncertainty and all his powers were concentrated on meeting the demands of each moment as it came, trying to find ways to evade the constant admission, "I don't remember . . ."

Sally found it hard to accept that every conversation began at the beginning again. Wildly excited by that first flash of recognition, she had assumed they would build on it, however slightly, at each encounter. This wasn't possible yet and she found it hard to get used to. Mike would place her, ask where she was staying, tell her he had been ill, talk about the weather. He was gentle, smiling, and gave no indication that he minded his present condition. Sally found that incredibly sad, but could at least be glad that he was unaware of her distress.

Sometimes he referred to Isobel. "She's never here," he would say naturally. "Always shopping or at her mother's, or taking the children out from school."

Sally asked how the children were; they never seemed to be at Edal Bank.

"Oh, they've been great," Mike said instantly, proudly. "I've been ill, you know, didn't know who the hell I was when I came out of hospital. Didn't know who the children were. But they've been great. Michael often helps me—" But a look of anxiety crossed his face as past and present failed to mesh in his brain. He peered at Sally uneasily, examining her face, then asked again with doubt in his voice, "So where are you living now?"

She knew he had lost track and that he was worried about it, so she chatted quietly for a few more moments and then walked on.

From Ann Jackson she learned that Mike was often alone at the house, even at night.

"It doesn't seem to bother him, though. Well, poor lad, he doesn't know what's going on, does he? And he'll never be any different, by all accounts. Every day's just starting all over again."

Sally refused to listen to Elsa Callander on the subject, or indeed any subject. On her first visit after Janey's death Elsa had spotted her in the village and was calling, "Oh, Sally, my dear, what frightful news!" while Sally was still yards away. "I was very fond of your aunt as you know—"

"I'm sorry, I don't want to talk about it," Sally had said flatly and walked on. Even Elsa could not insist, though Sally saw in the clutching movement of her hand that she would have liked to.

Sally knew she would have to come to a decision about the cottage soon. Sell, let? She couldn't keep three properties going indefinitely and Janey's solicitor was beginning to make noises. But now that she had begun to come here she dreaded breaking the link with Mike. She needed to be able to see him, however fleetingly, and assure herself that he was safe and in his own limited way contented. She was beginning to understand a little of his condition, and that was important to her.

Already she understood that the view of him which set village tongues clucking—disabled, neglected and perhaps cheated on by his wife, deprived of his children—ignored the true facts. Even if Isobel had formed some other relationship and he knew about it, sexual jealousy didn't exist for him. His brain would reject it, protecting him from emotions which would deplete his diminished resources. For him, survival—personal, day-to-day survival—was paramount, and for that battle he needed peace.

Where Michael and Kirsty were concerned he had no concept of time. He believed he saw them often, so that was good enough, harsh though it might sound. And how painful—and restricting—it must be for them to spend any length of time with him. He had no practical worries or responsibilities, and was secure in a familiar place with a simple, known routine and material needs met. As the children were at boarding school it would appear that finances weren't a problem.

Then Sally would remember what Nona had said about the need to reacquire social skills. Shouldn't that be happening for Mike? Had the task been abandoned as too much trouble or was he not capable of learning and readapting? Sally hadn't enough knowledge to be able to judge, but the question gnawed at her.

At Christmas a letter arrived from Nona. There were just enough words among the exclamation marks and dashes to tell Sally she was pregnant. After the first delight Sally felt a pang of loss; with Nona so far away she would miss the excitement when the baby was born. But it was more than that. It was the instant comparison, there before she could duck. Nona's life and hers. The knife twisting because her lover was lost to her, altered and maimed, beyond the reach of words.

Her mother also wrote, "thrilled to pieces" as she put it, and re-reading her excited letter Sally was amused and touched to find how easily it flowed, how much her mother had to share with her. They would be able to find a meeting place now, she was sure of it. I could go out there, she thought, as though it was a new discovery, meet Ray, see the baby—my niece. The doors were open.

Sally went to Drumveyn for Christmas lunch. She had already begun to get cross with well-meaning questions about her plans, hating her solitariness being underlined, when Pauly Napier turned up in the shop.

Pauly was impulsive, scatty, chaotic, but warmly generous and outgoing and Janey had been very fond of her. She stood there smiling, her toffee-colored hair wildly untidy under a broad-brimmed hat, wearing jeans and boots and some sort of poncho. "I don't want to butt in," she said in her direct way, "and you've probably got more exciting plans, but if not we'd love to have you for as much of Christmas Day as you could stand us for. Though we're quite a mob, as you know."

An image of Drumveyn as it used to be flashed across Sally's mind, the gloom and chill and atmosphere of censoriousness. But Pauly had changed all that, and Sally knew Christmas alone at the flat or at Grianan would be pretty desolate.

She was glad she had accepted when she found herself warmly welcomed by the large family. Many changes had overtaken the straitlaced household Sally had known. Reserved Lady Napier, Archie's mother, had become a different person after her husband's death a few years ago. She had married the factor and lived with him in a converted barn, happier than she had ever been to judge from her relaxed air and smiling eyes.

Her daughter Lisa, a contemporary Sally remembered as good fun as a child but rather moody later on, had returned to Drumveyn after her husband had mysteriously vanished and was now living in one of the estate cottages with an illustrator of children's books whose ex-wife lived next door and ran a kennels. They were all there, plus Archie and Pauly's two small daughters—adopted, Sally thought Janey had said—and the son of Archie's first wife. There was also a twelve-year-old Brazilian girl, whose connection with the family Sally wasn't clear about. There were a lot of dogs.

Andrew and Penny Forsyth, the Blaikies from Torglas and Robin Thorne from Baldarroch were there for drinks before lunch and Sally felt tension unwind as the familiar conversation flowed around her, its references and allusions part of life for ever. Lunch in the big beautiful kitchen wound on splendidly for hours, followed by a brisk walk around the loch in the dusk.

Kind Archie Napier, worried as they all were about Sally's isolation, took the chance to talk to her, as he had wanted to do for some time.

After some general enquiries about the business he said, "It must be worrying for you, knowing Grianan's standing empty. These big old houses are a nightmare to keep up. I just wanted to say—don't forget there are plenty of hands here to do any maintenance that's needed. You only have to ask."

"Oh, Archie, that's so good of you. I know I ought to do something about the place, but I've been putting off making a decision."

"Take your time. Just think about it when you're ready. We can keep an eye on things for you meantime. Janey was one of the great characters of the glen and we miss her."

Warmed by his down-to-earth kindness and grateful for Pauly's generous hospitality, Sally drove home after tea, refusing all offers of a bed for the night, feeling comforted and ready to face silent Grianan and its memories.

The talk and laughter and company had stirred her up however, and next morning she found herself too restless for the idle program she had planned. It was a brilliant day. There had been a light fall of snow and a hard frost, and a huge red ball of sun hung in the eastern sky. She suddenly felt a need to be at Edalmere; she had never seen it on such a day.

The Lakeland hills were a rich tawny shade in the sun, their tops frosted white. Parked cars at the popular spots indicated plenty of people were enjoying the crisp bright day but there was little moving on the roads. When she reached the cottage (no sign of life at the Danahers, hadn't they been together for Christmas?) she turned up the heating, put on boots and went up through the wood.

Unforgettable afternoon, here in the landscape she had shared with Mike, the rich blue of the lake vivid against dense green plantations and white ridges reaching away westward, turning every shade of pink and peach before metallic blue spread as the light died.

Coming down with the cold air biting her cheek-bones, toes and fingers warm with exercise, Sally felt an unexpected happiness. It had been a year of tragedy and grief. No one could replace Janey, nothing could bring back Mike as he had been, but she felt part of the fabric of life again, and that was good.

Hearing the car behind her Sally moved aside but didn't stop. Where was Isobel off to? Surely not going to Jedburgh today? As the car pulled up Sally felt reluctant to turn; Isobel would talk about Janey.

Kirsty was in the passenger seat, smiling shyly, winding down her window. In the driving seat, leaning to see Sally, was Mike, also smiling.

"Nice to see you. What are you doing here?"

Simple question, so like the questions he always asked when he saw her, but this time utterly different. He knew who she was. There was no doubt of it. His eyes, his face, his voice, all told her that. He was back.

"Mike." Sally clutched the edge of the window, her brain reeling. "How did you know—I mean, do you really remember me?" Impossible to avoid the word.

"Of course I remember you. It's a while, though, isn't it? Are you at the cottage?"

It's true. He does know me. He remembers. The thoughts jolted painfully around her brain. She felt a sting behind her eyes, a constriction in her throat. "Just for a day or two." She managed to get the words out normally, even managed a smile for Kirsty.

"Good. I'll come along and say hello later on. It's great to see you again."

"I'll look forward to it." Absurd, banal, yet what else was there to say? Sally stepped back from the car, waved and smiled as it drew away, then sank down shaking on the crisscross pattern of rimed grass on the bank.

Mike was driving again. He had known her. He had said he would come to the cottage. Blindly she walked on to the village, bought things there, though unable to think of anything she needed beyond milk and eggs. She met Ann Jackson but afterwards couldn't remember a word they exchanged. And for the rest of the day she waited, never going out of doors, shuttled between expectation and the anguished conviction that by now Mike wouldn't even know they had met.

The squawk of the gate jerked her out of her chair. She was so sick with nervous apprehension that she actually hoped for a moment it wasn't Mike. Then she heard his tread on the steps, his knock. It was an extraordinary moment—incredulous joy and agonizing uncertainty mingled. How much would he remember—what would he want—expect? He looked so much the same, yet not the same. He opened his arms and she went into them, seeing out of the tail of her eye at the last fractional second that his smile looked wrong, artificial and nervous.

His hug felt as though someone had explained the action to him and he was trying it out for the first time. Sally felt herself pressed for a moment against his now more fleshy frame but not received into his embrace. Stepping back as he released her she caught that strange smile again, the embarrassed smile of someone who has found a joke too explicit but doesn't want to be prudish about it. She realized he was uncomfortable, disturbed almost in some salacious guilty way by the contact. What associations were stirring, what long-ago strictures? And what anxieties as to what was expected of him?

But for Sally in that moment none of that mattered. Mike had come, had remembered for eleven hours that he had promised to come, taking a giant step out of the engulfing darkness of lost memory. The moment of true contact this morning had not been imagined. They were together again, she had felt his arms around her. But was it all right for him to be here? There was a new significance in that question now.

"Are the children at the farm?" she asked him.

"Yes, they're in bed. Michael was reading—reads till all hours."

"Is Isobel there?" So odd to use her name at last in this simple query.

Mike saw nothing strange in it. "No, she's never there. Can't blame her really, it's not much fun for her, with me in this state." He said it without bitterness, without any discernible feeling at all.

"You're sure the children are all right?"

"They're fine. They look after me half the time. But I'll go and check on them presently, when you've made the coffee."

"Two sugars."

"You remember that, do you?" He looked pleased.

"I remember you finding the sugar the first time

you came in." Could he possibly remember? Sally held her breath.

"Ah well, you have to know your way around all these damned cupboards of Ursula's," he said complacently. "You've tidied away a few things, though," he added. Sally found her hands unsteady as she took down the mugs. She had never imagined for one second that they would be together again in this room, laughing over however tiny a shred of shared memory.

When she suggested going to the sitting room Mike said, "Oh, God, no, I hate that room," and the sheer ordinariness of it made her feel for a moment that everything was back to normal.

She found his recollection was moving forward through the years. He accurately repeated stories about Teddy and Ursula which he had told Sally when she first knew him. The period of their own meeting was still patchy, though what he did recall moved and astonished her—that her wedding had been called off and she had come north to stay with Janey; that he had found her by the waterfall and she had helped him with jobs like clearing the beck; and that she had come to Edalmere often that first summer.

"Some nights we had, didn't we?" he said, watching her closely, and the uncharacteristic phrase and tone told Sally he was guessing. It was as though this area, sex, loving, was something his brain refused, perhaps because physical responses had not reawakened, or because such feelings would take too heavy a toll. When he referred to it he seemed to rely on role play, as though he felt vulnerable, dimly aware of something important but beyond his present powers.

"It was wonderful," she said gently. "Always. And

do you remember how we used to talk, for hours and hours on end?"

"God, yes." He seized on that gratefully. "We did, didn't we? About our travels . . ."

He was safe again, early memory sharp and clear. He could recall effortlessly jobs and journeys, people he'd worked with, place names, which year he was where. He would repeat the same story over and over again, with no idea he had told it a few minutes earlier.

"I was impressed to see you driving this morning," she said, breaking across the cycle as she got up to make more coffee.

"Oh, I'm good at that," he boasted. "That came back right away. I'm supposed to keep to the track, but I could drive anywhere, no trouble at all."

He talked differently in some subtle way. More childishly, which was perhaps to be expected. But his accent was surely different? Then it hit her. The voice he used was the voice of his youth, with the faint Irish accent that the years of travelling had smoothed away. It added to Sally's feeling of having to get to know a new person, while at the same time he was still overwhelmingly the Mike she loved.

As he talked, going over the same ground exhaustively, she realized he was getting increasingly rambly. She saw him frown once or twice and wondered if he had forgotten where he was. Perhaps exerting his memory so much was bad for him.

"I've no one to talk to, you know," he said more than once. "Not the way I can talk to you. Isobel and I didn't talk. She's never been happy here, hates the place, always rushing off somewhere."

"Well, if she's not there now, do you think we

should walk along and check on the children?" Sally suggested. Mike had forgotten his coffee and she observed with concern a faint sheen of sweat on his skin. If he got too confused she might have trouble getting him home, and once there it might upset the children to see him like this.

"They're fine," he said dismissively, making a curious hunching gesture with his shoulders as though shutting out a problem that was too difficult.

"Why don't we wander along the lane? It's getting fairly late."

He looked up at the wall. "You got rid of that damned cuckoo," he said with a glint of his old smile.

The small joke, remembered even through the fogs that were visibly gathering, reminding her that the inner self could never change, nearly destroyed Sally.

As they went slowly down the drive in the starlight he leaned heavily on her, yet gave the impression that he hardly knew she was there. He was newly docile in a way that she found unbearably sad. He muttered to himself as they walked in the darkness of the trees, and she was terrified that his brain had been harmed by the unaccustomed activity.

He didn't hug or kiss her when she left him at his gate. He had forgotten one did that and felt no natural instinct for contact.

"I'll come and see you tomorrow," he promised muzzily as he turned to go in.

She watched him go up the steps and fumble his way inside. She waited, listening for any sign that all was not well. A light went on. He'd be all right.

Along the dark track in the icy night she went, in the grip of a maelstrom of feelings. Her strong passionate lover, with his humor and tenderness and perceptiveness—how could this have happened to him? And yet against all odds they had been together again, had spent an evening in the cottage as they used to, sitting at the same table, talking of the same things. It was incredibly the same; it was agonizingly not the same.

He had said he would come back. All the next day Sally hugged this promise to herself, turning over every fragment of evidence that he had remembered their time together, longing to see him again. But she was obliged to accept that still, for Mike, a new day wiped the slate clean. He didn't come.

Chapter 18

Sally thought at first the Edal Bank number was engaged. It was only when she tried for the second time that she realized the sound was wrong. She checked with the operator. The line had been disconnected.

Even in the warm flat she felt chill fear flurry across her skin. Had something happened to Mike? She tried to rationalize, refusing panic. Perhaps he had taken to making weird or expensive calls and Isobel had had the phone cut off. But she couldn't quell the instinct that there was something ominous here.

Since that Boxing Day impulse to drive down, and the heart-stopping moment when she had seen that Mike truly knew who she was, she had phoned him quite often. The first time had been a strange experience. It was as though one small part of her went on resolutely tapping in the number while the rest of her protested that it was mad, wrong, impossible. She had looked the number up once, at the very beginning, in need of any scrap of knowledge about him. Unimaginable then to think of ever being able to use it but her brain had held on to it tenaciously just the same.

It was term-time so the children wouldn't be there. Isobel might or might not; she would never be able to work that out. Mike might not bother to answer the telephone, might have been told not to, might be afraid of it. But he had answered at last and Sally had been thrown into panic. They had never talked on the phone, how could he remember her without seeing her, how could she identify herself so that he would make the connection?

She had said in a nervous gabble, "Mike, hello. Do you remember someone called Sally, Sally Buchanan?" prepared to add, "I stay in the cottage along the lake," or "I used to help you mend bridges sometimes. . . ."

Mike had laughed and Sally had felt her limbs loosen in relief as she let out the breath she hadn't known she was holding. He had said easily, in that new slow voice of his, "Sally? Of course I remember you. Good to hear you. Where are you?"

He had chatted as though talking to her on the phone was entirely normal, saying every so often, "This is nice, isn't it? It's been a long time."

He had had no recollection of her recent visit or of going to the cottage, or of anything they had talked about that evening. He was back two-and-a-half years, when they had met, and he told her about his illness as though she would never have heard of it. "So when are you coming over?" he had asked, but in a casual social way which suggested that he remembered her as friend not lover. It was odd how the sexual element in him seemed to have been suppressed, or perhaps put on hold until his body was ready for its demands.

"I'm stuck here on my own a lot," he had explained, adding shatteringly, "Isobel's always up at Jedburgh seeing her mother and there's some bloke up there as well, she tells me. The children aren't here much. You should come over some time, it would be good to catch up."

It had all been so breath-takingly simple and matter-of-fact. "I'll come over to the cottage soon," Sally had managed to reply on the same note. "*Tha-at's* right, the cottage." He had this way now of drawing a word out as though facts were filtering back slowly. "Ursula and Teddy's cottage. You used to stay there, didn't you? Yes, come on over, we'll have a good long talk, I miss all the crack."

"I'll phone again, shall I?"

"You do that."

Whenever she did the conversation was much the same, but once or twice there had been some small sign that she was becoming an accepted constant in the slow journey back to normality. Once he had said, "Jesus, I need this. You can't think how good it is just to *talk*. Don't ever let go of the rope, will you?" and Sally had wept after putting down the phone in a passion of grief for what had befallen him, and for his immense patience and tolerance for the existence he now had.

Now this dead phone frightened her, as though the rope had broken in fact, and he was bobbing away from her on some dangerous sea. Could he have collapsed again, had a relapse, harmed himself in some way? There were so many terrifying possibilities for someone in his condition who was left so much alone.

Who could she ask? She winced at the thought of the gossiping tongues. Elsa Callander was out of the question. It would have to be Ann Jackson. God knew what she would make of such a question.

"Edal Bank? Oh, that's a downright shame, isn't it?" Ann was so eager to plunge into the details she didn't even stop to wonder why Sally was asking. "The Danahers have had that place for three generations, and young Michael loves it, wants to do just what his Dad did. Of course the job's gone now, well, it had to, didn't it, with Mike the way he is and who knows whether he'll ever be right again, but selling up when he still doesn't know whether he's coming or going, well, I said to Garth, that can't be right, can it. . . ."

Shaking, Sally let the spate pour over her, closing her eyes, setting her face grimly. Eventually she was able to ask, "Do you know where they've gone?"

"She's taken him back to Scotland. Of course, she never wanted to live down here, she made that plain enough. And the children are at school in Scotland, so I suppose it makes sense."

"They're at Isobel's mother's in Jedburgh?" Ann Jackson clearly wasn't switched to receive; it hardly mattered how direct the questions were.

"Oh, no—well, Isobel is, of course, she's been more or less living there these last months. But she's put Mike into a home, poor lad, somewhere near—oh, my head's like a sieve these days, what was the name now? I was talking to Mrs. Callander about it in the shop only the other day, she'd know right away. Let me see now. . . ."

Sally would have phoned even Elsa just then. A home. Mike, the tough, fit, active outdoor man in a *home*. What kind of home, where? She had to know.

"Oh, I remember, some name like Gilsborough, Gisborough, something like that. Not far from that place where Kirsty's going to school, St. Andrews. I do recall that because Kirsty was telling me about it herself last time she was here. . . ."

Sally prowled the flat, unable to settle to anything.

It felt shut in and dark. The bare trees, the slow slide of sunless water beneath the big window, the mathematical lines of the ploughed fields were drab and lifeless. She found herself longing for Janey, wishing she had told her about Mike. It was quite irrational; she couldn't have approved and it would have made no difference now; but there was a strong need to share this. On an impulse she went over to the computer. Nona knew most of the story. Sally's fingers flew in the marvelous release of knowing there was someone to whom the fears could be poured out, someone whose support was staunch, uncritical and now part of her life.

Then she went down to the car, fetched her road map and located Gilsburgh on the south shore of the Tay estuary. After that it didn't take long. Balmenie House. With a strange cold sense of simplicity she realized she could go there. By breaking up their home and abandoning Mike, Isobel had announced to the world that she no longer wanted him. Who was there to question it if Sally went to see him now?

Dull and gray, the main street of the little ex-mining town stretched away in the toneless afternoon light. Sally knew that her own dread was coloring her view of it, her longing to see Mike overlaid with a much stronger reluctance which she could do nothing about, but few places had ever given her such immediate and powerful feelings of distaste. She wanted to turn around and drive away. What was she doing here, anyway? she asked herself fiercely. This was an unforgivable intrusion into Mike's life. He was virtually a stranger now. He hardly knew who she was. Who was she to have a view on what should or shouldn't happen to him when her ignorance of his condition was almost total? And how could she assume that he would rather see her than any of the people at present around him? Perhaps Isobel was looking after him in the way that best suited his needs. She, after all, was the one who knew the limits of his present capability, and the prognosis for the future.

Balmenie House lay down to the left off the High Street and she had to make a couple of casts through a network of narrow streets to find it, a square solid house of dressed granite with big bay windows, its sloping front garden one obliterating stretch of concrete with a few straggling bushes on either side. Stark as it looked, at least there was no sense of enclosure.

As Sally rang the bell a surreptitious movement caught her eye—someone was peering out of the side window of the bay on her left. She was reminded with a sharp pang of Mike standing gray and still in the window of Edal Bank, an image she had never been able to eradicate from her mind and one she certainly would have done without now. But it was not Mike at the window; it was an old woman with wispy hair and yellowish skin and coal dark, hollowed eyes who had peeped out at her and now peeped again, her lips working in what looked like disapproval. What was she going to find here? Sally wondered, feeling her stomach clench with nervous apprehension.

A sound of yapping approached, then a woman opened the inner door of the porch and squeezed herself through a foot-wide gap while trying to prevent a couple of shrieking, scrabbling terriers from coming with her. "Come in, come in," she mouthed through the glass, and as Sally opened the outer door shouted, "They're quite harmless really," above the furious snarls.

Sally thought the "really" could have come more reassuringly earlier in the sentence. With a lot of growling and kicking and shouted commands, interspersed with deprecating smiles for Sally, they all worked their way across the hall and into a messy office.

"We're so pleased for Mr. Danaher that he has a visitor," Mrs. Lucas said, waving Sally to an armchair covered in dog hairs. Her manner was cozily fawning; her accent didn't sound like the one she would use in the kitchen.

"How is he?" What kind of answer can I expect from her to such a question, Sally thought helplessly.

"Oh, he's settled in extremely well, extremely well. Such a easy man, so pleased with everything." Why did such an ordinary statement make her sound so bogus? Sally hated her, with her sprayed hair and her spectacles hanging on a chain down the frilled front of her lilac polyester blouse.

"And it's all right to take him out? There's nothing I should be careful about?" Sally didn't know what she should ask.

"My goodness, he's not subnormal, you know, just suffering a temporary memory dysfunction. People often don't understand the difference." Sally had asked to be patronized, she supposed, but she hadn't asked for that sugary smile. "He has to adapt," Mrs. Lucas went on brightly, "get used to everything again. That's all there is to it. Otherwise he's just like you or I."

So trite, so complacent. What qualifications did she have, if any, for running this place? What right to pronounce on Mike and his state of mind?

"Then we'll go," Sally said crisply, needing this gratuitous delay to be over, this edgy exchange which seemed to be turning into a struggle for possession. The dogs let loose skirls of shrill rage as she stood up.

"Oh, he won't be far away, rest assured," Mrs. Lucas cried gaily as the racket subsided into a froth of sub growls. "He can't wait to see you. All done up in his best bib and tucker. If he's asked me the time once this afternoon he's asked a hundred times. Come along."

Sally's throat closed with nervous tension spiked with rage at the woman's fatuous smile as she followed her across the hall. Mike was waiting in a big, sparsely furnished lounge. Sally felt pure joy at the sight of him, never failing, then the small check of adjustment that was becoming familiar to see him as he was now, hair gray, face fleshy and smooth skinned, body thickened. This time there was an additional fleeting shock of distaste, followed at once by shame, because the hair was straggling and untidy and his clothes all wrong. He was wearing a clocked gray and white sweater stretched around his developing paunch and lightweight fawn slacks two inches too short. That one detail seemed to matter out of all proportion, filling Sally with angry pity. It was disconcerting too to see him standing in the emptiness of mid floor, passive, as though instructed like a child or a dog, "Wait there."

Dim figures huddled in meager leather-look chairs against the walls. Sally hardly saw them. For an aching instant the pain of finding Mike here in this incongruous place, so meekly acquiescent, stopped her in her tracks, and her own appearance here seemed outrageous and unjustifiable. They had been lovers once; they had agreed that she should walk away. They were nothing to do with each other any more; she should never have come.

Then Mike smiled at her, grinned, his eyes lighting up, and took a step towards her, shattering the unreality of the scene. As he moved, one of the smelly little dogs threw itself at him with teeth bared.

"Bloody animals," he said calmly, and lifted it aside with a well-timed swing of his foot.

The terrier yelled, more in surprise than anything else. There was a ripple of movement from the chairs. Sally laughed. Mike was Mike again.

"Mr. Danaher!" gasped Mrs. Lucas. "How could you? Poor little Gretchen, come to Mummy then—"

Mike winked at Sally. "She'll live. Are we off then? Where are we going?"

"Anywhere you like," she said, high on soaring happiness as he took her arm and steered her past a reproachful Mrs. Lucas, busy cuddling Gretchen and trying to pin her affability back in place.

"Not too late back, please," she fluted after them, attempting to re-establish control.

Mike didn't bother to answer and for a moment the illusion was there that nothing had ever happened to him. His unruffled air, his contempt for the horrible little dogs, his tall figure beside her and the way he smiled down at Sally with a fervent, "God, it's good to see you," as they walked away made it seem that he was himself again.

It wasn't so. Sally had thought she might take him to Cupar or St. Andrews and find somewhere quiet and comfortable where they could have tea and talk, but Mike resisted the idea instantly, looking worried. He wanted to follow a routine he knew and Sally hastily agreed. It seemed that every day—though she found he had no idea how many of them there had been—he walked into the town to fetch a newspaper, went back to Balmenie House to read it, then walked up the High Street on one side, down it on the other, had coffee at a grim little café, then went back to the house. After lunch there he went for a walk, sat for a while in the same café, and so back for supper, television and bed.

The walk he took her on depressed Sally quite unreasonably. They went down to the river and along a muddy path where they couldn't walk abreast, with pale, high reed beds on one side, on the other damp-stained council houses behind wire fences with concrete posts. There was a smell of sewage and rot; the tide was low and channels of pewter-colored water threaded the mud flats of the estuary under a threatening sky. Sally thought achingly of their sunlit sanctuary where the bright fall of the beck spilled down, the rocky ridge sweeping up to Helvellyn, its serrated teeth dark against a warm sunset sky, the smell of clean lake water as they dangled their legs over the edge of the old jetty.

They turned up a road through the council houses and in no time were back in the town. That was Mike's walk, to Sally a mere dim bad-dream background to the turmoil of feelings at being here, with him but separated from him because their minds could no longer find each other.

The café was steamy but not warm, the red formica table tops patterned with the lazy swipes of a greasy cloth. Her black coffee was stewed to treacle; you could smell it across the room. Mike's coffee was almost pure white; he didn't seem to notice.

Sally felt hollow, shivery, anxious, and too tempted to see a significance in being here with him which couldn't exist. She knew she was looking far too far ahead, unable to accept the moment for itself. She wanted to establish some basis for future meetings, be reassured that Mike wouldn't forget her, but on the other hand she longed, with an awful sense of guilt, to escape.

Mike's world was now Balmenie, the trivia of daily events there, the other residents, the food—a lot about the food. When Sally mentioned Edalmere he said, frowning, "Oh, that damned place," which surprised and hurt her for a moment till she saw it from his perspective, a perspective which didn't include their happiness together there. She didn't refer to its being up for sale, not sure if he would know. He asked her more than once how they had met but hardly listened to the answer, as though he found such facts difficult to relate to this new environment. He was more interested in hearing how she had found him here and seemed impressed that she had managed it.

She saw today more of how relentless the struggle was to keep a grasp on the simplest outline of his life. He would ask over and over again what day it was, attempting to place himself in a framework which no longer meant anything to him. He asked Sally several times when she had arrived and if she had been there for lunch. He went obsessively over the ground of where she lived, her job, Grianan, doing his best to pin down facts which were not part of his experience. When that grew too frustrating or tiring he would return to the known present and tell her again how he passed each day.

One thing was certain, he was pleased to see her, not because he remembered how they had felt about each other, but because he knew they had been friends.

"I never see anyone else, you know, from before," he said once. "And you can't talk to that lot, they live in a world of their own." He meant the other Balmenie residents. When Sally asked if the children came to see him he answered too quickly, "Oh, they're here all the time," and Sally knew from the anxious look that crossed his face that he was lying. She didn't ask about Isobel.

In spite of his dismissal of the people around him she was struck by his general tolerance. He didn't seriously criticize or complain. He seemed to have cultivated a new easygoing attitude and a way of shrugging off minor irritations, perhaps because he knew they were too sapping of vital energy and in any case beyond his power to alter.

"Who *are* the other people at Balmenie House?" Sally asked him.

"Oh, a bunch of has beens," he answered indifferently. "Dumped, like me."

"Mostly old people?" she went on, to gloss over the pain of that, though he hadn't spoken bitterly.

"Oh, God, yes, one foot in the grave." Sally was beginning to recognize this facile agreement as a trick he had learned to save himself the trouble of a more specific reply.

Then abruptly he became restless, asking her the time every couple of minutes, and she suggested that they should walk back.

"No, you're all right," he said quickly, but almost immediately asked the time again, and she saw the faint sweat that she remembered sheening his skin, and knew that anxiety was gripping him. She guessed that part of his brain was telling him that he liked being with her and didn't want it to end, but a deeper instinct was telling him that he had been out longer than usual and it was disturbing him.

"I'd like to see your room before I go," Sally suggested. "Would Mrs. Lucas twitter about that?"

"Nothing to do with her," Mike said at once, visibly relieved to realize he could go back to the house but not have to lose sight of Sally yet.

She wished she hadn't asked when she saw the room. It was reasonably big and well decorated, with a decent sized window. But it looked out on to the blank back wall of the bus station and the furniture was miserably skimpy for a man of Mike's size, crammed in to make the bedroom do duty as a sitting-room too.

Two details made her feel choky with misery as she drove away. While Mike was looking in a drawer for something he wanted to show her she had picked up his pillow and pressed it for a moment to her face. It smelled unclean, distasteful in a way that deeply distressed her. Nothing of him was there. And when Mike turned triumphantly he was holding his sketch book in his hand, full of soft pencil drawings of scenes she had been in with him and which had now been taken summarily from him. There were pages of birds, minutely observed, delicately drawn, coal-tits, gold-crests, a tree creeper at work. Mike appeared to find pleasure in the drawings but seemed to admire them as something which had nothing to do with him. He said they were his; he had been told that; the statement meant nothing to him.

"Couldn't leave this behind, could I?" he said, smiling with the sort of spurious brightness he had learned to use when there was nothing behind the smile.

Chapter 19

How could I have agreed to Mike coming by bus?
Sally reproached herself in guilty exasperation. She
could so easily have gone to fetch him, but Mrs. Lucas
had insisted on the plan, saying the doctor recommended it as part of Mr. Danaher's social rehabilita-
tion, and Sally had felt she had to accept that. The
Balmenie minibus would bring him to Perth and from
there he was to come on alone.

The moment Sally saw him she knew it had been a
disaster. His face was glistening, his hands making little dabbing movements, his eyes bright with the self-
conscious look of someone who has just screamed at
a shadow.

"Thank God you're here," he said, not touching her
but stooping to look closely into her face in trembling
need for reassurance. "I don't know what the hell I'd
have done if you hadn't been. Didn't know where I
was going or who I was going to see. Tried to get off
too early like a fool. They wouldn't let me of course,
they all knew I was around the twist. Thanks," he
called, raising a hand to the driver who nodded in
return, looking at them curiously.

In spite of the brave effort to make light of it Sally
could see how much Mike had minded this exposure,

and she put her arms around him quickly, hiding against him the distress she knew her face must show.

"That's nice," he said, pleased in a detached way, as though he found the gesture natural and agreeable but wouldn't have thought of hugging her himself.

He was carrying a holdall, with a small florist's package clutched in the same hand. "Brought you some flowers," he said, remembering them as his arms lifted in a sketchy reflex response to Sally's hug, though the rest of him stood immovable as a pillar. He said it proudly, sure he had done the right thing. Mrs. Lucas, it had to be, Sally thought. A dozen freesias, their cellophane wrapping tied with a shiny purple bow and crushed from being gripped against the handle of the holdall, which Sally guessed he had held on to anxiously for the entire journey. An image of him in ex-army combat jacket, rifle slung on shoulder, came back to her. Her eyes stung.

His relief to be safely there was almost tangible as they walked side by side down the winding vennel. Sally decided the question of the holdall had better be dealt with at once. "What's all the luggage about then?" she demanded mock-severely. "I thought you were invited for lunch."

"You didn't think I'm come all this way just for lunch, did you?" he parried scornfully, jokingly, but his grin and the look he darted at her were unsure.

"The flat has one bedroom, I'd have you know." She kept to the repressive tone as she led the way up the stone steps.

"Sounds fine to me," he replied jauntily, with a sudden genuine glimmer of the old Mike. He was clearly putting the ordeal of the journey behind him.

"And one bed," Sally said even more sternly, wondering what on earth she was going to do about this development.

"Better still," Mike replied, and she wondered what memories prompted the cheerfully suggestive tone. Not of her, she was fairly sure.

Mike was full of admiration for the flat and, listening to his comments, Sally found she no longer knew what his standards and tastes were based on now. "So you really think you're going to stay?" she asked, amused in spite of herself by his complacent confidence. She and Nona had managed, after all.

"What do you think? Anything to get out of that damned place." Mike's tone was joking too, but Sally sensed that a decision had been made in his mind and that though he wasn't quite comfortable with it he wasn't going to relinquish it. He wanted to stay, and couldn't afford to let any doubt creep in. Sally wished forlornly that he would say something to show that he remembered they had been lovers but knew she couldn't seriously hope for that. This was primarily about not going back to Balmenie, and after that perhaps about the idea of sharing a bed with a woman, being a bit of a lad. Male role play; remembered or relearned from someone? There had been the long months in hospital. She, as herself, didn't come into it, she knew.

"What about Mrs. Lucas? When does she expect you back?"

"None of her business." The instant flat rejection which he employed when something he wanted was threatened but he knew he couldn't cope with reasoned argument.

"Well, it is rather," Sally said mildly, not wanting

this to turn into an issue which might upset him. "Seriously, isn't she coming to meet you in Perth?"

"No chance," Mike said swiftly, as though he wanted to shift the responsibility for staying on to this hated figure. The quicksands of practical dealings with him quaked under Sally's feet. But why was she arguing anyway? She had been closer to this man than to any other person on earth. If this mattered so much to him then surely she wasn't going to refuse? It occurred to her wryly that three years ago this situation would have been the peak of unattainable bliss.

As she talked to Mrs. Lucas Mike watched her, smiling now, sure of the outcome. She would take him back tomorrow evening. As she put down the phone Sally was conscious of a great simplicity calming her. It was just Mike; just the two of them; it would be all right.

He was so happy that day. He didn't have to worry now about the journey back, and he was openly and endearigly cock-a-hoop to be back in everyday life in his own right. When Sally said apologetically that she would have to do some shopping (her normal supplies didn't run to male breakfasts) he was perfectly content. In fact it had been noticeable on Sally's visits to Gilsburgh during the last couple of months that he had developed an unexpected taste for urban surroundings, perhaps seeing them as an escape from his prison-like isolation in the house on Edalmere, or more probably accepting them as the new normality he was learning. He liked window shopping, and today he stood for minutes at a time gazing with fascination at the wares of gunsmith, ironmonger and wine merchant.

He ambled uncomplainingly around the supermarket, intrigued by everything, patient with the comprehensive patience of someone for whom time had no meaning, and when they left he took the shopping from Sally as though rather pleased with himself that long-buried social behavior was coming back to him.

He liked frequent coffee stops, loved just sitting and watching people. Sally wasn't sure if he needed to pause and be passive for a while or if it was just a habit he had acquired in Gilsburgh. Inevitably the first place he lived in, after home, would be a strong formative influence; she wasn't happy with the thought. Now Mike studied this new scene intently, with a sort of naïve readiness to like all he saw, and she realized that any worries she had had about filling the time could be forgotten.

What meant most to him, however, was taking her out to dinner. The whole pattern, though it was not something they had ever been able to do together, seemed to return intact and it moved her to see the evident buzz he got from the simple act of phoning to book a table, going carefully through the small ritual, throwing her a look of disingenuous triumph when he had accomplished it.

He showered and changed still with that air of "this is what we do," apparently taking for granted the intimacy of their getting ready together. Occasionally he would grin and exclaim, "God, it's good to be out of that place," but that was all the acknowledgment he made of a situation which Sally found unsettling in the extreme.

"How do you like this stuff?" he asked, slathering on aftershave. "My brother gave it to me years ago and I've never used it."

Sally recoiled. Had Mrs. Lucas packed for him?

Someone must have, of course. He was touchingly anxious about whether he looked all right and she saw how important all this was for him. She couldn't imagine the Mike she remembered ever caring for a second what he looked like. Though his clothes were not what she would have chosen she was more used to them by now and to her he looked marvelous. She had recently persuaded him to get his thick curly hair properly cut and it was good to see the shape of the long head again. He was smiling, a bit hyped up but tremendously happy, and tenderness for him flooded her.

She asked him to drive and was rewarded for her doubts about it by his huge grin, as thrilled as a teenager's, and by the smooth competence with which he took the car out of the tight yard and up the narrow streets into the town. There was a thrill in that for Sally too; a small feeling of being looked after which she had badly missed.

It was so good to watch his pride and pleasure that evening. Sally guessed it represented some major personal test to him, one he was immensely relieved to find he could pass. He loved it all—sitting on the terrace for drinks before dinner, the candle-lit crowded restaurant, the high gloss menu, but above all taking charge, making sure Sally chose just what she wanted, relaying her order to the waiter, choosing the wine, paying. When the moment came she was ready to chip in if necessary, not sure Mike would have any idea of how much he would need, but his wallet was well-filled and she was glad there was no need to spoil the moment for him.

She supposed the cash Isobel had realized by selling Edal Bank and its land, especially now that planning permission was available for building plots at the foot of the lake, was keeping him at Balmenie and the children at their boarding schools. Isobel did not intend to buy another house, it seemed, but was living with her mother again. And Mike, as he often said, had nothing to spend his money on. Sally understood that for him, this evening, putting down those notes was profoundly significant.

Equally important was the fact that for the first time since his illness no one knew he was disabled; there was no need for explanations or apologies. Sally's heart melted as she looked at him across the table, so proud of himself, so handsome, in spite of the physical changes that had overtaken him, in his new confidence and happiness. From time to time during that leisurely dinner, their talk flowing as easily as ever though often repeating itself, her mind would go forward with mild speculation to the night. Mike's kit was already in her room. When they had changed for dinner he had been completely unselfconscious about being there and it had been strange to realize that he was reverting to a familiar pattern shared with Isobel and not with her. Was he taking it for granted in the same way that they would sleep together? She found she couldn't worry about it. It didn't matter, there was no need to make any decisions about it. Only at a much deeper level she knew that in self-protection she was refusing to let her body wake with anticipation and longing.

"I enjoyed that," Mike said with satisfaction as he drove relaxedly through the quiet town. He had drunk very little and Sally had been relieved, not sure if he was supposed to or how much it would affect him. Probably he shouldn't have driven, but then nor should she, and she decided it was a risk worth taking. She knew it would matter to him, driving her home.

He delighted in all the small business of putting the car away, going in together, locking the door, putting on the lamps, making coffee. For him it was playing house again, resurrecting familiar actions associated with home, family, real life. Sally didn't figure except as the essential other, female, half. She didn't let herself mind that. This was his evening.

There was no discussion, no decision about who would sleep where. She saw that Mike expected to share her bed and she simply let it happen. It clearly hadn't crossed his mind that he wouldn't. He knew that they had slept together, though it was impossible to tell in what terms he remembered it. To suggest now that she slept on the sofa would puzzle and disappoint him. And why should she? What reason was there for denying him this?

One part of her went tidily through all the bedtime routine, composed and docile, feeling very little. Another part of her brain was reeling with disbelief that here with her in her room the man she had so passionately loved and had given up with such pain was sitting on the edge of her bed, loosening the knot of his tie with chin stretched up, unbuttoning his shirt, stripping off his socks—his wife gone, his home sold, his children kept from him.

So matter-of-factly that it was ludicrous—only there was no one to share the joke—they got into bed side by side and propped themselves on their separate pillows. With alarm Sally felt a fearful resistance grow in her body, which she recognized as a dread of being hurt, hurt by need and longing which would not be satisfied. This is not about you, she reminded herself savagely, and reached out to take Mike's hand.

Blessedly reassuring, it closed around hers at once,

a hand now soft and pale. but still long, shapely and warm. "Isn't this beautiful?" he said softly, and his choice of word, his intimate lover's tone, steadied her.

"It's wonderful," she agreed, her lips trembling, and turned to lean close and press her face against his shoulder. He moved at once, naturally, easily, to lift his arm and put it around her, drawing her comfortably against him.

The smell of the awful aftershave was unfamiliar, and his filled-out, unfit body was different, arousing none of the powerful feelings she had once had for him, but after all he was the same person, there had been love between them, and compassion filled Sally, a compassion charged with admiration for his courage and endurance. He had never let his essential self be destroyed by what had happened to him. And now, at this moment, how could she gauge what was going through his mind, what confused memories, doubt or apprehension, what crippling uncertainty as to what he should do? His patience, his quiet acceptance of what had become of his life, overwhelmed her.

She reached up to stroke his face, to kiss him gently, and felt his hands move in first, tentative, intent exploration and rediscovery. "Skin," he said. "Nothing like it, is there? Smooth, warm, wonderful skin."

He had put on pajamas bottoms; old habit or new? She didn't know. She had put on a nightdress and now at these words, spoken in delighted dreamy wonder, she slipped out of his arms, sat up and pulled it over her head. "There's more skin for you," she said, sliding down beside him again. She heard him draw in his breath sharply and then his hand moved to smooth over her breast and cup it gently.

"It's been years, hasn't it?" he asked. She had no

way of knowing if he was remembering making love to Isobel or to her, and that should have mattered but somehow it didn't; this meant too much to him.

"For too long," she said softly, giving herself up to the feel of his hands. It was an experience of such tenderness, such poignant sweetness, this breathless rediscovery of his of physical pleasure, that her own needs simply ceased to exist. Slowly, with an awareness so acute that she could feel it with him, he explored her body. For Sally as well as for him it was like being reendowed with the ability to experience these sensations for the first time, exciting and amazing all over again. And for Sally there was the added pleasure of being able to offer him this delight newminted, in this quiet room, in the tucked-away absolute privacy of this place, and of knowing that he trusted her. She was seized by a passionate determination to take care of him.

When she felt his emphatic erection she was first and foremost pleased for him. She hadn't expected it to happen and had feared his distress if he couldn't achieve it. Then she felt her own body melt in response and warned herself fiercely not to expect too much.

She had never before known such a desire to be receptive, totally and reassuringly, offering herself without any part of her awareness turned to her own sensations. Her body opened to him, giving, most tenderly welcoming. It was, as he had said, beautiful.

For Mike it was a brief, intent struggle, and there was no room in his mind to remember that Sally was even there. This was an act he desperately wanted to perform. When he achieved it he trembled and shook; in fact Sally thought he wept. She held him close, stroking the curly gray head, smoothing her hands down the shaking shoulders, drawing the duvet gently up his back, enfolding and comforting him.

"I never thought that would happen again," he mumbled after a while, his breathing still uneven against her neck. "Christ, I never thought that would happen again."

"Darling Mike, it was so good." It had been; not in the usual sense, for there had been no climax for Sally, or any approach to it, but no loving she had ever known had been more sweet or more intensely aware.

"Thought I was all washed up, you know. They'd written me off."

Sally's arms tightened around him. She couldn't speak.

"Just to hold a woman again," he said. "Just to lie like this . . ."

Sally could feel the tears running down the sides of her face. Would he feel them on his cheek? His slack weight crushed her; she made no move to shift it from her.

The next day Mike hardly spoke. Every so often he would ask where he was, listen and nod when Sally explained, but never seem reassured. She thought it wise to keep in his mind the fact that she would be taking him back to Balmenie House that evening, but when she reminded him he would frown and shake his head as though puzzled by the reference. Sally was terrified that all the new events of yesterday, and especially his making love to her, might have put back his progress for weeks or even months.

He had woken late, couldn't be bothered with breakfast and didn't reply to proposals about what they should do with their day or to Sally's increasingly perturbed questions about how he felt. He did nothing, just stood at the window and gazed at the river. He was there for hours, never so much as turning his head when she spoke.

Frightened and helpless, Sally thought of phoning Mrs. Lucas, but what was there to ask? Mike was coming to no harm, he wasn't aggressive or obstructive. If he objected to going back she would have a problem, and the prospect loomed before her all day. But when the time came, after crawling silent hours when all Sally's bright suggestions finally died on her lips and she could only sit anxiously watching him, he accepted it obediently. She had packed his bag for him but he didn't even ask about it. He said nothing on the drive down to Gilsburgh. Sally asked him once if he remembered the house where he was living but he just shrugged. What have I done to him? she thought in panic. She was even tempted, in her dread and ignorance, to tell Mrs. Lucas that she had let him do too much, see too many new places, stay out late, drink. eat rich food, make love . . . The catalog, listed like that, horrified her with her own irresponsibility.

Mrs. Lucas didn't give her the chance to say any of it, luckily. "Oh, he just has these days. Gets a bit down in the dumps, don't you, Mr. Danaher?" (Did she call him that when no one was there?) "Perfectly normal—or perhaps I should say nothing to worry about. One good day, when he's just like anyone else, then off we go again, hardly knows where he is."

Sally drove home in a turmoil of remorse and anxiety. Would Mike be better off if she never saw him again, if she left him to the repetitive round he had adapted to and now accepted? His brain, as he had explained to her himself as though reciting a well-rehearsed lesson, would never function fully again. The damaged cells couldn't regenerate. Was it wiser and kinder to do as Isobel had done, give him a stable background without responsibility or demands, and leave him there in peace? Then Sally remembered the inertia and passivity of the inmates of Balmenie House, the drabness of the horrid little town, the reed beds and mud flats of the estuary which she found such an incongruous setting for Mike. She thought of his pride as he sat across the table from her at dinner last night, and how alive his face had looked. She remembered the rapt tone of his voice, tinged with the little touch of humor that was so much his, as he murmured, "Skin . . . I'd forgotten . . ."

How could she abandon him?

Chapter 20

Mike phoned late on Thursday evening asking, "What time are you coming to pick me up tomorrow?"

It was a huge thrill to hear that ordinary question, to think that he had reached the point of being able to phone by himself and make his own plans. Sally was in tearing spirits as she got up at six the following morning to wash her hair, put clean sheets on the bed, shove in a load of washing, then race around hoovering and tidying away the strewn work which she had intended to get through this weekend.

She also had to do some horse trading about the shop being looked after on a Saturday. She had had trouble finding even half-adequate help since Nona had left and now employed a conscientious creature called Tessa who did everything she was told and nothing she wasn't. She served customers in an unsmiling silence which made Sally want to apologize for her all the time, but she checked the cash as though her life depended on it and seemed actually to enjoy tedious chores like photocopying, unpacking orders and stock taking. She was very punctual; arriving and leaving. Sally was sure that one day she would shut the shop with someone in it.

It took over an hour to get to Gilsburgh and Mike

seemed to think she was late. She knew it only meant that he had been watching for the car all afternoon, but still felt slightly piqued after the scramble she had had.

"Now you keep him as long as you like," Mrs. Lucas caroled after them, waving and smirking.

Yes, nice one, save on the food bills I suppose, Sally thought sourly as she drove off. She detested the woman.

Mike settled in at the flat with every appearance of being at home, putting his belongings exactly where they had been the previous week, beaming and openly exultant to be back. His pleasure was infectious and Sally felt herself unwinding as she cooked dinner and he watched *High Road* with a child's absorption. It didn't occur to him to offer to help but when Sally asked him to open a bottle of wine he was clearly gratified, as though knowing this was the man's job. Otherwise he expected food to be put in front of him, plates taken away. Sally would never know if this was what he had been used to with Isobel or if it was the result of being helpless after his illness and now looked after in the residential home.

There was no doubt that he reveled in the feeling of ordinary home life which being in the flat gave him. He talked about it later when they were lying close in the big bed. He hadn't attempted to make love—Sally thought he had forgotten to—and there had been a bleak moment when she had realized that it wasn't going to happen, a disappointment made sharper by knowing they wouldn't be able to discuss it. But she pushed that aside. Mike's satisfaction to be there with her, to have his arms around her, was unmistakable.

"This was always one of the best things, wasn't it?"

he said with a sigh of pleasure. "Just lying like this, talking."

"It was," she agreed. She hoped he meant with her but there was never any way of knowing and that was something she was just going to have to get used to.

"God, it's good to be here in a proper house though, and out of that awful place," he added more forcefully than he usually let himself speak, crushing her to him with a little shudder.

"Do you really hate it?" Sally asked with surprised concern. He always insisted that Balmenie suited him but she knew by now that this could be part of the protective mechanism he had developed to keep any form of stress at bay.

She felt him shrug. "Oh, it's not that bad, I suppose. And I can't expect much else, can I, the state I'm in now?"

"Oh, Mike." The image of him reduced to a meaningless existence in that dreary place was always with her, but what better answer was there?

"Well, let's face it, I'll never be good for much again," he said with the lucidity she had noticed was always most in evidence late at night. "Can't work, can't look after myself, can't look after the children. Can't even go shopping in that damned little town without getting myself lost. I found myself sitting on someone's garden wall the other day and hadn't a clue where I was or how I'd got there. I was scared to death. Started looking for the car, would you believe, and I haven't had a car for years, have I?" He wasn't sure.

"What did you do?" It was difficult to speak.

"Asked some bloke where I was. He must have thought I was a right eejut. But he had a look in my wallet and the address was there. He saw me back— was probably terrified I'd turn screaming bonkers on him at any moment."

"Don't." She crushed her face into the hollow of his shoulder, shivering. He used all these crude terms freely now, though she was sure they would never have been part of his normal vocabulary. Who had used them to him?

"Hey, come on, it doesn't happen very often. And we never thought I'd get this far, did we? I nearly didn't make it at all, don't forget. I'm just glad to be alive. No, that place is all right, it suits me very well in fact. I can walk up into the town on my own, fetch a newspaper, have coffee. . . ." As he settled into the well-worn account of his daily routine Sally knew he was burying the memory of that alarming moment. He had to be satisfied with the hand fate had dealt him. To allow himself not to be posed too many unanswerable and threatening questions.

Sally had to go into the shop on Saturday morning as Tessa, asked to help at short notice, had only been able to do the afternoon, but Mike went along too and seemed quite content to hang around chatting to customers, carrying the odd box out to a car, offering to make coffee every few minutes but rarely getting any further than putting on the kettle.

Once Tessa had arrived to take over, not looking too amenable, Mike wanted to "go out." All the things they had done together last weekend, at least on the first day when he had been so happy, were evidently still clear in his mind and he wanted to repeat them.

It was a pattern that established itself, with his urgent need for recognized patterns, with each weekend that he came to stay. Though he loved the flat, prowling around every morning when he got up to pick up objects and ask the same questions about them again and again, wanting to know how long Sally had been there and if it belonged to her, he nevertheless found it confining and would soon grow restless and eager to be off in search of movement and people.

At least it wasn't necessary to find new things to entertain him. His short-term memory, though improving, was still poor and the same sequence repeated over and over again satisfied and reassured him. Bar lunch in Aberfeldy or Pitlochry, slow-paced shopping, going out for dinner—all that he loved. He particularly liked going into Perth and would wander up and down the High Street for hours, looking in the same shop windows time after time with inexhaustible fascination. Sally would get bored, hating the repetitiveness, the clogging drift of Saturday shoppers, the mess, and then be horribly ashamed of herself.

That shame was to grow, swiftly deepening to a guilt that dogged every waking moment. Mike took it for granted that these weekends were now a regular part of his life and that she would turn up every Friday to collect him. At least he appeared to take it for granted. Sometimes Sally suspected that deep down he knew this wasn't what had been intended, but wanted this escape so badly that he simply closed his mind to any disturbing doubt.

How could she tell him that he couldn't come? He was so vulnerable but she knew would instantly hide his hurt under that easygoing acceptance he had been forced to learn. And she *wanted* him to come. All the same, a sense of being trapped in this situation grew in her with a speed that shook her. From excited pleasure at hearing his voice saying he was coming to stay, from whipping around eagerly to get all the boring domestic stuff out of the way so that all her time would be his, she began to feel harried and caught up in something she wasn't ready for.

Her normal week had to be crammed into four and a half hectic days while the rest of the time went into slow motion, geared to Mike's pace and capacity. Hurrying through work that couldn't be done in the shop, getting her hair cut, going to the dentist, putting the car in for MOT or repairs, writing to Nona (a contact that was very important to Sally just now), keeping up with all the ordinary household chores, became increasingly hard to manage. And she was getting tired. Mike's daily progression from morning sluggishness to a varying degree of alertness through the day meant that he was at his best late at night and liked nothing better than to talk well into the small hours. It was beginning to take its toll on Sally.

She knew this driven sense of never quite keeping up had a lot to do with Grianan. She hadn't been there for weeks and the question of what should be done with the place loomed more and more worryingly at the back of her mind. She had to make a decision soon. It was shortsighted and irresponsible to let neglect overtake it, and Janey would have hated to see the present state of the garden. So would Piers. But the weeks seemed to slip through her fingers at a frightening rate.

She had suggested more than once to Mike that they should go up to Grianan together but to her surprise he had developed a deep resistance to the idea.

"It's away at the back of beyond, isn't it?" he would say frowning. "No point in going all the way up there, is there, plenty to do here." Or, "Isn't the house empty now? Be a bit depressing, wouldn't it?"

Whenever Sally mentioned Grianan he would need to be told again that she had lived there as a child, that it had belonged to Aunt Janey (placing Aunt Janey, whom he remembered as Ursula's sister visiting the Edalmere cottage) and was now hers, and he would nod, pretending to take the information in but Sally knew rejecting it for some reason. He had perfected this trick of switching off, his face going blank in a way that reminded her uncomfortably of her first glimpse of him after his illness.

Puzzling over this resistance to Grianan she wondered if he was afraid that it would remind him of Edal Bank, wincing to imagine the associations with that once loved place which must now cloud his mind. She knew he would never go back there and for her too the place had taken on a different aspect, the magic overlaid by tragedy. She had already put the cottage on the market. She didn't tell Mike. That sort of practical decision had no relevance for him.

One weekend he didn't come to the flat and she hated herself for seeing it as a respite. His brother had come over from Ireland and he took Mike away for a few nights, but from Mike's vagueness about it afterwards Sally deduced that he had found it hard to relate his brother's sudden appearance to his present life.

Sally took the chance of the weekend on her own to accept a standing invitation for dinner at Drumveyn. She hadn't had the chance to see much of Pauly lately, but it was good to drink a deep draught of her warmth and friendliness, see the children before they vanished to bed, sit for hours around the big table in the kitchen talking after dinner with Archie's mother and Tom, her husband, and a friend they had staying with them, a relief worker briefly home on leave who, when persuaded to talk, took them into places and conditions quite alien to the safe and beautiful world of the glen.

It was good to see other faces and turn her mind to larger issues and new subjects, but afterwards Sally felt deeply guilty at the sensation of release and freedom it had produced, especially as Mike revealed a most unexpected sense of rejection.

"I haven't been here for weeks, have I?" he asked, frowning as he looked around the flat.

"Two weeks," Sally said lightly, holding his hand in both hers, minding his confusion.

"It's been a lot longer than that," he said definitely, and from that he refused to be budged.

"You only missed last weekend," Sally insisted, vainly she knew, but this was important to her. "You were with your brother."

"Colin. I hardly see him nowadays, you know."

"Were you close when you were younger?"

"Oh, about average, I suppose. He's all right."

"Have you ever thought of going to stay with him? Or living with him?" Sally asked tentatively when he had chatted for a while, not about the days spent with Colin last week but about growing up in Kendal and about Colin's house and business in Carlow.

"God, no," he said at once. "He hasn't got room anyway. He's just made a separate flat for my mother." An instant snatching at any reason which would be regarded as acceptable to protect him from such an unnerving change.

"Wouldn't you like to see your mother?"

It had frequently occurred to Sally that Mike's family showed remarkably little interest in his circumstances. Perhaps Isobel had convinced them that she had made the best possible arrangements for him "in his condition."

Mike shrugged. "Probably just upset her. She's pretty frail, hardly gets out at all these days."

It wasn't always easy to know what "these days" meant to him. "Is there something wrong with her?"

"Arthritis. She's always suffered from it. Colin says she's had to have full-time care for years now. Live-in." He often repeated phrases as though he had recently heard them without knowing what they meant.

She couldn't detect much feeling for his family there, but she knew she must take into account the fact that Mike would automatically reject anything that looked too daunting or taxing. The thought of another change or a journey to somewhere that had belonged to a different and distant part of his life would seem understandably alarming.

For the same reason, she knew, he rarely referred to the children. He was convinced that they were better off without him (had almost certainly been told that by Isobel), and because this was painful he avoided talking about them at all. When he spoke of the past with Isobel it was always of the time before they were born.

It was something Sally had to learn to deal with, hearing his memories of those early days. He was incapable now of the discretion any man would normally employ when talking about one woman in his life to another.

"She's grown so hard," he would say. "She used to be such a gentle, shy girl. Very quiet, with a lovely little private smile. And that glorious hair, like fire in the sunlight. That's how I first saw her, you know, on that beach, she looked amazing. She'd been dumped by the boyfriend she was traveling with, left without any money or anything, poor girl. She badly needed someone to look after her. . . ."

Oddly enough, in spite of the tender reminiscent tone, Sally found it didn't really hurt. It was too honest. Instead it filled her with a piercing sadness for all this man had lost.

"Where was that?" she would ask. She had heard most of this story before, bits from Janey, bits from him, and had pieced together a picture which she had made herself accept.

". . . Malaysia, on my way back from Australia, having a look at those fabulous beaches on the east coast. Coral reefs full of beautiful fish, you could spend whole days snorkeling. I'd worked my way down from Kota Bharu nearly to Pekan when I ran into Isobel. Some state she was in, so she was, poor little girl . . ."

A tone of nostalgic love Sally knew she would never quite get out of her mind.

"She never could cope with much really," Mike went on once, on a more matter-of-fact note. "She certainly never reconciled herself to living at Edalmere. Hated the isolation, always wanted me to find a decent job somewhere more civilized, with a decent salary anyway. She wanted a social life, friends around her, morning coffee, golf, shops, hairdresser. In fact, mentally she never left home. Now she's got this new man there. Well, not so new, it's all been going on since before I was ill."

"Since before you were ill?" This must be part of

his usual problem with sorting out an accurate time-scale.

"Oh, sure. She told me when she came to talk about getting married again. Edward, that's it." His tone was full of satisfaction that he had pinned down the name that had been evading him.

Sally felt the breath rush out of her body. "Married? Mike, how could she get married?"

"Why not? I'm no good to her. She'll be far better off with somebody else, anybody else come to that," he amended with a rare bitterness.

"But Isobel's married to you." Sally still felt breathless, shaken.

"Oh, they've organized a divorce, Isobel's lawyers. Ages ago. They just had to wait till I could sign to say I agreed."

Sally was up on one elbow, gazing down at him in shock and struggling incredulity. "But Mike, was that what you wanted? Did they give you a choice? How was that ever allowed?"

"Seemed a good idea to me," he said shrugging. "I'm all washed up. Isobel doesn't give a damn about me, hasn't for years. She just wanted out. She only put up with Edal Bank and me and my unambitious job for the sake of the children, as she told me every day of my life. Edward's a good bloke. He's been to see me a couple of times at that place. He can give her everything she wants and take care of the children too. Good luck to them."

Sally could still hardly take in that he had known all this, that it was final, already accomplished and she hadn't had the least idea of it. Mike sounded unperturbed, indifferent even, but she ached to think of the hours and days of wretchedness that he must have gone through as all this penetrated his awareness and he discovered what his illness had cost him.

This bombshell—though as always there were reservations about the accuracy of what he had told her—made Sally's brain reel as she tried to take in the implications. How long had Edward been on the scene? And her own sacrifice in walking away so that Mike's marriage and family should be unharmed, had that been meaningless after all?

If Mike and Isobel were divorced, something once imagined only in despairing fantasies, what would happen to Mike? He seemed sure that Isobel, and now Edward, would go on looking after him financially. Could that really be their intention?

One thing was clear to Sally however. Mike had not related the fact of his divorce to his relationship with her, and for that she was thankful, needing time to adjust to this new and startling situation. It unquestionably added to the pressure she was under. Everything except Mike seemed to have been pushed to the sidelines of her life. Her need for her own space grew as she felt her responsibility for him increasing. The flat felt too small, or Mike too large for it. He had started leaving things there all the time and Sally despised herself for resenting it. Also, she was increasingly aware that the problem of sharing a bed with him was something she would have to sort out soon.

The truth was that sleeping with him had become a torment. He rarely made love to her and when he did it was intense and effortful, his concentration focused exclusively on himself. Sally knew it was the only way it could be for him and she wanted to give him this pleasure, but what she found hard to endure were the many many times when he would caress and arouse her and then simply forget what he was doing. He had woken her body to its old need for him and didn't satisfy it, could never satisfy it.

She was concerned too about his growing dependence on her. She knew she must, for both their sakes, take a long, steady look at where they were heading. How long could she cope with this two-tier life? She was harried by guilt at no longer giving one hundred per cent of herself to her work. And how did she truly feel about Mike now? Pity, compassion, tenderness, affection, but was he the man she had loved?

Then shame would shrivel her. Hundreds, thousands of people went through this sort of trauma and survived. Was she really so cowardly, so selfish and ungenerous, that she could refuse Mike the time and company he so desperately needed?

Driving to see clients or going up and down the A9 to Gilsburgh, often her only chance to think things out, she would turn it all over again in her mind, despising her hesitation, her weighing up of day-to-day trivia. But life is made up of trivia, the inner argument would run. And Mike wasn't really, in cold fact, anything to do with her. They had been lovers once but he was not that person now and those feelings had not survived. He was not her responsibility. She was racked by her own meanness of spirit but couldn't help feeling that she was being pushed headlong into something for which she was not ready.

How was she to say to Mike, "I'm sorry, you can't come again," leaving him to an uneasy shadow world which would hold his brain in limbo for ever? And he would know why. It was unbearable to think of him accepting her disappearance from his life with that shrug which was the only way he had left to deal with things which hurt too much. He had no other weapon available to him.

As she grew more tired, feeling enmeshed in something too big to cope with alone, Sally was shocked to find herself growing impatient with Mike himself. In an attempt to relate to the world around him, which was virtually new to him each day, he incessantly asked what time it was, what day it was, where they had been that morning, what they had done yesterday. Sally understood why he asked, couldn't think of a single person she knew who would mind such a small thing, yet sometimes it drove her nearly to tears with frustration.

She told herself this reaction was really all about the much larger issues which were crowding her, but she still couldn't control her irritation. Then she would look at Mike, so patient, so ready to please. She would see the heavy unfit body, the gray hair, the scars left on his forehead by the terrible sequence of operations, and she would be filled with scalding self-contempt, would go to wrap her arms around him, hide her tears against him. How could she be so ungiving, how could she worry for a second about her own unimportant little life? And she would cast about for ways to look after him better.

Mike swung, as she had learned, from good days to bad, with every so often a day so marvelous that it seemed total recovery must be just around the corner. So on good days that summer they turned into tourists, inspired by Sally's being given two free tickets to the Highland Wildlife Park near Kingussie. The day was a huge success, Mike not only fascinated by all he saw (and making none of the strictures about animals in captivity, however skillfully their environment had been adapted to their needs, which he would have made three years ago), but responding with surprising enthusiasm to being in a new scene. It made Sally reflect as she drove home that, deeply as they had been in love that first summer, they had shared little beyond the bounds of the lake, the fells, talking and making love. Now they enjoyed all kinds of new things, visiting castles and art galleries, craft shops and glass factory, the theater and salmon ladder at Pitlochry, and on fine Sundays the splendid gardens of Perthshire's big houses.

When it rained, or when Mike was having one of his down days, it was harder. He would watch any rubbish on television, always at a volume which maddened Sally. He wouldn't read as he never knew where he had got to and found it understandably frustrating to go continually over the same few imperfectly remembered pages. On the other hand, he didn't like Sally getting absorbed in some challenging piece of work, or doing anything which excluded him. He didn't say so, but she would recognize the signs in his increased restlessness and constant interruptions.

On these days of depression and inertia Sally knew by now that his body was husbanding its resources, his brain refusing an overload of anxiety or information. It was hard at such times to believe the positiveness of the good days, and even harder to accept that he couldn't pull himself out of it.

The pressures on Sally's own life were aggravated at this point by two crises. The flat was broken into and burgled and Tessa said she was leaving. It was a bad week and Sally couldn't face having Mike at the weekend. Also it seemed to her that perhaps this would be a chance to break the rigid routine for valid impersonal reasons. She phoned Mrs. Lucas and asked her to explain to Mike why he wouldn't be able to come, but to assure him that she would be there to pick him up the following Friday.

Chapter 21

"Don't give yourself such a hard time," Nona wrote. "You're not thinking straight. I'm just about to do it for you so this will sound brutal, OK? He's not the guy you loved and he's not your job. This shouldn't be about his wife dumping him, it's about what <u>you</u> feel. It's you I'm worried about. If you let yourself get committed to him, what are you looking at? Ten years of taking care of him? Twenty? Thirty? And his condition might detererate. Come on, Sal, you know that's not on. And you can't ask this, but I can. What's in it for you? Said I'd be brutal. And the answer is nothing. You could never expect normal two-way comunication. And what if you meet another bloke? How about kids? I know you feel you've got involved and can't walk away, but if you want my advise, which you probably don't, I think you should cool the whole thing. You need your own space. Make sure he knows you'll go and see him and take him out, but not on a regular basis. He won't know if it's been last week or last month, will he, honestly? Bet the old cow who runs the place reminds him to get him off her hands. I'd have a word with her . . ."

* * *

Sally might smile briefly at the spelling but she knew Nona was right. Even the bluntness of the phrasing was welcome, since in one form or another she had thought all this for herself. There was no way she could look after Mike for the rest of his life. She had her living to earn, her own life to lead. She would establish some pattern of seeing him which would suit them both; the rest was not up to her.

A loud thumping at the door shot her heart into her mouth. She was still twitchy after the burglary. Nothing much had been taken except the share of the Buchanan family silver which Janey had given her when she got engaged to Julian and insisted she should keep. But a window had been broken, a mess left behind and she was feeling slightly vulnerable.

But burglars don't knock at doors. From the roughness of the banging she thought it must be Jed, tanked up, and her heart sank at the prospect.

An unexpected figure hung back from the door, one step down, ducking his head and turning a filthy cap in his hands. He was usually to be seen shuffling around the square poking in the litter bins, drunk if he could manage it, talking and singing to anyone who would listen, but quite harmless. His favorite occupation was watching the buses come in. Sally knew he was called Tam Ritchie but she had no idea where he lived and she had never seen him outside the square.

He mouthed at her, stretching his dirty scraggy neck up at her like a goose, blinking nervously with red watery eyes. There was no threat from this familiar figure.

"Tam, what on earth is it?" Did he know something about the burglary?

"I seen him. I seen them tak him awa'."

"Who have you seen?" But she knew. "Tam, what's happened, tell me."

"They wouldna' listen to me. Naebody listens to me."

"Tell me who you saw, Tam." Sally made a big effort to keep her voice calm and not fluster him.

"Yon pollis laddies, they just tellt me to be on ma way. And where's that, I says to them, where's ma way, tell me that?"

The police. Christ, what had happened? Sally turned to dive for her bag. "I'll take you up to the square, Tam, and you can tell me what happened."

"I kent him the moment I saw him. Yon big lad ye're aye ganging aboot wi'. Getting off the bus, he was. And ye werena' there, were ye, ye werena' there."

"Did something happen to him? Is he hurt?"

Tam was having trouble getting into the car, catching his foot, tipping forwards so that Sally caught the foul whiff of him as he fell against her. She jumped out again and ran around to stuff him in furiously.

"Look, just tell me what *happened*. I need to know. Where is Mike now?"

"The pollis have him awa' wi' them. I tellt ye," he said aggrievedly, sniffing and wiping his nose on a disgusting sleeve.

"Is he hurt?"

"Nah." He sounded contemptuous. "How would he get hurt? Dinna' be daft. He was just stravaigin' aboot like he didna' ken where to go."

Sally dropped him in the square, heaving him out ruthlessly, but pushing enough money into his hand to put a blissful smile on his skinny face as he trotted off to the nearest pub.

Sally raced up to the police station. The duty sergeant had recognized Mike and had just been phoning the flat. Mike was in an alarming state, shaking and muttering. He clutched at Sally, hanging on to her arm tightly, and she nearly buckled beneath his trembling weight.

"Now are you sure you're going to be all right with him?" the sergeant asked dubiously. "Wouldn't you be best letting one of us give you a hand?"

"Just to the car, thanks."

"How about at the other end? Someone can go down with you, you know, and help get him into the house. He's a big lad."

"It's very good of you, but truly, I'll be fine." All she wanted was to take him away, have him safe and alone with her, to hold and soothe him.

"Well, mind you give us a ring if you have any trouble. There you go, then, sir, you'll be fine now." The sergeant gave Mike a friendly pat on the shoulder, uncomprehending.

As Sally drove home Mike leaned forward, peering out of the window, still muttering to himself, evidently baffled by what he saw. She talked to him quietly, telling him where he was and where they were going.

"Now we turn down here, you remember this, don't you, the lane and the river, and this little courtyard? You've been here lots of times."

He didn't recognize any of it, shaking his head and frowning as she led him up the steps. Once in the flat he didn't look about him but stood apathetically waiting to be taken to the next place.

"You're safe now, everything's all right. We're home, Mike. Come and sit down and I'll make tea."

"They were staring at me, you know, all the people." His voice sounded muffled, uncertain. He put a hand to his head and Sally felt fear plume up in her.

"No one's here now. There's just the two of us. You're quite safe, darling, darling Mike." She drew his head down to her, wishing she could fold him inside her, protect him utterly.

He wouldn't stay in his chair but followed her about as though on a string, needing her nearness. She made him hot sweet tea which he gratefully gulped down, and she held on to his hand as the Balmenie number rang.

"But Mr. Danaher's up in his room," Mrs. Lucas insisted with instant defensive indignation. "He's been there all evening, I can assure you."

"He's here, Mrs. Lucas, right beside me, sitting on my bloody sofa."

"There's no need to take that tone," Mrs. Lucas protested, more willing to take offense than to admit guilt. "His television's been on all evening, I heard it myself."

How could she argue about it? "Mr. Danaher is *here,* for God's sake. He walked out of your house, where you are paid to look after him, and he got himself to Muirend where he was found wandering about and was picked up by the police—" The iron control Sally had started out with was cracking.

"Well, I can promise you, Miss Buchanan, his absence would have been discovered at once when he didn't come down for his hot drink. Everyone has a hot drink at ten, I make it myself every night. Mr. Danaher's always down for that. I really don't see how you can possibly hold me responsible for—"

"It's your *job* to be responsible!" Sally longed to get her hands around the woman's throat.

"I will need to know of course when you intend to bring him back." As though Sally had taken him away in the first place.

Take him back? Sally looked at Mike, motionless beside her, eyes shut, the sweat of fear still on his skin. She put the phone down before she began to shout and rave at Mrs. Lucas, pouring out on her not only righteous anger but a much deeper sense of guilt and failure.

Mike took ages to pull out of it. He wouldn't eat, wouldn't talk about anything except that horror of being lost and helpless among strangers in a strange place.

"I'm a useless bastard," he said at last, sitting forward with his head propped on his hands. "No bloody use to anyone." Sally knew that some recollection of how he had come to be there was seeping back.

"Come to bed, come and sleep and forget all about it. Tomorrow it will seem as though it had never happened." Please, please let that be so.

"Where's my room?" he asked in a groping anxious way that filled her with an agony of pity for him.

"Just here. You'll remember when you see it."

"Don't leave me," he begged, jibbing as she started to lead him to the bedroom.

"I'll be there," she promised, tears audible in her voice. "I'll be there with you, don't worry. I won't go away."

"They were all looking at me, you know. They know I'm crackers."

He slept quite soon, to Sally's relief, exhausted, but his sleep was restless and broken and often he called out in muddled terror and she held him, stroking and soothing him to sleep again. Towards morning he sank at last into a sounder sleep and she felt more hopeful for a while herself.

When Mike woke he knew at once where he was and Sally hugged him in passionate thankfulness. He thought this was an ordinary weekend visit, and though he was noticeably silent and subdued he was a long way from yesterday's dark confusion.

All night Sally had worried about what to do with him today. She had at last taken the step of agreeing to have Grianan valued and was due to meet Janey's solicitor—her solicitor—there this morning. Tessa had agreed to look after the shop. The whole plan was in place. What concerned her was that Mike had shown such a reluctance to go there whenever she had suggested it before. Would it be bad for him today to make him do something he would dislike? Then Sally realized that it wouldn't matter to him where he went. So long as he was with her he would be docile and unquestioning. It was hard to get him moving though. He took ages to dress and shave, always a bad sign, and roamed aimlessly about, looking intently at everything and picking up objects at random but not seeming sure that he recognized them.

They were late leaving and Sally felt rattled as she swung up the glen road. She knew it was more than anxiety about Mike. She was hating the step she was taking, but what else could be done with Grianan?

They were well up the glen, Mike passive beside her, before she even noticed what a marvelous day it was. The white froth of the bird cherry was browning now, but gorse and broom spread great swathes of blazing gold, rhododendrons were mounds of color from palest pink to crimson, and tall purple-blue cranesbill edged the road. When she wound down the window the scent of hawthorn met her in a wave of sweetness, bringing a rush of nostalgia for Edalmere. Yet Mike was here with her; the nostalgia was no longer for him, but for then, for that time, for themselves as they had been.

In spite of the sharp pang her spirits rose. Why on earth didn't she come up here more often? Nowhere in the world was more lovely than Glen Ellig on a sunny morning of early summer. A year since Janey's party, she thought in disbelief, her eye caught by the tapestry of greens where Archie Napier had planted new trees on Drumveyn. Three years since she had met Mike.

She glanced at him and was glad to see that he was looking about him with awakening interest. She put her hand on his thigh and his came down over it. Sometimes when she did that he took no notice, and this morning she was especially glad that he had responded. She still didn't know what her touch or touching her meant to him.

The solicitor who had looked after Janey's affairs for many years had recently retired and the partner waiting for them on the gravel sweep in front of the house was John Ballantyne, a smooth-skinned, plump and arrogant younger man, who made it clear through a lot of urbane waffle that he thought Sally had messed him about quite long enough on a decision to sell. There was also more than a suggestion that he was doing her a favor by being here on a Saturday morning, though Sally knew he had been fishing in Glen Maraich for the past week. She foresaw that any selling blurb concocted by him would set her teeth on edge.

Mike followed amenably at their heels, looking

about him admiringly as they went through the dusty rooms, while John Ballantyne pursed his lips, shook his head from time to time and tapped his teeth with the sort of biro that comes in a fancy box twinned with a propelling pencil no one ever uses. His darting eyes assessed and disparaged and even rooms Sally had thought quite presentable turned shabby, faded and ill-cared-for under his calculating gaze.

He said things like, "Of course, in this condition you couldn't expect . . ." and "Properly maintained, we'd have been looking at a great deal more as I'm sure you realize . . ." and drew in his breath in a hiss of actual pain when Sally led him into the hinterland beyond the kitchen. She was glad of Mike's quiet approving presence. His rangy frame, these days so much heavier, looked at home in the big well-proportioned rooms and she was glad to see that he obviously liked the house now that he was finally here.

"Well, we should be able to get something together," John Ballantyne said, with a finely tuned edge of doubt in his voice just this side of rudeness. "Of course major refurbishment would be required and that would naturally affect any offer we could hope for. Difficult size as well, too large for a family home in today's terms, and as a commercial enterprise it has never been properly adapted or equipped."

Sally had never been more thankful to see any car disappear down the drive.

'If that's all he can say I should get someone else to sell it for you," Mike recommended, easy and relaxed beside her, his face turned up to the sun which was now getting hot. He sounded very matter-of-fact, as though they could discuss all the pros and cons together and he would come up with sound advice.

"I think you're right," Sally agreed, laughing and giving his arm a little squeeze. It hardly seemed possible that this was the man who yesterday had wandered helpless and afraid among Muirend's unthreatening shoppers. "Let's wander around the garden, shall we?"

"It's some place. And you own it?"

"I do." Though probably not for much longer, she thought with a bleak tug of loss.

"But why haven't you brought me here before?" Mike asked as they went in the sunshine down the ragged grassy paths and she felt peace flowing through her in a warm tide.

"Because you wouldn't come, you obstinate so and so," she told him laughing.

"I wouldn't?" But a small grin told her he remembered something about it. "And to think I've been missing all this."

Everywhere was the richness and profusion of new growth. From a distance it all looked marvelous. White cushions of snow-in-summer lined (or choked) the paths, lupins speared up through the weeds in ranks of color, poppies splashed vividness and Janey's azaleas were a dream of exotic scent and beauty.

"And this is really yours?" Mike asked again, wonderingly.

"All except that cottage. It was left to a friend of Aunt Janey's. A boyfriend," Sally amended, smiling through the ache of memories.

"Why doesn't he use it? It's a gem."

Sally gazed at the neat, contained little house. How could a stone exterior say so plainly that its soul had fled? The poetry and the music. Would Piers ever come back? Suddenly she realized she could tell Mike about it, could tell him anything. He loved stories, was greedy for every detail of her life, and the tolerance and kindness that had always been part of him were much more in evidence now. And it was his memory that had been damaged, not his powers of understanding. Even so, she found that she had underestimated them. Telling him about Piers, the hurt showed more clearly than she had intended and Mike saw it.

"You should find him," he said, looking closely into her face, his own showing open sympathy. "You should tell him how you feel."

"I wish I could."

"Poor little Sally, you've had a rough time, haven't you, one way and another? Come here." His arms went around her, and as she leaned gratefully against him she reflected that it was the first time since his illness that he had comforted her, and it was good. But then perhaps it was the first time she had let him see that she needed comfort. Did it feel good for him too?

Presently, close and easy pacing, they ambled on, looking, smelling, feeling, stopping often to talk. Later they foraged for food and took what they had raked together out on to the lawn, kept roughly cut by Jed's son Scott—very roughly, Sally observed—and ate with their eyes on the sunlit bowl of the glen where the fine day had brought out all the busy machines to wuffle and bale.

"Why didn't we come here before?" Mike asked again and she was so pleased to see him enjoying Grianan that she didn't care how often he said it. She had assumed that as soon as her business with John Ballantyne was finished Mike would have been hankering to be off to town and his favorite pub for lunch, and she would have minded being dragged away on such a day.

"We could stay, you know," she suggested with sudden inspiration, a strange excitement quickening at the thought, instantly followed by anxiety that it might confuse Mike to sleep in yet another place.

"Could we do that?" he enquired, sounding eager. "I wouldn't mind a walk. I used to love being in the hills. I haven't been anywhere like this for ages. Have I?" The familiar little check of doubt.

"Not for a long time," Sally said gently, then became brisk because that was too sad a thought just now. "We'll have to go down to the village and get something better to eat than fusty oatcakes and tinned pâté that probably belonged to Marchmain in the first place."

"Who the hell's Marchmain?"

"The cat."

"We'll go shopping."

Seeing him look amused and teasing, the hazel eyes alive, Sally was swept by old feelings and hastily crushed them down. "The beds will be damp," she warned him.

"So? And what do you mean, beds?" His arm came around her and his grin was cocksure. Sally knew in that moment where they would sleep, where it would be right and good to sleep. Nothing about this would offend Janey; she would welcome them.

They went down to the village shop, and because it was Saturday afternoon there was no bread left, no cream, and no fresh vegetables or fruit, so they bought a pile of frozen rubbish and didn't care. Later they went up the hill in the lazy warmth of late afternoon and Sally was struck by how natural it felt to be here with Mike, on home ground, after all this time and against such odds.

Maybe because everything was a bit makeshift he seemed to take it for granted this evening that he would do his share. Glancing at him as he flipped over chicken legs sizzling in butter and herbs, or twisted one of Janey's bottles of Niersteiner deeper into the peat-flecked ice he'd battered from ancient metal trays, Sally was moved to see his patent satisfaction at dealing competently with these ordinary tasks.

Only once did grief come with a tiger's spring. They had decided to have dinner in the little sitting room where it was still warm enough for the French windows to stand open, and unthinkingly Sally had gone to put on some music. She didn't check what tape was in, and solemn and majestic there poured into the room the "Procession to the Minster" from *Lohengrin*. It was as though Janey had stepped into the room and Sally turned with an inarticulate cry, tears filling her eyes.

Mike was there in an instant, reaching to stop the tape, knowing without being told, hugging her close. "Your aunt? Oh, Sally, poor little love. Music can do that, can't it? Scents and music. Nothing bites so deep."

For the second time that day she had turned to him and he hadn't failed her. It was good, later, to be with him in the big bed with all its plump enfolding softness, the bed where Janey had slept with her lover, Piers, and where in all probability she had been born. This night Mike was not Sally's lover, and she didn't mind, lying with her back tucked against his side, her arms holding close against her breast the arm he had wrapped around her. He had been too exhausted by last night's harried dreams and fitful sleep, and by all the day's new scenes and thoughts, to think of making love to her. But she smiled in the soft darkness of the summer night, unworried, wanting nothing for herself beyond this closeness and the perfection of the day they had shared.

They breakfasted in the little paved corner outside the sitting room, very late, still drowsy in the sun that was already pouring down into this sheltered nook. Mike seemed to have got brown in one day and looked wonderful.

After a while they wandered down to the azalea garden, Mike taking Sally's hand as they stood with closed eyes to drink in the intoxicating fragrance. Then they went on, down to the wild end of the garden, and on every side Sally saw jobs crying out to be attended to. Along a netting fence a mass of wild sweet peas grew, their mauve perennial flowers one of her childhood favorites. This year, given no help, they were sprawling forward across the weedy ground. She crouched down and began to lift the tough stems and hook the tiny tendrils, so frail and tenacious, around the wire.

"You'll be there all day," Mike protested, but he knelt to help her all the same. "I've always thought the bloke who designed the grappling iron must have grown sweet peas. Look, perfect."

The sight of his long fingers so delicately handling the minute green curls, the amused comment, so normal and simple, the sun on her back, the sense of sanctuary that Grianan gave, suddenly came together in a moment of blinding clarity and certainty. This was the place for Mike, for them. She had one vivid pang of regret for the successful enterprise she had built up and put so much into, then she knew it didn't matter. The flat, the shop, her own trivial concerns simply weren't important. What was important was this man, who needed her, whose life had been torn apart, everything he knew and cared about snatched from him.

Sally stood up, a great calm filling her, her eyes on his long back as he worked patiently at the fiddly task.

"I'm going to keep Grianan," she said.

"Yes?" Mike turned his head to look up at her, still holding a stem against the wire. Then he nodded. "Good thinking," he said.

"I'm going to live here."

He straightened up, letting the sweet peas fall, the small hands opening with unheard shrieks of anguish. He looked at Sally in that new intent way of his, as though he sensed that something was coming that mattered.

"I'm going to sell the flat and the shop and move back here." She felt breathless, shaky, but very very sure; she knew without any doubt that she could give all this up for him.

Mike took her hands, his eyes delighted. "Sounds good to me," he said. "This is the place you really love."

"Yes it is." She felt a big beaming smile spread across her face. "Mike, I've been such a fool."

How she longed to say there and then, in the peace and sunlight and the swamping relief. "And you're going to come and live here with me."

But first that had to be arranged.

Chapter 22

A very villa-ish house for Scotland, incongruous among its sturdy granite neighbors on the outskirts of the town, with freshly painted white harling, a big curve of bow window and half the slated roof sweeping low with a couple of dormer windows looking out of it. A neat short drive the color of breaded haddock led to a tiled porch. A clean little Fiesta and a clean little Metro were parked outside. Female cars. The garden was very bright and very tidy.

Like the spider which plasters bits of its surroundings on its back as camouflage, Isobel was wearing at noon on a warm summer day silk dress, tights and high heels, plus a very irritating charm bracelet. She was painstakingly made up and the glorious red-gold hair was piled into a careful edifice then tweaked out messily. She was very thin, tense to the point of hostility, and at the sight of her Sally's own nervousness vanished.

She had always been intimidated by Isobel, or by her image of her—the beautiful gentle girl Mike had longed to look after, his wife, the mother of his children. Now Isobel seemed oddly out of her depth, as though by running home to her mother's house she had sacrificed status and identity. Certainly she was wary and defensive, and hopelessly uptight. Also, Sally found as she struggled to open some line of communication between them, not very bright.

Sally was here chiefly because of the children. The divorce was now final and she had already taken legal responsibility for Mike. His brother had come over from Ireland to see her at Grianan and had admitted that after the brief holiday he had spent with Mike he had known that he couldn't cope with looking after him. When he had had a whisky or two and relaxed a bit more he had confessed that his wife had refused absolutely to let him offer to do it. Having her mother-in-law, now severely incapacitated, living with them in supposedly self-contained quarters was as much as she felt she could cope with. Colin broke down as he said goodbye in mingled guilt and gratitude that Mike would be adrift no longer.

What Sally wanted today was to establish her own contact with Isobel, so that arrangements for the children to see Mike would be made in a spirit of cooperation and, if possible, goodwill.

"Thank you for letting me come," she said, as they settled in a room so full of gleaming repro that it seemed there must be another one just like it in different colors on the other side of a partition. "I thought it would be a good idea for us to meet."

Isobel's mother was present, very nervous but, Sally suspected, ready to be aggressive. Sally saw in her exactly what Isobel would become, the lovely hair a rusty gray, the light skin pallid, the eyes anxious.

"Oh, that's all right, Mike doesn't mean anything to me any more," Isobel cut in quickly, surprising Sally, who hadn't thought that was what they were talking about. Since Mike and Isobel were divorced matters had surely moved on from there.

"He's just not the same man," Isobel was hurrying on defensively. "Not the man I married. He'll never be normal, you know that, don't you? He's impossible to live with and he'll never be any different."

Her tone was so callously dismissive that Sally felt anger spread through her, realizing with disbelief that Isobel's viewpoint was entirely subjective. How she, Sally, might feel about such a comment, hadn't entered Isobel's mind. She wanted only to justify herself for running out on an ill and mentally impaired husband.

Sally was about to tell her that she had been to see Mike's present doctor and the neurosurgeon who had operated on him, both of whom had made sure she knew Mike would never make a complete recovery but had been equally emphatic about his capacity to achieve an acceptable quality of life. Then she saw that Isobel's mind was closed to this idea, and also found that she herself didn't want to enter into any discussion with her about it.

"Such an appalling time she had with him," Isobel's mother was confirming, almost to herself, in case an input from her would not be well received. "No one knows who hasn't been through it, no one." She hadn't been through it, as far as Sally knew.

Sally attempted to steer the conversation to the question of the children but Isobel didn't seem to hear. Perched with half a buttock on the edge of a red and cream striped sofa, drawing hard on a cigarette but exhaling immediately with a jerky sideways turn of her head, tapping ash off every couple of seconds, she let it all pour out.

"I had the house to look after, stuck away up those miles of track, and the whole responsibility for the children, I nearly went mad up there by myself. And paying for Mike's care, these places cost the earth. I know his father would have liked Michael to have the house but how was I supposed to cope till he was old enough? And with Mike's brother living in Ireland, and his mother needing looking after as well, it was just a nightmare. . . ."

Sally had imagined, or done her best to imagine what all these problems must have been like for Isobel, and even now a sort of exasperated fairness took the edge off her anger. It must have been a nightmare indeed, and Isobel had not been strong enough to cope. It would be on her conscience for ever.

". . . and that awful place, no neighbors, miles from anywhere, impossible to get a thing. And it wasn't a marriage any more, that part was out of the question, of course . . ."

Good.

". . . I know people think I should have stood by him, but I did, I did everything for that man when he came out of hospital. Everything. It's easy to talk if it's not you that's stuck there, day after day. The only thing I could do was sell up. . . ."

Sally had explained to Mike that Edal Bank had been sold and he had shown no interest at all. In a way he had seemed relieved and she realized that this development was too large for him to confront. Listening as Isobel's querulous voice ran on in what was clearly a well worn defense, with supportive murmurs coming from mother, she waited for some acknowledgment of what Mike had lost and suffered. But gradually it dawned on her that when Isobel had agreed to her coming here it had not been about Mike or the children. It had been about her own need to absolve herself from blame.

Before Sally could get around to the practical question of the children's visits to Grianan, a black Jaguar came scrunching across the orange gravel and a moment later a man walked into the glossy room with the firm tread if not of possession than certainly of unquestioned right to be there. The boyfriend, Sally thought with reviving interest, surprised and intrigued by his appearing like this.

He came straight to her with energetic directness, hand outstretched, immaculate blue and white striped cuff emerging from dark gray sleeve. "Edward Rokeby." His warm tone and hearty smile suggested a course in interview techniques, though he gave no impression of falseness. He was short, compact, buzzing with a current of power which Sally could actually feel as he shook her hand, his grip hard and brief. She was sure in that second that he read all her frustration, Isobel's tense self-absorption and her mother's fluttering doubt as to whether he should have come.

"I thought you had meetings all day." Isobel sounded far from welcoming, and the sulky tone suggested they were well into a relationship.

"Change of plan, change of plan." A man with no time to waste, a man with shrewd eyes which met Sally's with a message that surprised her, a message of understanding and reassurance. He had known she was to be here and why. He had intended to turn up at this precise moment, she was convinced. Whatever his degree of involvement was, he had not trusted this interview to Isobel.

Sally's hope for workable solutions over the children reawoke.

Isobel's mother began twittering about whether to offer coffee or sherry or even perhaps lunch, or was it still a little early? Edward hustled her into action with what was evidently accustomed authority. They had prawn cocktails—tomato ketchup mixed with mayonnaise out of a jar masquerading as Marie Rose dressing—a concave mushroom flan and mandarin gateau. Sally imagined Isobel's smooth pale hands and long red nails tearing open packets.

"It's a great relief to Isobel, as I'm sure you will appreciate, to know that Mike will be properly looked after," Edward—now officially tagged as the fiancé—assured her, calmly ignoring Isobel's indignant glare. "He's had a bad time of it, all in all."

Isobel opened her mouth but he shot her a look from which his cultivated *bonhomie* was suddenly absent, and she shut it again, wriggling her thin shoulders and allowing herself a pout of defiance.

"I think Grianan will be a good place for him," Sally said neutrally. "He seemed to like towns and lots of people about at first but maybe that was just part of the relearning process. He doesn't seem to miss them now anyway."

"He doesn't know where he is, and that's all there is to it," Isobel stated flatly, with instant automatic possessiveness. Her tone was just short of derision that Sally imagined she could know how Mike felt about anything. That was her province. "You may think he knows, but in actual fact he hasn't the faintest idea."

Sally kept her eyes down till she had made sure her voice was going to be under control. She had not been prepared for this utter dismissal of the idea of Mike as a functioning human being. Don't fight her. Remember what you came here for. "Well, Grianan will certainly be ideal for the children, whenever they want to see their father. You will let them come, won't you?" In spite of herself her voice grew urgent, and it was to Edward she turned, not Isobel.

It was Edward who answered, with great firmness, "They will most certainly come. You needn't ever worry on that score."

"They loathed going to Gilsburgh," Isobel leapt in petulantly. "Half the time Mike didn't even know who they were, you know that. It upset them and there was nothing for them to do and he wouldn't go anywhere else with them. . . ."

Oh, Mike, I know, poor love.

"And it did distress Kirsty, you know that. It was dreadful for her, poor wee girl," Isobel's mother chipped in almost eagerly. How did she know, had she been there?

Edward frowned quickly. Sally wondered at the power of female helplessness combined with glorious red hair. It seemed to her that Isobel, weak and self-centered and, it must be said, not conspicuously intelligent, had cornered two admirable men. What were the prospects for this marriage? Sally wondered in passing.

It was Edward who came out to see her off. Isobel hovered for a moment in the porch, waggled her fingers in self-conscious farewell and turned to go in before Sally had reached her car.

"We shall be married in a month's time," Edward said quietly.

Sally turned to look at him, not sure what he was telling her. Perhaps that he would take charge? "It will be all right, won't it?" she asked, more urgently than she had intended.

"I guarantee it. The children really miss their father, especially Michael. I shall look after them and make sure they get everything they need in material terms, but it's Mike they love."

They stood with the car door between them and their eyes, almost on a level, met unsmiling, expressing mutual concern, finding mutual reassurance. "It was good of you to come back today," Sally said quietly.

Edward nodded an acknowledgment, making no fudging excuses, and Sally saw in his eyes his decision to say the next thing.

"I think, if you'll allow me to say so, that at the end of the day Mike is a lucky man."

Sally could find no appropriate answer to that, an extraordinarily generous compliment in the circumstances, but she felt her face light up. There had been no one till now to give her that encouragement.

"Keep in touch," Edward said, nodding. "If there's ever anything you need to discuss you can always contact me." A die-stamped card.

Sally knew that at last she had an ally. "I'm so glad we've met."

He smiled, the kindness in his eyes genuine, patting her arm. "Drive carefully."

He had known she would want to put her foot down on the way home. Not only to get back to Grianan and Mike but to get the taste of Isobel's callousness out of her mouth. Yet in a strange way Isobel had become unimportant today, her power finally gone. As Sally crossed the Forth Bridge and headed up the motorway her mind ranged forward contentedly, conscious of a firm base of happiness beneath the flow of thoughts.

The Edalmere cottage had been sold. She had taken the first offer that came for it, ignoring John Ballantyne's protests. She had never been back to it. Ann Jackson had gone in to empty cupboards and take anything she wanted. The rest of the contents had gone to the sale room.

The boathouse flat was on the market. Now that she was back at Grianan Sally wondered how she could have been content in it for so long. In retrospect it seemed dark and confined. But it had been a refuge which had served its turn, and it had been the place where she had got to know Nona.

The business she minded giving up more than she had expected. It had been a positive thread which had held her life together, and in spite of all the difficulties and distractions she had made it work. It had been swiftly snapped up and she was glad that after the effort she and Nona had put into it, it looked as though it might survive. But she had no serious or lasting regrets; Mike came first.

From that moment in the sunny sleeping garden at Grianan, watching Mike peacefully hooking up the wild sweet peas, when she had known with absolute certainty what she wanted, she had never looked back.

All doubts, all the practical objections put forward for her good by Nona, had simply fallen away. Who else did she want to be with? Who else did she want to look after? She had loved Mike more than she had ever loved anyone and he was Mike still. Deficient in one small function of the brain, the emphasis of his personality altered, but still that person.

Having stipulated to Mrs. Lucas, with a firmness even that insensitive busybody could not ignore, that she herself must be the one to propose the new plan to Mike, she had put it off and put it off, gnawed by apprehension not only on her own account but fearful that Mike would reject the plan or be worried by it in a way which would retard his progress. Hesitating like this had given Sally plenty of time to discover what it would mean to her if he didn't agree. In the end she had got into such a state of nerves about the whole thing that she had become appalled at what she was suggesting—wrenching his life arbitrarily into a different course, making herself responsible for his welfare and happiness for the rest of his days. What meddling arrogance.

They had been at Grianan for the weekend and she had been due to take Mike back to Gilsburgh that evening. She had kept to the pattern he was used to so that no hint of change should unsettle him before it was certain there would be no insurmountable legal or practical obstacles.

They had just finished watering the small patch of ground which they had planted with lettuce and spring onions and a couple of rows of spinach and broccoli. One of the victims of Sally's neglect had been the garden hose, left out all winter, and they had been going back and forth with watering cans. Mike was very patient about that sort of thing now, the instinct to find a more efficient method to do a job, once so fundamental to his character and training, completely dormant.

Sally had felt harried, with a sense of time closing in on her, angry with herself for having let the whole weekend slip by again without saying anything, but feeling it would be a bad idea to launch into the subject in the car on the way down to Gilsburgh. At a deeper level of course she hated having to take Mike back at all.

The outside tap on the greenhouse wall wouldn't turn off properly. She had seized it with both hands, quite unreasonably infuriated by the petty setback. It went on dripping and she had gone down on one knee to put more beef into her efforts. It had been a dry summer; water was precious. But it hadn't just been that. All her churning doubts and fears had focused on this one obstinate object. Drop after drop squeezed out, falling on the cracked grid below. God, something else that ought to be seen to, she had thought in despair. Her own inadequacy had seemed suddenly too great to bear. She had hit the tap a violent blow with the metal watering can, a gesture of complete futility, jarring her arm. A stronger spatter of water had rewarded her and she had realized to her horror that in a couple of seconds she would be in tears.

"Hey—*hey!*" Mike's voice had protested behind her, amused but concerned. A hand had appeared over her shoulder, shutting off the tap without apparent effort, then both hands had gripped her arms and lifted her to her feet. "Come on, what's all this about?" He had turned her towards him, smothering her anger in his embrace, bending his head over hers. "You've been like a lit fuse all day. And do you think you could let go of that damned can?"

Giggling with the slight hysteria of averted tears, she had let it clatter at their feet, butting her head against him.

"You going to tell me what's eating you?"

The moment had come and she had seized it. She had arched away from him to look into his eyes, supported by the circle of his arms. "Mike, would you like to come and live here, at Grianan, with me?" She had thought so carefully of how she would lead up to it, asking if he was really happy where he was, if he'd prefer to live somewhere more rural, if he would like perhaps to stay here with her for a week or two to see how it worked out, but out the suggestion came, unequivocal and not to be recalled.

He had stared at her for a moment, a curious blankness in his eyes as though he was in shock, and she had had a moment's terror that she had done some irreversible damage, set back his recovery for weeks or even months. Then his eyes had come alive, those arresting green-brown eyes, a joyful light leaping in them followed by a relief so overwhelming that he had tried to hide it from her, pressing his head hard down against hers again, and she had felt the tremor of intense feeling which ran through his big frame. She had heard his breath drawn raggedly, harshly, and had known that he was weeping.

"Mike, darling Mike." Her own voice had wavered, her throat aching. "Oh, Mike, don't, it's all right. Everything's all right. You can decide whatever you want, we can talk about it all . . ." She had stroked his bent head, soothed and comforted him, shaken to pieces at his reaction.

After a moment he had lifted his head, his painful grip on her relaxing. "Damn fool, aren't I?" he said, with an attempt at a laugh. "But did you mean it, Sally? Were you serious?"

"Yes, absolutely serious."

His eyes had been wet with tears but eager with the beginning of an incredulous excitement. "Is it what you want yourself?"

"More than I've ever wanted anything."

"But—live here? What about the flat?"

"Sell it."

He had stared at her, drawing a long shaky breath. "Live here with you. Christ, I can't believe this is happening." He had released her and taken a couple of jerky steps away and back. Sally had had a sudden detached view of the two of them standing in this scruffy corner beside the derelict-looking greenhouse and the compost heap green with weeds, the coils of cracked hose around their feet, the amber light of evening flooding across the garden, their lives changing direction.

"But are you sure it's what you want, Sally?" Mike had repeated urgently. "I am no bloody good to anyone now, you know that. I shouldn't let you lumber yourself with me."

"Be a darn sight easier living with you here than rushing up and down to Gilsburgh all the time," she had told him cheerfully, seeing the fear that was overtaking him as he began to think through the realities. "We want to be together. That's all we have to worry about. We can just take it one day at a time, as you say yourself."

"Yes, but it's different for me, that's all I can manage," he had pointed out, with a small rueful smile she had been glad to see. "It's hardly the same for you."

"Why not? I'll be here, at home." And safe, she had thought, in the way only Grianan can make me feel.

"Bloody hell." He had looked around him and Sally had seen the tension draining from him. "What a prospect," he had said softly.

"We probably ought to be on our way now, though.

It's getting late. You can think about this during the week and then on Friday—"

"I'm not going back." The instant panicky flat defiance had sharply reminded her that he was not equipped either to think anything over or to argue his case reasonably.

"It won't be for long—" she had begun. But she should have known better by this time.

"No point in going back there, is there?" A little attempt at jauntiness there that she had recognized; a casualness which could not hide his alarm. "And anyway, who's going to care?"

Sally had suddenly glimpsed what it would be like for him to be back at Balmenie House alone, not counting off the last few days in relief and anticipation as anyone else could do, but worried and unsure, terrified that he had imagined it all, fighting to keep hold of his fragile grip on time.

And what difference did it make, after all? Mike was right. Who was there to care?

She had looked up at him and laughed in relief at the simplicity of it. "I'll phone Mrs. Lucas."

"Yes?" Mike's skin was glistening faintly in the familiar ominous way. What had she put him through in the last few moments?

"You're right, Mike. Why should you ever go back?"

"Christ, Sally." His arms reached for her again and he crushed her to him. "I thought I'd go mad in that place. Sometimes I thought I was mad. I wanted to top myself. I used to think, Is this it, for the rest of my life? These doddering old fools around me, this smarmy woman patronizing me, this dismal little town, the mud, the smell of the river—sometimes it seemed as though I'd never get it out of my nostrils."

Sally hugged him, shocked, stunned with guilt. He had suffered it all because he had known there was no alternative that he could demand. What sort of courage was that?

Watching him adapting to his new life Sally couldn't believe that she had waited so long to bring him here, or remember what else she had ever thought had mattered. At Grianan, where Mike had felt at ease from the first moment, he was secure and occupied in an environment he enjoyed and understood. He was never alone, which had been a dread Sally hadn't fully grasped but which he now described in terms that made her wince.

She had wondered if he would like to have his own room but he'd simply laughed at her, picking her up and swinging her round exuberantly. "Are you joking? Separate rooms? No chance, you're not getting away with that."

As simple as that. And how much she would have minded, she knew, if he had chosen otherwise. For she had long ago moved on from the needful, restless, will-he-won't-he torment of his first visits to the flat. She wanted him there, wanted to sleep with her body against his, to wake and find him beside her. She would have been miserable alone, knowing that he was sleeping somewhere else in the house.

Even if Mike had never made love to her at all she would have wanted to be with him. But the change which moving to Grianan made in him had affected more than his mental stability. He was leading a more active life, eating and sleeping better, and he looked fit again, the incipient paunch gone. Sally had grown used to his hair being gray but now it had more life to it, the flattened dead look gone, and his skin was as brown and freckled as it had ever been. The hideous clothes of the Gilsburgh days had been jettisoned and the long limbs once more in cords and working shirts had all the old appeal for her.

Occupied, belonging, secure, Mike was at last able to look beyond his own struggle to survive and take more notice of other people again. Sally had seen flashes of this—his perception of her longing for Janey and her guilt over Piers—but now this new awareness was evident in his love making, bringing a return of tenderness and sensitivity which she had never thought he would be capable of again.

It was good to watch his growing assurance as he found himself in a scene he could deal with, and where he felt he had a role. It was a self-generating cycle of confidence and improvement, and Sally loved those quiet days when they were always together, watching him rediscover lost skills and pleasures, seeing his concentration span increase in leaps and bounds.

One day as they were working together on making the greenhouse weatherproof once more, she was startled and moved to hear an almost forgotten sound. Mike was whistling as he expertly thumbed putty into place around a new pane. Sally hadn't heard him do that since before he was ill and she stopped work to stand still, filled with joy. It was hard to forgive herself for having made him wait even one extra hour for this, but he was safe now.

Chapter 23

Once Sally had made the decision to live at Grianan she hadn't looked much beyond establishing Mike there happily. In financial terms there was no immediate worry. The capital she had realized was, hopefully, reasonably well invested. Edward Rokeby had said he would from now on maintain and educate the Danaher children and Sally had blithely accepted the offer on Mike's behalf. Mike himself had his disability benefit and his share of the proceeds from Edal Bank and its adjoining land, and he was adamant about both going into the kitty. Finding how deeply this mattered to him, Sally had agreed. They could live quietly at Grianan, pottering away at the endless jobs such a place threw up, establishing a new routine for themselves and a sense of permanence and peace. Sally saw Mike as her job now.

It didn't work out like that.

Michael and Kirsty were the first to come, Michael in particular stiff and shy with Sally, very grown up and masculine and, she guessed, terrified of any new development which would take his father further away from him still. Kirsty, more outgoing and with much of her father's practical adaptability, relaxed a couple of hours into her first visit and never looked back.

Sally had been apprehensive too, about occupying them as much as anything else, so it was a relief to find that they reveled in the place, glad to be back in the type of environment they were used to and had badly missed. Another thing she was thankful for was that, in spite of Isobel's assertions that they had hated going to visit Mike in Gilsburgh, their father's limitations didn't seem to worry them at all. They simply took no notice of them, each showing a ready kindness towards him and truly impressive patience with the way he endlessly repeated himself and wandered off in the middle of doing things and wanted to be told over and over again what he had done yesterday.

Sally made no special plans for these visits—other than providing favorite food. She just went on with whatever she was doing, letting the children be with Mike or go off on their own, swim in the river, get out the old croquet set, have the run of house and garden, disappear up the hill or to Glen Ellig farm. They liked best of all to hang around Scott Maclachlan, who quickly became their hero. Sally wasn't too sure what they would learn from him but at least he was tolerant of them. She let them wear what they liked and get as scruffy as they liked, which as she could well believe was not the case in their grandmother's house.

She loved watching Mike with them. He kept to a light touch but sometimes she caught in his face an incredulous gratitude that he hadn't lost them, that the tamped down feelings which he had not been able to risk showing could be expressed again. He had not fought to see more of Michael and Kirsty because he had known he could offer them nothing—and because Isobel had told him that it upset them to be with him,

Sally learned with bitter anger. But he had missed them deeply and his satisfaction to see them so much at home at Grianan was one of the great pleasures of the new life they were establishing.

An even greater joy for Sally was the fact that the old chemistry was alive between her and Mike again. Time had absorbed the shock of the changes illness had made in him. Sometimes, with a sort of remote surprise, Sally could remember Nona's fears that one day she might meet a man with whom she would want a "full relationship." What man? Impossible to envisage wanting to be with some hypothetical stranger when she could spend her days and nights with Mike, whose body was familiar and satisfying, whose voice and smile and touch were as essential to her as breathing.

For touch had become as natural to him again as it had ever been. The unease with sexual contact which had been part of the terrors of the early stages of his illness was long forgotten. Now he would hold Sally's hand, slip an arm around her, show his need for her nearness just as he used to. At night he held her in the melding ease of lovers, where bones and angles and elbows never obtrude, and when he made love to her they were in tune once more in their own private world of pleasure, not swept up in the wild need of their early loving but wrapped in a restored mutual tenderness which meant more to Sally than all the old urgent passion.

Any guilt that beset her these days was for having been so blind to his needs. He had lived through a nightmare at Gilsburgh, a nightmare endured with a self-discipline phenomenal in his condition. All he had needed was to belong and to feel of use again, and those needs Grianan could fulfil, at the same time providing that other essential for him, calm. Because he was no longer trying to fit into a timetable arbitrary to him but governing the activities of everyone around him, he gradually abandoned his obsessive questions about what time and what day it was. When he had bad days, which he still did, and which Sally had learned to see coming from his reluctance to get up and his extreme slowness in dressing, they could be got through quietly. There was no pressure on him to do anything he didn't want to do.

On such days he wouldn't touch jobs he had been engrossed in the day before but would wander and stand at windows, silent and withdrawn but not apparently disturbed. Sally learned that these were recuperative periods, protecting his brain from the threat of overload, and once she had understood this they didn't alarm her.

Far outweighing them, in any case, was the joy of seeing the first flicker of humor return, a link once so important between them whose absence had changed the tone of their relationship more subtly than any other. Mike had begun to tease her again, just standard male put downs about the time it took her to change a plug or the rough and ready job she was satisfied with when she slapped some paint on the greenhouse door, and though she defended herself hotly she secretly relished the signs that he was no longer taking her for granted as the competent figure-in-charge.

And jokes reappeared, however feeble.

"Don't rush me, must listen to this, my tune." Elaine Page singing "Memory." Mike winked at Sally as he saw her register it and she laughed but was intensely moved. That he had come this far. She had never loved him more.

People were gradually becoming necessary to him again, not to watch and wonder at as if their antics belonged to some existence he could never share, but to be with on equal terms. When Scott appeared to scrat around a bit in the garden, which he did whenever he was short of cash, Mike liked to work alongside him and Sally would hear them chatting companionably. If Jed came to help with something major like clearing the soakaway for the septic tank or shoring up a roof, he and Mike would tackle the job together as a matter of course.

Sally had been wary of how Jed would react to Mike, wondering if male jealousy would surface. She found she had misjudged him. He took Mike exactly as he found him and they got on extremely well, working easily together, blethering away for hours about glen concerns and occasionally going down to the pub for a pint when a job was finished.

Jed still sent Sally the occasional signal of possessiveness. She didn't mind. He was part of her growing up at Grianan and, more recently, he had been there for her at a lonely time. He would always mean something to her and they both knew it.

Mike soon seemed to know half the glen. He would chat to everyone he met and people who were at first careful and sympathetic soon forgot that there was anything wrong with him. Outwardly no one could have told at first meeting that there was. The self-conscious air and the trick of looking closely into people's faces were gone. Only when he was with someone for any length of time did the faulty memory show. When for instance they went to Drumveyn, for a barbecue lunch by the loch so relaxed that no one left till seven, Sally was conscious of him becoming increasingly wandering, repeating things he had just said and clinging determinedly to anecdotes from the past where he felt sure of his ground.

She knew no one would mind. He was safe here with people who would never by word or look make him aware of his deficiencies. Pauly especially was perfect with him. Her father was a neurosurgeon, and being able to talk to her about Mike's illness had been a great new release and source of support for Sally.

As she and Mike drove home, his relief at his own success was boisterous and gloriously conceited and Sally laughed at him, as pleased he was.

"You're just a huge show off."

"I've always been popular."

As though from a different life she recalled her jealousy for the lively gatherings of his Lakeland friends, the reasonable certainty that there had been other affairs. "Oh, please."

"I think I need a wider stage though. How about opening Grianan up for guests again?"

"Not you, too." Every person she had talked to today seemed to have asked her about it.

"Have you thought about it?" Mike was serious now.

"It certainly wasn't part of the plan."

"It's a possibility, isn't it?"

"Not really. I'm no Janey, remember."

"You don't have to be, do you?"

"But people came to Grianan because of her—and because of the food, of course. You know I'm not in that league. I'm not even interested in cooking."

"Someone else could cook. And the guests loved the place as well, you told me so yourself."

"They'll all have found somewhere else to go by this time."

But later, coming in from a last wander on the hill together before bed, she had asked abruptly, "Mike, do *you* think I should open the place up again?"

"Well," he said, in that new easygoing way of his, "it seems a bit of a waste, just the two of us here, doesn't it? This big house in such a perfect setting. And you're used to being busy. Don't you think you'll get bored after a while?"

"You're worried that I've given up a meaningful career selling envelopes for your sake?"

He laughed. "To the point, as ever."

"Seriously, do you think something like that?"

"I think eventually you will need more than your present existence to occupy you, and I think this place could be better used. And I'm sure the guests still miss it, whatever you say."

Sally laughed. "I've often wondered if the other hotels read those postcards." All through the year there had been a steady trickle of messages saying things like, "How we miss Grianan, we can't find anything remotely like it," or, "This place isn't a patch on Grianan—food's frightful and water's always hot . . ." And they sent their love. Sally knew it was a reaching out to Janey through her but she knew it was genuine none the less.

"Maureen would come and cook."

"How do you know that?"

"She said so." Mike's cheerful grin nearly distracted Sally from the whole conversation.

"You've discussed this with Maureen?"

The grin widened. "And with Connie."

"But Mike, listen—" She followed him across the kitchen and clutched his arm in her need for his full attention as he went to draw the kettle on to the Aga hob. "Wouldn't you hate it? People around all the time, me rushed off my feet and always having to put them first and work to a timetable? And it never stops, you know, there's no such thing as time off."

Mike put his hand over hers, smiling at her sudden urgency. "Sweetheart, I like people, I always have. And you could have as many or as few as you liked. We don't have to make a living out of it, though a place like this ought to bring in some return. And it stops in the winter, doesn't it?"

"Are you trying to persuade me because you feel it would be good for me?" As she spoke it struck Sally how impossible it would have been to have put such a question to him even a few weeks ago.

He looked down at her hand, clasped in his. She saw his struggle to find words. "I don't want you to feel you have to look after me. I don't want to be a passenger. Damnation—" She could see the words slipping away from him because this mattered too much. Her heart ached for him and she put up her free hand to stroke his cheek.

"Darling Mike, don't worry about it now, we can talk about it another time."

"No, no." His grip tightened on her hand. "Just slow down," he muttered to himself, then went on with taut effort, "Sharing. Contributing. Doing this together, where we live."

That overriding need, to feel that he was making an input again. Suddenly Sally realized that it was all supremely simple. "Then we'll do it," she said. "No reason in the world why not. A new enterprise together."

"Do you mean it?" Mike looked attentively into her face for a moment, then seized her and they clung together in exultant excitement.

Sally knew she should have brought the washing in long before this. There was more than a hint of autumn in the dusky air and the sheets were probably wetter than they had been an hour ago. That damned scullery tap blowing its top just as Maureen was starting dinner may have been hilarious but dinner would undoubtedly be late. Good job Mike had been on hand to deal with the crises with his usual calm competence.

As Sally started down the crooked steps a light caught her eye away to the right. Jed out lamping? But this light was nearer and not moving, a square patch steady through the screening trees. The garden cottage. Had someone broken in? Or—?

Her heart beating fast, she dumped down the laundry basket and began to run. It didn't occur to her to be afraid of what she might find, or to fetch Mike. She slowed as she approached, doubt assailing her. The door wasn't closed and she could hear music. She paused, head cocked. How often had she listened to that evocative haunting sound, lying beside Piers in this room of pure color and spare beauty. Simon and Garfunkel, "*El Condor Pasa*."

Relief and delight swept her forward. He was standing by the unrolled futon, sorting out a pile of belongings which he had emptied on to it from the backpack at his feet.

"I thought you would never come back."

She was across the room, shaking him, clutching him. He rocked under the attack and steadied her, gasping. Then, her eyes shut against tears, Sally felt his hand hard behind her head, pulling her cheek to his.

"Oh, Sally, bless you for that," he said, his voice muffled. "Let me look at you." He held her off, smiling, his cheek wet from hers. "Tears too," he said softly.

"I thought you'd gone for ever."

"Time," he said, "I just needed time."

"I thought you hated me—"

He shook her gently, frowning. "Never. Never in the world. But there were a lot of feelings. We'll talk about it, I promise."

Sally looked at him, at his sensitive face, his dark eyes which she had last seen stony with pain, and she felt a core of guilt and remorse deep inside her melt away. "Yes, we must talk."

"We will," he repeated definitely. "There'll be plenty of time."

"You're staying?"

"I'm staying."

"We're open again," she told him, grabbing at any bit of news, hearing the childish elation in her voice and not caring.

"I know," he said, eyes smiling.

"How d'you know?" she demanded indignantly. "Connie? You've been in touch all the time? The miserable wretch, why didn't she tell me?"

"I asked her not to."

"She could at least have said you were coming."

"She didn't know, truly. And are you enjoying having guests here again?"

Sally allowed herself to be deflected. The truth was

she had never imagined how much fun it would be. Feeling very tentative, she had written around the guests who usually came in late summer and autumn, hoping that some might not have arranged an alternative holiday yet. The response had been startling, not only in immediate bookings but in enthusiasm and good wishes and plans for next year.

"You thought you'd keep the numbers small?" Mike had mocked. "I'll be building an extension at this rate."

Sally didn't ask on what terms Piers had returned but it seemed that he intended to take up where he had left off. The only thing she insisted on was that he was paid. Janey had fed him and let him live in the cottage; that had been their deal. But now the cottage was his property. Sally had Mike to back her on this and Piers had to give in.

In his wake another figure from the past re-emerged, not quite so welcome. Marchmain came stalking into the sitting room one day, tail aloft, a malevolent gleam in his eye which Sally remembered of old. Fortunately he thought poorly of the computer, the different music, the lack of cigar smoke. Perhaps he even missed the rugby. For whatever reason he elected to take up residence in the garden cottage. Sally very much approved.

She and Piers found their chances to talk in the late autumn days when he began the job of reclaiming the garden, which they hoped to have fully productive again next year.

"I know you think I failed Aunt Janey." At last it could be said.

"I was too hard on you."

"Because you loved her."

Piers straightened up from his digging and looked at her with a sudden penetrating scrutiny.

Sally met it as calmly as she could. She felt Piers would always be part of their lives and she wanted this out in the open and accepted.

For a moment the shutters of the intensely private person seemed ready to come down and she regretted what she had said. Piers read that in her eyes and took a deep breath.

"Yes, I loved her."

Sally touched his arm in quick grateful acknowledgment. "And you thought I didn't love her enough."

"No, I thought you were going to realize too late just how much you did love her. And I wanted you to see her pain and understand how deeply she minded about leaving you, the most precious person in her life."

He smiled wryly at Sally's reaction of surprised denial. "Oh, Sally, of course you were. I just wanted you to look past yourself. That's why when I heard you'd given up everything to look after Mike, and were opening the doors of Grianan again and letting life come back to it, I knew you had learned that and it was time to come back."

Stark truths, but oddly acceptable to have them put into words by him. There was a feeling of completeness to have him there again, quietly in the background of their lives, and for Sally there was a special pleasure to be able to share words and books and poetry once more, a world largely closed to Mike now.

They got on well, these two so different men. Slow moving, without urgency, talking or silent for hours as inclination or Mike's mood swings dictated. They gradually worked their way through the maintenance jobs so long neglected, Mike supplying muscle and professional know-how, Piers his craftsman's skills.

They all shared their amusement at the guests, who one and all declared themselves ready to accept any changes but universally longed for everything to be exactly as it had always been. Outwardly it was. Nothing had changed in the rooms, or in the pattern of the days. Packed lunches were put out on the same table in the hall, dog bowls left on the corridor windowsill by the kitchen door, the same boots and tweeds stank out the boiler room. Even the food was almost the same.

"Janey used to have to chase Maureen all the time," Sally had worried to Mike. "She'll never keep the standard up if she's on her own."

"That was when there was someone to do the chasing. Tell her you know you can rely on her to produce the goods and she'll surprise you."

He was right. Sally stressed her own inadequacy (though she thought Maureen needn't have agreed about it quite so readily) and Maureen felt the mantle of Janey had fallen on her shoulders. All the energy formerly channeled into outwitting and circumventing the boss now went into outdoing her.

Mike was perfect with the guests. Janey had always muttered about the way they expected her to sit and chat to them, and Sally was discovering just how impossible it was to make the time for such indulgence, but these first arrivals particularly, since they felt they had been specially invited, yearned for personal attention and a feeling of involvement. Mike loved that side of things. He had all the time in the world for wordy old generals and even more for their flirtatious old wives.

Sally knew it was early days and that the pleasure would almost certainly pall under the pressure of sheer hard work, but for the time being it felt so much like having a houseful of friends to stay that it seemed outrageous to accept their checks.

It was Mike who persuaded her to ask her father to come. He understood her deep-seated reluctance but knew too that it was a shadowy and unsatisfactory area of her life which should be dealt with.

"You don't have to be on top of each other all the time. In fact you hardly need to see one another if it doesn't work out."

"But he hates me." It was a last minute cry of protest, voicing the old buried fear.

Mike didn't bother to answer it, just throwing a long arm around her, pulling her in close, saying, "I'm here, remember, you're not on your own."

With her father too, when he came, Sally realized that she had been missing the obvious. As a member of the medical profession, who better to understand Mike's problems and help her to understand them? Why hadn't she written or talked to him about it all long before this? And his pleasure at being at Grianan again surprised and shamed her. She had held on to it fiercely as her territory after her mother had gone, her place and Janey's, but now she saw that her father would readily have come here with her if she had given him the chance.

They still talked with difficulty. Her father could infect her with his own communication problems in seconds flat. But they did fumble towards a new frankness.

"It's meant a lot to me, you know, being here again," her father said awkwardly, one day when he had found her madly plucking pheasants which she had forgotten they needed for dinner and had most uncharacteristically started to help her. "I hope it's been acceptable to you—that is, not upset you in any way?"

"It's been good." He should not have had to ask such a question.

"This is a pretty special place, Sally. It has a spirit very much its own."

"Janey's spirit."

"Yours now." He studied her, his gaunt face sad. "I've missed so much of you. My own fault."

"You needn't miss any more of me." How crass that sounded. She hurried on. "I mean, I do want you to come here, whenever you want to, if you'd like to."

He smiled and she had a startling glimpse of the father who had loved his small girl, and been adored in return. "I should like to."

They plucked on, slow and not so slow.

"And Sally—"

She looked up, the urgency of his voice arresting her.

"—about Mike. Don't have any doubts. He's the right man for you, I'm sure of it. And he'll give you every ounce of himself, always. Sorry, that's probably unacceptably intrusive—"

"No, I'm glad you said it."

He was the right man. Her weighing up of the pros and cons of living with him seemed incredible now. Once the pressure of trying to cope with him and her own separate life had been lifted, so all the impatience which would in turn torture her with guilt had evaporated. There was never conflict or even minor arguments between them. No man could have been more generous, loving or tolerant. And, as her father had said, everything Mike was or had was hers.

They were on their way one Friday afternoon to collect Kirsty from school for the weekend when Sally opened a fat letter from Australia which she hadn't had time to look at when Postie came. It contained yet another photograph of Nona's grinning darkhaired son to join the rest that had been winging to Grianan since August. "Oh, look, isn't he heaven?"

"Would it be all right if I looked later?" Mike asked with mild irony. He liked to drive in the glen though they changed over before Muirend.

"Oh, and goodness, guess what—"

"Tell me."

"My mother and Bill are thinking of coming over next year. My mother asks if it would be all right if they came to see us. Oh, how *awful* that she thinks she has to ask. How truly awful. Of course they must come."

"Phone her."

Two calm words and all the panic went.

"When's Nona coming over, more to the point?" Mike went on. "She is some eyeful, that sister of yours. Is she in that photo?"

"No, tough. Mind you, Ray's pretty attractive, aren't you looking forward to meeting him one day?"

"Not particularly."

"Oh, and listen to this . . .." She read on eagerly.

"Try out loud."

"Sorry, but this is such a turn up. Danny, my eldest brother," the word easy now because of Nona, "is having a year's traveling before university and wants to know if he can come and work at Grianan for a few months, do anything. . . ."

Her voice tailed away as she looked up from the letter, caught up in amazing new visions reaching forward through the meshes of relationships and friendships, through the unexpected twists of time's plotting.

"It's Grianan," she said. "It's Grianan, isn't it?"

Mike pulled into the lay-by where they always changed places. He reached over to pull her into a headlock as he would have done Michael.

"What's Grianan?" he asked, giving her a little shake.

"Let go, you big brute." Breathlessly Sally dragged her head free and shook back her thick hair. "I mean, making everything possible, drawing everyone, together. I used to think it was Janey."

"It's you, you absurd woman. It was Janey and now it's you. You've stopped holding people off."

"Giving not taking," she amended grimly.

"That too." Mike leaned over and dropped a quick light kiss on her temple.

She knew that it was true. As soon as she had opened the doors everything and everyone she cared about had come flocking towards her. She turned her head and pressed her lips to the back of the hand that lay on her shoulder.

PENGUIN PUTNAM

online

Your Internet gateway to a virtual environment with hundreds of entertaining and enlightening books from Penguin Putnam Inc.

While you're there, get the latest buzz on the best authors and books around—

Tom Clancy, Patricia Cornwell, W.E.B. Griffin, Nora Roberts, William Gibson, Robin Cook, Brian Jacques, Catherine Coulter, Stephen King, Jacquelyn Mitchard, and many more!

Penguin Putnam Online is located at
http://www.penguinputnam.com

PENGUIN PUTNAM NEWS

Every month you'll get an inside look at our upcoming books and new features on our site. This is an ongoing effort to provide you with the most interesting and up-to-date information about our books and authors.

Subscribe to Penguin Putnam News at
http://www.penguinputnam.com/ClubPPI